DRAGON SOURCE

REUNIFICATION BOOK ONE

GLENN BIRMINGHAM

STET PUBLISHING, LLC

Interior graphics by Crystal Gafford of Crafty as a Coyote.

Published by STET Publishing, Denver
WWW.STETPUBLISHING.COM

PAPERBACK EDITION
ISBN 10: 1-64392-007-3
ISBN 13: 978-1-64392-007-8

To the child I was,
You were told you'd never be smart enough,
good enough, fast enough.
Enough.

And to my readers who still need to hear it:
You are Enough.

1

THE WORDS

ARTEN

The dreams were strong. They came almost nightly now. Dreams of burning, of light, of floating on a demon wind. She awoke with syllables in her mouth, shaped on her tongue, ready to sigh out on hot breath. When she tasted them, they were unlike any language she knew, and as soon as she tried to capture them in her mind, they evaporated. On this morning, the Words strained to escape. They seared her throat and demanded release.

She didn't know what would happen when they were released, beyond the sense of dread that gripped her. Dread that was stronger than the compulsion to give them voice. For now, but for how much longer?

She clenched her jaw and sprang for the basin of water beside her pallet. Her legs tangled in the rough blanket, twined around her from her nightly thrashing. She fell. Her jaw thunked against the woolen mat and the floorboards underneath sighed with the impact.

A single syllable jarred free.

The near-dark room dimmed to black, and she shivered

as the sheen of sweat on her skin evaporated in an instant. The Words scented freedom and leapt to the front of her tongue, dancing on her lips. She lunged the rest of the way to the basin, shoved her face into the frigid water. The abrupt cold shocked the Words free. They escaped into the clay bowl, boiled to the surface. They licked her eyes and cheeks in their passing. She shivered again.

She clung there, arms clutching the now empty basin as she panted. She trembled from fatigue as much as fear. Only when she pulled her face away did she see it—the line of dark char on her woolen mat, where the first syllable had escaped.

It's true... Saviors protect me, it's real... But it was too late for that. The demons had marked her.

Her stomach turned over and clenched. She fought the bile down but couldn't stop the shaking that rattled her to her core. She couldn't pretend anymore—she was going to die.

EVENTUALLY, she summoned the energy to crawl back onto her pallet. She stared at the ceiling unseeing, her stomach knotted, her skin on fire. She didn't notice when dark shifted to light. She barely noted her mother entering, could hear nothing of what she said. Her mind registered a voiced question, which she vaguely wished to answer but managed only a groan. She couldn't make her jaws unclench, like her body was trying to prevent more Words from escaping.

When the healer arrived—was it midday?—she was wrung out. His hands were icy on her forehead and cheeks, his eyes foreign and too-blue, like glacial melt. She dragged herself out of her hazy torpor, seeking shelter in their cool depths. Then he turned away and the heat flared again.

"...fever," she heard him say to her mother. His voice was as distant as the clouds. She tried to listen. "—nothing I can do unless she gets worse. Then we might know what kind of sickness has taken her." The icy eyes shifted back and pinned her down. They were hard, his face worried with a suspicious frown.

Does he know? Her heart pounded.

If he did, he said nothing. Then he was gone, and she faded.

THE SUN WAS all wrong when she awoke. She rubbed grit from her eyes and pushed herself up on one elbow. She trembled from this small effort and wanted to collapse back onto her pallet, but the scent of water drew her up. Her fingers found an earthenware mug and brought it to her lips. It was too heavy. She drained it, gasped with relief as it drenched the parched layers of her tongue and throat. She fell back, coughing, as moisture returned. The cup was taken from her hands. She instinctively clutched after it.

"Let me fill it," her mother said in a voice usually reserved for keeping Arten and Deric from pinching each other at Temple. The cup was taken again, and an arm reached under her shoulders to prop her up against the wall. The cup was returned and drained twice more before the desert in her mouth was gone.

"Thank you, Mother," she croaked, and then startled at her own voice. It was rough and too deep.

Her mother's brow had a vertical crease, and it shadowed her eyes. The woman said nothing, but her jaw tensed briefly. Arten heard the unspoken: *We can't afford for you to be sick.* Guilt and shame flushed through Arten.

There was no need for her mother to say what she was thinking—Arten already knew it. It was really better that way. She tried to be strong but hearing the words in the confines of her head was much easier to bear than when they actually came out of her mother's mouth. She chided herself, and it sounded in her mother's voice: *At least I won't impose upon them much longer. I only have to slip up once, then they'll know about my Taint, and I'll burn. Father will be sad to lose another, but he'll be better off without me. They all will. Not that I deserve the honor of the pyres.*

It was Arten who broke the heavy silence, finally. "How long...?"

"Three days."

"Three days?" she yelped. "But that means..."

"Yes," there was a grimness about her mother's mouth. "Your father has gone without you. He took Deric. We hired a boy to mind the shop." The expense of that hung between them, oppressive. "Rest and get well," she commanded. There was a hardness in her tone that belied the sentiment. She bustled around for a few moments with brisk efficiency, then left, sliding closed the thin panel that divided Arten's room from the outer bedroom where Deric slept. Arten heard Deric's door rattle closed, then heard the muffled padding of feet in the room beyond. She listened until she heard the soft creak of the stairs, her mother descending into the shop.

Arten lay back and groaned, forced her muscles to relax. *Three days...* They couldn't afford a shop boy for one day, let alone three. How were they to manage? Her stomach churned around the knot of guilt. But there was nothing to do but rest for the moment. She was too weak to stand much less run the shop. So, she pulled the blanket up over her head and tried to sleep.

It eluded her. When she closed her eyes, she saw the healer's eyes, his suspicion. *He knows, he knows, he knows.* Every jangle of the shop bell that trickled distantly through the floor, every clatter of hooves passing in the lane, set her heart racing. Were they come to fetch her away? *Don't be silly,* she tried to tell herself, *the venerated doesn't have a horse.* But the healer might. He might throw her across his horse's withers and take her to the temple, turn her over to the venerated. Or he might bind her hands and drag her along beside him as he rode, so people would know she was Tainted. A hundred scenarios chased each other through her mind, each ending in chains and fire.

When her mother came back and left a plate and full basin of water at her bedside, Arten feigned sleep until she had gone out again. Her palms were slick against the clay mug, but the water was soothing to her still-fevered body, and the food sat comfortingly in her stomach.

"Get up, get dressed."

Arten groaned. Morning light shafted though the crack in the sliding door, edging past the fuzzy silhouette of her mother, hands busy pinning hair on her head with brusque stabs, her face in shadow. Arten didn't need to see her face to know that she was frowning. She inched herself up the wall on weak arms, nightclothes sticking to clammy skin, sleep and fever heavy in her limbs.

"I'm not going to dress you, you're not a child. If you don't move any faster, you're going in what you're wearing." Her mother disappeared back into her bedroom, became an intermittent shadow that flickered across the beams of sunlight as she moved about. Arten heard the sharp clack of narrow-heeled boots and the susurration of satin. All wisps of fatigue fled her mind as she understood what her mother's preparations implied.

She had been under the fever for three days. That made today the ninth day—Saviorsday. Her stomach turned and clenched, and she feared she would purge it, then immediately wondered if that wouldn't be such a bad thing. "I don't think I feel well enough to go today," she called, endeavoring to sound as weak and sickly as possible. It was alarmingly easy.

"Nonsense," her mother said, sliding the door wide and emerging from her room into Arten's. She looked like one of the five saviors standing there, the morning light softening the hard angles of her crossed arms, the sharp lines of her face, burnishing the coppery folds of her dress and illuminating her hair so she glowed like an ember. Arten knew that today that ember would burn, not comfort. "Get up," she said again, lips thinned.

Arten knew she was going to lose the argument, but she tried anyway. "I might spread the fever. It's not a good idea for me to go today."

Her mother's look narrowed, the vertical crease appearing between her brows. It had been the wrong thing to say. "A burning liar won't ascend," her mother quoted quietly.

She suspects, Arten thought, panicked. Her eyes darted to the telling ashy scuff on the rug and quickly away. She drew the blanket close up to her chest, fingers clutched in it to hide their trembling. *Did the healer tell her? Did I say something while I was fevered?* Her mind spun uselessly. *What do I do, what do I do?* It kept spinning as her mother hauled her to her feet and shoved her into her best dress, despite her earlier threat. She risked only brief glances at her mother, while she sat her down and scrubbed a brush through her hair, equally anxious about drawing her attention as she was about what her mother was thinking. How much did she suspect?

"That will have to do," her mother declared at last, grimly. "It's a good thing your father isn't here to see you disgracing us today." Before Arten could more than register the pang of guilt, her mother dragged her up from the bench, her hand a steel band around Arten's upper arm, and propelled her through Deric's room, the common area, down the stairs, and out into the bright world. Arten tripped over the threshold, nearly tumbled down their three stone steps, but her mother's grip tightened and kept her bodily on her feet. They marched down the dusty lane at a pace that had Arten's breath stinging and her shoulder aching when she lagged or stumbled and her mother yanked her onwards.

They lived only two miles from the temple, but the walk was interminable. When other families began to join them on the road, Arten's mother hissed at her, "Make an effort at least, Arten! These are our neighbors." Arten tried to stand straighter, to paste a neutral smile on her face, but it was all she could do to keep up. With every person who greeted them, who paused to comment on how ill she looked, she felt a stab of fear. Could they see her secret? Would they reveal it or help her? Who could she trust? The congregation of the faithful drew a close net around her as they approached the temple.

The temple was a humble stone building encircled by a broad flattish lawn, neither of which were large enough to hold the entire village anymore. Because her family was on the east side of the temple, they attended morning services. The western half would displace them in the evening. Tall narrow windows were set with stained glass in the thick, ancient stone, and a small dome perched above the exact center of the building. How had she never noted before the rusted iron girding the dome or the ruby flames that burned along each pane of glass?

Nestled near the entrance of the temple property were two small, squat buildings. They were covered in vines, and the surrounding underbrush had nearly reclaimed them, but she had played in and around them enough to know they were there, to know what purpose they had been built for. They pulled at her today, as she and her mother passed. She suppressed a shudder. She dragged her eyes away, focused on the temple, on the rough lawn under her feet, on the good-wishes of their neighbors for her health, on the careful way her mother avoided answering questions about her illness.

When they finally passed through the temple doors, Arten felt a well of relief. The temple was safe. Here, she was protected by the five saviors. Within these walls, no demons could dwell. As the heavy doors scraped closed, sealing her in amongst her neighbors and friends, she looked to the altar, her eyes drifting up to the dome above it. To the manacles that hung from the ironwork there, chains looping like curtain swags, clinking faintly in the breeze that filtered through the slats in the high stone.

She released her tension in a long, soft breath through her teeth. *The saviors will protect me,* she told herself. Almost believed it.

Despite her exhaustion, she threw herself into the devotions. Prayed with the venerated, prayed more fervently than she ever had before. She threw her fear against the refrains and affirmations, a pleading, a bargain. *Let the five protect us from the Taint. Let the righteous bear witness to the sacrifice, and let the suffering renew our world.* She prayed silently to be saved from the Taint, for the purity of her soul, for the honor of her family. She embraced her neighbors and offered blessings with a fixed, frantic smile, even as a small part of her mind asked, *Would you turn me over if you knew?*

The press of bodies, the fervor of her prayers, the heat of summer pounding on the stone walls, that was what caused her perspiration. Not the fever. Not the Words. When the breeze filtered down from the dome and licked across her brow, she imagined it was one of the five saviors looking upon her with pity and compassion. Tried to push away the images of a possessive god caressing her head, claiming her.

THEY BROKE AT MIDDAY, when the altar was fully shadowed by the dome, and filed out of the temple. She swayed on her feet, but her mother's grip kept her upright, steered her through the crowd as they socialized and traded news with the neighbors. Arten knew that the pretense of enjoying the exchange mattered. So, while her mother pretended to care about their neighbors, Arten pretended to be well and meek and uninteresting. Her head ached from the sun. Her stomach began to cramp with fear again now that they were outside the safety of the temple walls. She did her best not to look towards the small outbuildings, to pay attention to her mother and be dutiful. But she could feel them, wrenching at the periphery of her vision, tugging at her thoughts, lancing spears of cold dread down her spine despite the heat.

At long last, they were called to confession. Arten waited

at the foot of the altar, eyes fixated on the relics of the five saviors that hung high above, while her mother was closeted with Venerated Vachel. She normally would have crept to the wall behind the pillar and pressed her ear to that one stone near the floor, where the mortar had been chipped out by some enterprising person, long before she discovered it, in order to overhear what her mother was saying about her. It was better to confess things the venerated already knew. To surprise him with sins he was not prepared for was never pleasant. He'd only struck her once, but his words were worse than any blow. Today, though, she knelt at the altar and cast her prayers to the five saviors. Prayed that she was wrong.

The richly carved wooden door opened, her mother emerged, head bowed piously, and perched on a bench to reflect as Arten was called back.

"Blessings, child," Venerated Vachel smiled as he welcomed Arten into the small confessional room, the picture of serenity. The door snicked closed behind her.

"Thank you, Venerated," she replied, as was expected, "and upon you." Her back was already slimy with sweat.

"Something weighs heavily upon you, does it not?" he pried gently as he settled into the more comfortable of the two chairs in the room. Arten seated herself after, perching on the very edge of the finely-crafted chair.

"What do you mean?" she said, glad he couldn't know the pounding of her heart at his words. She couldn't exactly lie. He had a knack for sniffing out lies.

"I understand you have been ill with a fever."

Does he...? Her blood roared in her ears, and she almost missed what he said next, had to replay the sounds as he looked at her expectantly.

"These trials are reminders of how closely demons

dwell, and help strengthen us against their attacks," he had said.

"Yes, Venerated," she said, showing him the same false piety her mother so recently paraded, even as the word *demon* pealed through her as strongly as the temple bells, and something deep in her writhed in response.

"It is especially important, during these times of trial, to take council from those who offer it, as I am about to."

"Yes, Venerated."

"With your father and brother away, your mother must bear the burden of your illness alone. It is a difficult time for you both. You must help her as much as you can. Since Deric cannot be here, you must recover quickly and do your best to fill your brother's role." He must have misinterpreted Arten's frown, because his tone sharpened, "Selfishness and sloth invite the demons in. You must be compassionate for your mother's trials, as she is with yours, though you do not deserve it. You must not be mean-spirited, but generous in offering yourself to her service..."

Arten kept her face neutral, her answers obliging, as he continued on in that vein for some time. She felt the familiar weight of guilt at the reminder that she was undeserving of her mother's care. The venerated knew her secret, knew the curse she brought to her family. He reminded her constantly. As though she could ever forget.

When he felt she had been sufficiently warned against the evil of which her heart, thoughts, and actions were capable, and the dire consequences of anything but absolute submission to her mother, he rose. Her stomach jumped as he spoke a blessing over her, a spasm of relief.

There had been no mention of Taint. She practically floated out of the room. The only narrowed, suspicious eyes were her mother's. Arten quickly blanked her face. Happiness was not permitted to her. They marched home, her mother once again dragging her by the arm as the heat and the day's emotions turned her legs gelatinous. Even the pain from that grip was muted by the gentle buzz of secret relief zapping through Arten.

She didn't tell him, she thought, staring through the road dust unseeing. *Does that mean she doesn't think I'm Tainted? Does that mean she's protecting me?* Something visceral and wrong clanged through her at the thought. *No, I'm unworthy of her protection. Either she doesn't know, or she's waiting for proof. Perhaps she's waiting for Father's advice. Father will know what to do.* That was a comforting thought. She clung to it for the rest of the trudge home, curled up around it on her pallet. She just had to make it another few weeks until he returned, then he would tell her she was being silly, that she wasn't Tainted. She wouldn't burn.

I just have to make sure I show everyone how normal I am until the next Decaday, she thought just before sleep crashed around her. Three weeks that may as well be an eternity.

THE NEXT DAY, whether from her natural toughness or her desperate prayers throughout the night, she was strong enough to ease her way down the stairs to the shop. Three days of expense on her behalf. Something in her stomach writhed at the thought. Fortunately, there had been no dreams. She had been terrified that her weakened state would prevent her from fighting the pull of the Words. But they had not come. A mercy from the saviors, or a sign that the Taint was a figment of her mind?

She sat on the tall stool behind the long counter inlaid with broad panels of clear glass, an extravagance and evidence of the superiority of her father's shop. Mikneilson's counter was half as long and was made only of wood (that was infrequently polished). She rested her cheek and fore-arms on the glass, moving by inches to find cooler spots on the smooth panes. She was sweltering in the heat, longed to be outside where at least the breeze could reach her.

Her mother had specifically forbade her to leave the shop for any reason until she returned. Arten had not thought to bring in enough water to even use that to cool herself. Why was it so hot this early in the season?

She thought of her father. He would still be on the road, wouldn't reach Laird until tomorrow or the day after. She imagined him, sitting in the driver's seat, head shaded with his battered summer hat. It was midday, and he would be stopping soon to give the horses a rest, to catch a quick nap in the grass under the wagon.

Deric was probably already napping in the bed. He would spend the break drawing the horses or some of the local birds or an interesting cloud. She felt a stab of jealousy. *She* would have been pestering her father with questions every waking moment, because he knew everything. Not wasting the time sleeping. Or she'd have been sitting in the back, snuggled against aromatic grain sacks, listening to her father recount his merchanting adventures. And in the afternoon, she would have taken her turn at driving, feeling the dance of harness through the reins, attuned to the secret messages the horses sent each other and herself if she only listened properly. If only she were there.

You've always been jealous that Deric gets to mind the shop. Now that you've been given the opportunity, you're still jealous of him, she scowled at herself, the words echoing in her moth-er's tones. Her normal job, stocking the shelves and counting the inventory, was less glamorous than tending the customers, taking money, giving change, measuring goods by weight, length, and count. She should be excited that she was going to be able to do these things to her heart's content for the next three weeks. But she hated he was taking her place at the fair. It was the one thing she looked forward to every year. The one time she could be unrepentant and feel joy.

Besides which, she justified her unhappiness further, *I still have to do my normal job. I'm doing twice the work, and he's having all the fun.* She ignored the logical retort that normally *he* would be stuck doing two jobs and, instead, focused on all she was missing. The merchant's fair where people from all around gathered to buy and sell their goods. Exotic spices from foreign lands, cattle and sheep and horses, soap and candles, fine porcelain dishes and dainty cups, beads and jewels, little mechanical gadgets she didn't understand, powders and potions, bolts of cloth both luxurious and plain. So many marvels, such interesting people.

The crowds, the bustle, the opulence of it—she loved everything about the fair. Learning to barter for the goods, to identify a good price, how to tell quality, when to demand proof of ownership. Sleeping in the wagon bed, under the stars or under the canvas awning while the patter of rain lulled her to sleep. The dusty drive out there, behind their unmatched team, jouncing on the driver's seat. The slow drive back, wheels groaning under the weight of their purchases.

A glitter of bells announced the arrival of a customer. Arten peeled herself off the glass, scrubbed at the marks of her face with the corner of her apron, and contrived to look alert as the woman rattled out her demands at an expectant clip.

The afternoon stretched on in fits and starts, and Arten

wilted. By the time her mother returned and closed the shop for the night, Arten was too miserable to want to do anything but shuck off her damp clothes and sleep. Even the thought of food was unpleasant.

"Arten, come in here," her mother called from the small office. Arten slithered off the stool and padded over to the doorway. Her mother sat at the narrow desk, pulling out the stiff-bound ledger books. The room looked so much bigger without her father in it. His head brushed the underside of the stairs when he sat at the desk, and he always looked like a foot crammed into last year's shoe. "Well," she snapped, eying Arten with an expectant frown, "bring the sales ledger!"

"I don't—what sales ledger?"

"What sales—don't tell me you didn't record your sales today..."

"I—I didn't know I was supposed to," Arten said in a small, faltering voice. She wanted to melt into the floor.

Her mother emitted a strangled noise that conveyed precisely her disappointment and irritation. "Well," she said, and Arten quavered inside at how calm she was trying to sound. "You must simply do a complete inventory tomorrow to find the items that were sold, and then contrive to remember to whom they were sold and the amounts of sale, which you will write down, so we can reconcile the accounts and tender tomorrow night." Under her breath, she added, "This is going to be a nightmare. Jahn will have something to answer for when he gets back." Arten pretended not to have heard, since the words were not for her ears, but it sparked something in her. Some ember of defiance, a coal of anger.

She held it close, the motion of her breath in her chest nurturing it into a lick of flame, a steady blaze. Later, it helped her find the energy to eat, the heat of her anger demanding sustenance, and when she lay in bed that night, she knew it was the writhing of her conviction in her chest, definitely not the Words. She would prove her mother wrong.

The next three weeks would be the easiest of her mother's life. And when her father returned, he would hear nothing but praises for how well Arten had done in his absence, how she'd done a better job than Deric, as though this weren't her first time tending the shop. And her father would nod silently, but his eyes would show the delight and pride he couldn't express. When she dreamed that night, it was about small moments of victory, where she impressed her mother with her business acumen, where she dazzled customers with her salesmanship, where Deric sulked at being outshone.

BY THE MORNING, the fire had banked into a controlled smolder in her gut. She knew she didn't have the skill to accomplish her goal on her own, but she knew someone who did. And it was partly her own pride, and partly the knowledge that her mother wouldn't approve of her being indebted to Leif that made her keep silent on the plan she'd made. She would need some help to get word to Leif, and she'd have to hope her mother didn't find out.

She forced herself to be patient and silent through breakfast, though the plan crackled inside her and jangled in her leg. She watched as her mother brought out the tender box, the sales ledger (which Arten noted with sharp eyes today), and opened the curtains. Watched as she unlocked the front door, set the shingle in the window.

Listened as she was admonished not to leave the shop for any reason, to remember to record the sales today, to do the inventory, to give correct change. Waited as her mother disappeared down the lane, towards the town. Until the underbrush at the far bend swallowed the last trailing glimpse of her skirt.

Then, only then, did she dare to act on her plan. She took down the shingle, threw the lock, and sprinted out the back door. She slipped through the split-rail fence, pounded across the open horse pasture, through the fence on the other side. She flew through the woods, woods that were more home to her than the rooms above the shop, trees and rocks greeted her, each old friends.

When she arrived at the neighbor's house, she was alarmingly winded. Her side burned and ached, and she hunched over the hand she pressed there, trying to find relief, as she waited for an answer to her urgent knock.

The young man who answered the door took her in with a glance and shouted over his shoulder, "Maruko, it's for you." He crossed his arms and leaned on the door frame, scowling at her. She thought he was trying to look imposing. *Mother has a thing or two to teach him.* "You look like dung," he said.

"At least that's new for me," she hissed back around her panting. "You've been smearing it on your face for years."

He fingered the patchy attempts at a beard and mustache he had been trying to cultivate since it first sprouted. She almost thought she saw a twitch of a smile at his mouth before his fingers covered it. She heard Maruko moving about upstairs, and the sweet, "Just a minute!" that floated down. She sank onto the flagstones and propped her back against the doorpost to wait and catch her breath, her feet splayed out in front of her.

"You shouldn't sit like that, it's not ladylike," he said.

"Well that explains you the past few years," she sniped. "Do you ride side-saddle, too?" He snorted, but then surprised her by sliding down the inside of the doorjamb. He stretched his newly-long legs out, one foot inside the house, the other heel shoved against her thigh. She tucked her leg up to her chest, moving it away from his foot, and ignored him.

Once, he had been everything to her. When she was six, their family had moved here from another town. He had been ten and seemed so smart—knew things even her father didn't know—and so sad. She'd been hiding in one of her secret places, avoiding Deric, when the new boy next door had crashed through the bushes and thrown himself down not two body-lengths away, and proceeded to cry quietly into his arms.

Maybe it was because she remembered the way Deric had cried after their sister... or maybe it was because he had been bullying her lately, or maybe it was because she saw someone else who was lonely. Whatever the reason, she decided right then that she and this boy were going to be friends. And they had been.

Maruko had tagged along, but it had always been the two of them, fast as glue. Until he turned fifteen and decided he was too grown up to hang around with little girls, and her world had broken. Maruko had actually punched him in the face when he said it, nearly broken his nose. It had been her and Maruko ever since.

"Heard you were sick," he said casually, interrupting her thoughts. He sounded almost like he cared, almost like he hadn't rejected her completely.

She didn't respond. He was just trying to bait her, to get her talking so he could mock her or make her angry.

He'd never forgiven her for laughing when Maruko knocked him on his ass. She remembered the expression on his face—shock, pain, dismay. Betrayal. *Well, he deserved it.*

"Heard you're running the shop while your dad's gone," he tried again. Again, she didn't respond.

"Hey," in a new tone, "are you actually marrying Leif?"

"What?" She jerked her head around to look at him. He looked concerned, intense. Not the aloof, laughing superiority he wore so casually these days. "What are you talking about?" she sputtered.

"Is it true?" he pressed, leaning forwards, fists balled before him.

"No! Why would you think that?" In her alarm, she forgot her resolve not to engage with him.

"I heard—" he started, but his eyes darted to the stairs, where Maruko was descending. His eyes flicked back to Arten, and then her friend was gone and the man was back. He stood, turned his back to her. Her gut wrenched unexpectedly.

"Get lost, Juro," Maruko said, sweeping past him.

"As you command, little sister," he said with a mocking bow as she passed. As soon as Maruko cleared the threshold, he shut the door in their faces.

Arten swore at him, heard his muffled laugh through the door.

"I hope Jerko didn't bother you," Maruko said.

"He's been worse."

"Doubtful." Maruko sniffed and Arten huffed a laugh. "So, what brings you here at the demon-sworn dawn? I take it something important."

Arten had been distracted by Juro's question, but she shook it off and made her request. "I need you to write a note to Leif Mikneilson for me and take it to him this morning."

"Is that all?" Maruko snorted. "Very well. I expect you will tell me why this is so important."

"Later," Arten promised, anxiety growing in her to be back. What if her mother had forgotten something and turned around? What if a customer came and the shop wasn't open and word got back?

"What is your message?" Maruko asked with long-suffering patience. When Arten had relayed it, she sighed and rolled her eyes, but turned back to the house. "I'll write it while Juro gets the horse ready. He'll take it over after he drops you back home. Don't even try to protest. You look terrible, and I'm not letting you traipse back through the woods in that state. Just wait here."

Maruko went inside, barked some orders at Juro, who came out, stalked stiff-legged past her to the barn. Arten leaned against the house, silently grateful for Maruko's offer. She had been avoiding thinking about how tired she was, what the sprint here had taken out of her.

The day stretched in front of her, already too short to contain all she would need to do. Standing in the soft shadows of post-dawn, in the breeze that still remembered night, it was difficult to feel the urgency and conviction that had driven her here. Too soon, Maruko emerged with a folded scrap of paper and called harassments to Juro to expedite their departure. They bickered when he brought the horse out with no saddle, only a bridle and saddle pad.

"It's fine," Arten interrupted, "Let's just go," she said to Juro. He smirked at her, then mounted up with agility that shouldn't have surprised her, took the note from Maruko, then offered her a hand up. She put her foot on his boot, grabbed his hand, and he hauled her up behind him.

"Let's see if you can still ride, little sister. Hang on!" He laughed over his shoulder and leaned forwards.

"I'm not your sis—" she snapped but clenched her teeth around the rest as the horse lurched below her, jumping into motion, far too fast on cold muscles. She heard Maruko cursing him for ruining the horse as they disappeared not onto the lane, but into the woods. He merely laughed, loudly enough for his sister to hear. Arten clutched fistfuls of his shirt in her hands, focused on staying balanced.

Once they were out of sight, Maruko's curses still ringing through the woods at them, Juro slowed the horse to a walk with a pat and an apology to him. The sounds of the woods and the wet snorting of horsey breath filled the silence between them. Arten wanted to ask him about Leif, what he might have heard and where. She was steeling herself, building up her courage, but he spoke first.

"You can see I don't ride side-saddle," he said. She would have expected disdain or smugness in his voice, not the questioning tone she heard.

"Neither do I," she said, not really knowing why. Not knowing what assurance he was looking for.

"Jerko?" he asked.

"I'm surprised this is the first time you've heard that," she said, more harshly than she intended.

"How long?"

"Since you turned into a giant ass." He didn't say anything to that, and when it was apparent he wasn't going to, she fidgeted and blurted before she lost the nerve, "What did you mean about Leif?"

"Hmm? Oh," he muttered distractedly. "Is it true, then?"

"No. Why would you think it?"

"Just—Forget I mentioned it, okay?"

"No. Tell me," she pressed.

"I'm not—" he began, but she cut him off angrily.

"This is my life, Juro! Tell me what you know!"

His shoulders drooped, and she tried to peer over them, to see his face, but he'd grown too tall. "A couple weeks ago, when your parents came over for dinner. They talked. I'm... Well, I'm old enough now that they didn't send me away after dinner. Your mom mentioned that this fall you'll be eligible to receive offers. She wanted to know if I knew anyone who would...be interested. But then your dad said he wouldn't stand to set you up with just anyone, and that Leif was the only one he would consider. It sounded like he wanted to unite the families, form a merchant empire, or something. He talked about it like it was...settled."

Her stomach clenched. It was hard to breathe. She'd known it was coming, she'd always known. The day when she would be sold to a marriage. She hadn't forgotten how old she was, hadn't forgotten it was almost here. But knowing her parents were actively planning for it, knowing she was being excluded from conversations about her fate... Somehow, she had expected more time, had expected no one would want her, useless as she was, and that would keep her safe.

A hand closed over her own. "Arten," Juro said softly, "that hurts." She looked down, saw her fingers clawed into his sides, jerked her hands away.

"Sorry," she muttered, wrapping her arms around herself. "What did you say, when she asked?"

"I didn't say anything. I was too angry."

"Why?"

"Because my best friend's parents were sitting there talking about selling her like—like a horse!" He growled, his body rigid. "Saying things like, 'She needs a strong husband to tame her,' and, 'The sooner she has children the better.' It was disgusting!" he snarled.

She was shaking. Didn't know why. The only thing she could think was, "I'm not your best friend."

"Yes, you are," he snorted, shaking his head, then continued more softly, "You always have been. I've just been stupid these past few years."

"You're still stupid," she said, but she didn't mean it.

"Yeah," he agreed quietly. "Here, we're about to go up the hill. Give me your hand." He reached back and, one at a time, drew her hands forwards, clasped them around his middle. "Hold on," he said, closing his hand around her own fisted ones, his forearm tight against hers.

"I know how to ride," she groused.

"I know," he said but didn't release her hands. The hill was steep, and she needed the anchor he provided. Once they leveled out, though, she didn't try to pull away. She left her cheek resting against his back, remembering how easy things used to be between them.

"Do you think I need to be tamed?" she asked.

His hand spasmed over hers. "I think," he ground out, "if anyone tries to *tame* you, I will thrash him. Or better yet, I'll set Maruko loose and let *her* thrash him." It startled a weak laugh out of her. His thumb brushed over hers as he squeezed her arm against him. "Arten," he said, gravely, "*can* we be friends again?"

She thought about it. Considered all that had come between them, considered how altered he had been since they entered the woods. "Can you be friends with a little girl?" she voiced the old hurt, the one that still wounded her, the only thing that mattered.

He tensed, and she thought he sounded guilty as he

responded, "I can be friends with *you*. You're not a little girl. Not anymore. Maybe you never were."

Something in his words struck her, and she felt a moment of dread, "Are you going to offer for me?"

"No," he said, and a tension she didn't know she'd been carrying left her in a rush. "I will not marry anyone under twenty."

It was a strange conviction, and before she could stop herself, she asked "Why not?"

"Because," he said, and she could picture the grimness on his face, "anyone under twenty can still be sacrificed."

The world slowed. Her heart hammered.

Does he know? He can't know, we haven't talked in ages... What if Maruko told him? No, Maruko doesn't know either. Only the healer, only Mother...they're the only ones who have seen anything. So, what does he mean by saying that? The bitterness, the quiet anger... if it wasn't about her, then—?

But they had arrived, and he had slipped off the horse, was offering her a hand down. She accepted his help, his hug.

"See you soon," he promised as he remounted. "I'll drop by with his answer." Then he was off, and she put Juro, Leif, marriage, and the Taint from her mind as she squared her shoulders and entered the shop.

SEARCHING

STEKIN

Five days ago, he had awoken from his sleep, senses screaming at him. A flash, only a flash, had come from the northwest. Not a misfiring, not this time. It had been so much stronger than any time before. He had wasted not a moment in departing, collecting only what he could carry, only what he could access in the dead of night. The sacrifice was small. He had left behind only some clothing, little comforts for his daily existence like his paltry collection of books and his accrued yet unpaid wages. By now he was accustomed to uprooting his life in a moment, and regretted only that he had not been able to bid farewell to the very few people whose acquaintance he enjoyed.

He had stayed too long there, and had gotten comfortable, self-indulgent. Walking all day, scavenging for food and water, sleeping uncovered were hardships that now made his body protest. He would need to hunt soon or purchase some food. When he left, he had avoided the road, which swept southeast before it split and branched into something that would take him northwest. It was no fault of the road builders. The city was built along the bed of a long-dry canyon, and there was only one exit anyone would consider. The detour would have taken him days out of the way, so he opted instead to wing above the canyon walls and make his way directly northwest.

The arid grasslands he had crossed had been less hospitable than he anticipated. The days were hot, the nights frigid, the bounty of the land meager. He had started traveling at night, so the movement kept him warm, and sleeping during the day. Last night, he had crossed into rocky, rolling hill lands and though his nocturnal vision was superior, there was enough treacherous terrain to make it dangerous to continue until day. This morning, he had awoken damp, hungry, and sore.

Despite the inconveniences and irritations, there was no question in his mind of turning back or delaying. He had been chasing this for too long, and it had been so strong this time. He would find the source, he *must* find it. And before it was discovered.

Perhaps I should have kept wandering after the last glimmer turned out only to be that artefact, he thought, trudging up a particularly steep hill, thorny ground-cover tearing at the skin of his sandaled feet. Once he had disposed of the artefact, he had debated moving on but had decided to rest in the canyon city for a little while, to rejuvenate himself from the long search. That had been three years ago. When he was honest with himself, part of him had stayed from despair, and another part stayed because he was certain he would see no further activity for years to come.

Until five nights ago, the despairing part of him was certain the source had been found and eliminated. If the initial surge, which had drawn him from his distant home, had been due to power manifestation, as was his original theory, he had valid reason to despair, for it was nigh on impossible for the source to exist this long unnoticed. However, if his second theory was correct, power would not manifest for years yet. What, then, had caused the flash? It was the same energy, the absolute same, as the one that had drawn him to this part of the world nearly thirteen years ago. The same as the second flash, eight years ago.

I will find you, he promised the source. A diamond beast stirred inside him. Bound that promise to his soul.

3

AN OLD FRIEND AND AN IMPENDING OFFER

ARTEN

Despite her intentions, Arten barely made it through the day. A full inventory usually took her three days, and with customers and the general flagging of her energy, she had only made it a quarter of the way through the store by closing. She had wracked her brain, however, and thought she had a complete list of all items sold yesterday written down in the sales ledger alongside the items sold today. The moment her mother laid eyes on it, she knew her efforts had not been enough.

Her mother *tsk*-ed over the incomplete inventory; over her handwriting, which was proclaimed all but illegible; over her arithmetic, which was incorrect.

"Lady in green hat?" she snapped, "What am I supposed to do with this? Arten, you are utterly useless. How am I supposed to apply this to a customer's account if I don't know who that customer is?" All in all, the day ended up a disaster, and her mother was more justified in her disappointment than ever.

Arten curled around herself that night, on her pallet, her

confidence wavering. *Stop it*, she scolded herself. *Leif has agreed to come and teach you tomorrow. You're better off concentrating on what to ask him.* She tried to turn her thoughts in that direction, but they strayed. *I wonder if he's agreed to offer for me. If he's part of the scheme, or if it's all his parents' idea.* It would be laughable if it didn't terrify her so much. Leif was a few years older than her, old enough to know what he wanted, and for the past year he'd been completely smitten with Deric. *Being married to someone lusting after my brother would be awkward at best. If only Deric would notice him, maybe they could get married and save me the hassle.* But Deric was too thick and bitter to think about anything beyond getting out of this house and finding a patron in Denauth. *And Leif's family would never let him marry an artist, if they're anything like mine.*

She stilled as a cough from her mother's room reached her ears. When it was certain her mother wasn't getting up, she drifted back to her thoughts. *Maybe it will be better to marry Leif. He's safe. I know he doesn't want—that, with me. And as far as kids go, well, I don't need to figure out an excuse for that until I'm 16. That's ages away.* When she thought of confronting her parents with that future lie, though, it was Juro she pictured at her side, not Leif. Juro, who still wanted to be her friend. Who had called her his best friend. Juro, who wasn't going to turn weird and offer for her in the fall.

The world felt a little more right after this morning. Like a piece of herself she'd lost had been returned, and she hadn't realized how much she'd needed it. Would he stick by her, though, if he found out about the Words? She thought he would, because he'd said...

But between one thought and the next, sleep entered and wiped her clean.

Leif came by the next morning. Arten practically pounced on him, badgering him with questions.

"Demons!" he cried, holding his hands up desperately, "I can't teach you all that in one day! And I've only got about an hour before I need to get back." Something in her chest sank, and it must have showed on her face because he added quickly, "I'll tell you what I can in an hour, and I'll come by later, after dinner and we can plan the rest. How does that sound?"

"After dinner? Won't your parents object to you being out so late?"

"Well, uh..." he stammered, face flushing. He tugged at the collar of his tunic, eyes searching for anything to look at but her. "You see..."

"So, it's true," she said, the pit in her chest flopping a little. "Are you going through with it? The offer, I mean?"

"My parents expect me to," he said glumly.

"Do they know about Deric?" she asked.

"What? No!" he yelped, then looked at her, eyes wide and alarmed. "How do you...?" She just shrugged. It was obvious to anyone except, it seemed, their parents. "And, ah, what do you think about...?"

"I think it's not fair that we're being forced into this situation. You, at least, have some choice in the matter." By his face, though, she knew he didn't feel that way. "We'll worry about it later," she soothed. "It's months away. We'll figure something out."

"Yeah," he agreed flatly, but forced an upbeat tone as he changed the topic, "So what you need to know about credit accounts..." and launched into an explanation of how credit worked. She was soon engrossed in the conversation, which was much more interesting than marriage by any accounting.

Leif was a good teacher, she decided after he left. He'd had an answer for every question she'd had. He'd been kind and hadn't laughed at her or belittled her when she didn't know something. If anything, he'd been excited, happy to share his knowledge, like it was a rare treat to do so. He'd left her with a few little scripts—how to ask the customers for their account information, how to suggest they come back tomorrow if she couldn't determine the status of their account and needed to check with her mother—and some reminders of what they'd discussed.

Her mother spotted them on the counter that evening and snatched one up before Arten could stash them below.

"Who gave you this?" she demanded, preparing to be angry.

"Leif," Arten replied.

"Ah." The way her mother said it, the secret smile, hidden a fraction of a second too late... If Arten had had doubts about the proposed alliance with Leif before, they were completely dispelled now. "He has excellent penmanship. You should try harder, Arten, yours is atrocious."

Something surged inside her, and she pushed it down. "Yes, Mother."

"Bring the sales register, let's see how much you've mangled things today."

"Yes, Mother."

"Did you finish the inventory?"

"Not yet. I'm halfway through."

A huffed snort. Silence as her mother zipped through the sales ledger, made notes in the appropriate registers and on the customer cards. "Well done," she said quietly at the end. She didn't sound particularly happy about it.

When Leif arrived after supper, Arten grabbed his hand and hauled him outside before her mother could more than squawk an objection. She dragged him down into the woods, far enough away from the house that she knew her mother wouldn't be able to overhear them.

"Demons, slow down!" he hissed. "It's dark, I can't see where I'm going."

"It's okay, we can stop now." She sat on the ground, back leaned against a lichen-flecked rock, and tucked her knees up to her chin.

"What was that about?" he demanded, standing angry and stiff in front of her, fists on his hips.

"She—I don't think she liked that you taught me about credit accounts," Arten admitted, hating how shaky her voice sounded. "I don't want her to stop us."

"I offered to help you not break my neck for you," he said, still angry.

She apologized and said, "We can go back, if you want."

"No." He sighed and dropped down beside her. "*My* mother expects me to be wooing you. If she finds out from yours that I ran away five minutes in, we'll both be in trouble." He rubbed his forehead, like an ache was lodged there. "Ask me your questions."

Arten did, and he set about answering them. His voice was pleasant, easy to listen to, no longer prone to those unpredictable swings.

She awoke with a start, jerking upright from where she'd sagged against Leif's side. "Oh, sorry," she said thickly, then yawned.

"Didn't mean to startle you," he said quietly. "You must

have been exhausted, so I just let you sleep for a bit. But I should be getting back."

"Oh, yeah. Sorry," she said again.

He stood, rolling his shoulders. "Don't worry about it." He gave her a hand up, then brushed the dirt off his trousers. "I heard you've been sick," he said, offering her an excuse.

"Yeah." Her voice was still muzzy. They walked back in silence except for her pointing out places for him to watch his step or head. They parted at the door.

"I'll try and drop by tomorrow morning," he said. "Good-night, Arten."

"Thanks. And goodnight, Leif."

She staggered up the stairs, sat through her mother's censure, and didn't have to feign exhaustion to get out of the lecture that threatened to follow.

THE REST of the week passed quickly. Although Leif didn't come by again, he and Arten shared written correspondence, as couriered by Juro. Juro also wrote out Arten's half of the letters, much to her embarrassment. For some reason, it was acceptable to have Maruko write for her, but not her brother.

"Want me to read it to you?" Juro grinned and leaned over the counter on his elbows to peer at the note she was struggling to decipher.

Arten huffed an annoyance and jerked the paper out of his sight.

"So, is it a love note, or what?" he pressed.

"I don't know, I haven't gotten past the first line, with you interrupting me." She turned away and went back to reading the note. Even with Leif's fine handwriting, it was a laborious process for her. Arten hadn't had much use for reading, outside of labels on crates and products, which were mostly reminders of what she already knew. And her family was not so wealthy as Juro's to be able to afford books and paper for pleasure. The few books they had, aside from *The Wisdoms*, had to earn their keep. Her mother had taught her, as a child, to read, insisting that education separated them from the poor. But after Tizzy, Arten's education had abruptly ended.

"Hey!" she protested hotly as a hand reached over her shoulder and whisked the note away. Juro stepped out of her reach and took the contents in with a glance.

"Ah, it *is* a love note!" he proclaimed with a pained look. "Listen to this drivel..." he adopted a simpering, love-addled tone as he read, "My dearest Arten—"

"It does *not* say that! It just says Arten."

"My dearest Arten," he repeated more loudly, "you are *absolutely* right that keeping the registers is *vital*. I am *happy* to share with you what I know. I *look forward* to seeing you next Firstday, when I will have *a few moments* free. Yours eternally, Leif"

"You're absurd, Juro," Arten rolled her eyes.

Juro frowned and tossed the note on the counter. "Not very exciting for a love note." He sniffed.

"You wouldn't know a love note if it was stuck to your face," Arten laughed.

"Well! I'm certain I could do better than that," he scoffed.

She just shook her head, folded Leif's note and tucked it into her apron pocket, along with his others. None of them love notes.

"Do you want to send him a response?" Juro asked, straightening.

"No."

"Alright. Well, I need to be off." She felt a flash of disappointment. "There's been a ruckus of some sort at the farm, and it seems I'm needed to do some manly labor." Arten scoffed. He grinned. "I'll see you tomorrow, though. Maruko has even deigned to wake up early enough to walk to the temple with you and your mom. How's that for generosity, hey?"

"Walking two miles with a grouchy Maruko. Sounds like the perfect way to start the day," Arten muttered.

Juro grinned. "I will relay your excitement to her."

"Don't you dare!"

He smirked. "Only if you promise to come over in the afternoon. Your mom can't possibly object."

"Sure she can," Arten grumbled.

"Well, I'll just have to charm her then."

"Since when do you have charm?"

"I've always had charm, Arten. It is just that you have always been immune to it." He grinned at her. "Oh! I almost forgot. I have something for you." He pulled a book out of the pocket of his tunic and plunked it on the counter. "Maruko said you'd like it." His grin took a mischievous cast and he made a hasty exit while she puzzled over the title.

The Mummy's Embrace. What was a mummy, and what was an EM-brah-see? *Well, if Maruko thinks I should read it...* She opened it and began the torturous process of reading. It had been printed on a press, so the letters were clear and precise, but by the end of the day, she was still only a short way into the story.

Later, as she began closing up the shop, she was dismayed to see how shabby it looked. The floors and shelves were dusty, items were disorganized in their bins, erratic in their stacks. Bolts of cloth stuck out in their cubbyholes where she had not pushed them flush, drawers stood similarly cracked open. The glass of the counter was smudged and cloudy from sweaty hands and arms. She had been so focused on the inventory, learning how to interact with customers, keeping the sales log up to date, checking and double-checking that the credit accounts were in good standing, all the day-to-day things she'd never had to do before, that she had neglected the shop's basic upkeep. In the short time before her mother arrived, she tidied in a flurry. She was cleaning the glass on the counter when her mother entered.

"Good to see you finally putting some work into the place," her mother said as she took down the shingle and locked the front door. Arten stowed her cleaning supplies and grabbed the sales book. Trotted behind her mother as she swept into the office. Arten had already laid out the account books and canted the customer cards in their file drawer so they could be pulled quickly. She thought she'd gotten everything prepared correctly today. Yesterday, she'd forgotten to have the tender box pre-sorted by denomination, which had resulted in wasted time.

She couldn't wait until Leif explained to her what each of the registers was for, how they worked together. She only knew the pattern her mother followed and how to reduce the time she spent searching for things. Firstday, the day after tomorrow, that's when she would learn. If she survived the temple tomorrow.

The thought had sweat prickling on her back. She hadn't thought of the Taint in days. The Words had been silent, her dreams clear. What did that mean? Had she imagined them? No, the scar on her rug was real. She once again felt the roiling bubbles against her cheek as the Words evaporated the water from her basin. So where had they gone?

What if they're waiting, biding their time? She shivered, imagining them erupting tomorrow, in the middle of service, with half the village as witness. It took her a moment to realize her mother was staring at her expectantly, that she was blocking the doorway, and they were done.

She moved through the rest of the evening in a daze. Retired to her room early but was afraid to sleep. She was irrationally convinced the Words would try escape that night. She turned and rolled, stilling only as her mother went through to find her own bed, feigning the elusive sleep. The cicadas were too loud outside. Their singing grated on her, agitated through her, mocking and damning. At length, she decided she would be better off staying awake.

She slid open the door between her and Deric's rooms gently, then closed it again. She paused to ensure her mother had not been alerted by the sound. Did the same with the door to the common room. The moonlight streamed in strong and bright. Tomorrow night, it would be full. Her father's chair under the window beckoned her. She crept over and climbed into it. It smelled of him, made her long for his return. *Only two more weeks*, she comforted herself, curling into the cushions.

She pulled out the book, resting it atop her knees, and began to read. In the dark, with the cicadas and the tree frogs outside, and the occasional cloud throwing the room into shadow, the tale was much scarier than it had been in the shop this afternoon. When the wind gusted and the house creaked, she jumped and her heart raced. She pushed herself to read faster, anxious to know how the characters got out of danger.

She blamed the twisting in her gut on the story. *Definitely the story, not the Taint.*

She didn't finish by dawn and crept back to her bed exhausted and agitated, but also relieved that she'd made it through the night unscathed.

HALF AN HOUR LATER, she was stuffed into her Saviorsday dress, yawning and scrubbing at her face with her hands, the scent of dew and bark and wet hedges in her nostrils as she stood in the lane, waiting on her mother to finish locking up. Maruko and Juro rounded the bend and called out to her. Maruko looked about as tired as Arten felt and blinked to keep her eyes open.

"`Morning," Arten greeted. Her mother's thin-heeled boots crunched on the gravel of their drive, announcing her arrival.

"Shall we all walk together, then?" Juro said smoothly.

"A splendid idea," her mother replied, smiling. She could be charming when it suited her. For people outside the family. Maruko had always thought Arten exaggerated when she relayed some of the things her mother did. Arten wondered if Juro had believed her.

They walked four abreast, Maruko leaning heavily on Juro and Arten's arms. Maruko was yawning almost as often as Arten did. Arten was glad to have Juro there, since it kept her mother's attention fixed on someone other than her. Arten only distantly followed their polite conversation about Juro's father's latest letter and its descriptions of the faraway places he was visiting.

"I can't believe Juro talked me into this," Maruko groused.

"What?" Arten said through a yawn.

"Walking to temple. What was I thinking?" she groaned.

Arten blinked and shook her head. "I thought it was your idea to walk with us today?"

"How long have you known me?" Maruko snorted. "You may be like a sister to me, but I don't love you enough to give up an easy ride in favor of blisters."

Arten frowned, opened her mouth to ask why they were walking in then but was interrupted by Maruko answering some inquiry from Juro.

The walk, the bracing air, worked to enliven Arten, so as they approached the temple, she was more-or-less alert. Not alert enough to notice what caught her eye about the stone outbuildings. Not until she was sealed inside the temple, behind the great iron doors, seated between her mother and Maruko. Not until the priest had begun leading them in prayer, a prayer of Midsummer cleansing, an enjoinder to be grateful for those who sacrificed themselves on the pyres.

Only then did she recognize the difference she'd seen. The buildings had been cleared of vines. The underbrush was cut back. The iron gates were closed, the locks shining and new. Someone had prepared the cells.

Something stabbed hot talons into her gut, started scrabbling up, up. Her hand found Maruko's. She clung to it with desperate strength. Sweat beaded on her forehead, on her torso, gathered into thick droplets and rolled silently down. She dared not wipe it away, lest the motion draw someone's gaze. Her mother's. Venerated Vachel's.

She cast her eyes to the temple dome, seeking... What? A reminder of the comfort she'd always found inside these walls, the promise of safety the temple had always offered. She saw the relics, clinking in the breeze that could not reach her. Saw them for what they were. Not symbols of peace and safety.

Restraints.

Were the cells prepared for me? she wondered frantically. *Will they pull the relics down and bind me in front of everyone?* She was breathing in shallow, silent pants through her nose. Her chest tightened around the thing trying to escape. She dragged her gaze down, to the altar, to the venerated. Divided her will between keeping her expression neutral and pressing down against that force scraping under her ribs.

It only distantly registered when Venerated Vachel introduced the Dedicate Brecarian. Who would be staying amongst them until Midsummer and presiding over the services.

And only when her hand cramped and stung, much later, toward the end of the service, did she notice that Maruko had been gripping *her* hand just as hard.

ON THE WALK HOME, Maruko grasped her hand again, but gently. "Are you okay?" she whispered.

Arten managed to shake her head minutely. "Are you?" Arten whispered back, tried to still the trembling of her fingers.

Maruko gave her a small, tight smile. "No," she said, "but let's pretend otherwise, so my brother's plan doesn't go awry."

Before Arten could voice her question, Maruko turned away and jumped into the mincing discourse between Juro and Arten's mother. Arten listened as the brother and sister began steering the conversation, carefully guiding her mother into agreement, so subtly that her mother never seemed to suspect she was being maneuvered. In the end, it was as though her mother, not the Swain siblings, had conceived the idea that Arten should spend the rest of the day with them, and (it *would* be nice to have an evening to herself) would it be too great an imposition for her to stay the night?

So Arten did not turn into the semi-circle drive that arced around their store and home but continued down the lane to Maruko and Juro's house. The siblings kept up their calm, easy conversation, Arten scuffing along blankly beside them until the front door shut behind the three of them.

Then, as if shedding a larval skin, Maruko wilted, her knees going weak, hands trembling. Juro caught her before she sank to the floor, held her as she shook with silent tears. His eyes were dry, but there was a rage on his face Arten had never seen before. She looked away. The awkward, isolated feelings that rose in her were strong enough to drown out all others.

At length, Maruko said, her voice shockingly steady, "I'll be alright, Juro. I just...need to lie down." With an apology to Arten, Maruko disappeared up the stairs, the soft hiss of her bedroom door echoed down into the silent foyer.

"I'm going for a ride," Juro announced, his anger undimmed, stalking to the door. "You can come if you'd like."

"I don't want to intrude," Arten said in a small voice. *On whatever this is...*

He stopped himself, wiped a hand down his face. The motion seemed to drain him. When he looked at her again, there was only an old pain that stared out at her, a pain she'd rarely seen. "You won't. Come on, little sister." He extended a hand to her. When she accepted, he gave her the same pained smile Maruko had given earlier.

She helped him groom his horse in silence. Swung up behind him bareback. Stared at the crisp wrinkles across the back of his white shirt, where he'd creased it leaning back against the stone benches in the temple. They threaded through the woods. Everything inside her was still, waiting. Thinking. Remembering.

Remembering that it had been midsummer when he'd flung himself into her thicket, seeking the freedom to cry. Remembering that his father had always managed to be away at this time of year on business or holiday. Remembering those infrequent moments of small cruelty, like the one that had driven them apart, had always been near the longest day of the year.

Anyone under twenty can still burn, he'd said. *Someone he knew was sacrificed,* she realized. *A sister? Why has he never said? Neither of them have ever said...*

Understanding resonated through her. And fear. She wrapped her arms around him, banding them about his chest, her face pressed into the soft cotton along his spine. He stiffened, relaxed by degrees. A hand covered one of hers. She hoped he would mistake her tears for sweat. Tears that were as much for herself as him.

Will my family be this stricken when I burn?

No, she knew they wouldn't. *After Tizzy...* She couldn't finish the thought. *They'll be relieved.*

"Ready?" Juro asked grimly. She raised her head, saw that they had reached the Falson's meadow. Long and narrow, perfect for footraces and a brief gallop.

She adjusted her grip and seat. "Ready," she said. They ran. When he turned the gelding in an abrupt about-face, she lost her seat, hadn't regained it by the second turn, and slid off onto the hard-packed ground. She'd fallen clear, and it hadn't been a long fall with as deeply dug-in as the horse had been. Still, it smarted. Juro pulled up, was circling back to her. She waved him on and set about rubbing feeling back into her hip while he made a few more circuits. When the horse's neck was flecked with foam, the pair slowed and transitioned into the fluid dances that only well-bred horses could manage, and only the moderately wealthy could afford to spend time learning. Even though it was a reminder that she would never attain that skill or be his social equal, she couldn't help but smile as she watched.

If I didn't know better, she thought, as he coaxed the gelding into some leaping moves she'd never seen before, *I'd think he's showing off.*

When they side-stepped up to her, the horse was well-lathered, his nostrils limned with red, his eyes bright and alert. Juro looked much the same. He jumped down and started walking to cool the horse down. She fell in beside him.

"He moves like a dream," she said. He looked pleased, gave his mount a solid pat on the neck.

"Sorry for dumping you."

"My own fault. You needed it more than me."

"Yeah," he agreed, the light on his face dimming. Before she could mentally kick herself, he said, "I could use a swim."

"You do smell."

He grinned at her.

They made their way through the woods to the creek. It was shallow and rocky in most places, but there was a sharp bend where a deeper hole had been scooped away out of the sandy bed, perfect for swimming. Arten stretched out on one of the sun-warmed rocks while Juro swam. Once, she would have stripped down and jumped in with him, but they were both too old for that now. She kept her eyes averted, listened to his splashing, to the trickle of the creek over the rock and whisper of a breeze through tree leaves. Her eyelids drooped, closed. She slept.

Her dreams came fast and deep. She was uncoiling, unfurling, stretching out from the cramped, dark place where she'd been waiting. It felt so good to expand, to relax into space that was large enough to contain her with no corners, no walls, no frailty. She tasted the wind, scenting the heat of the sun, the memory of snow burned away. She expanded, filled her lungs with it, tight as a drum. Imbued her own scent into it. Opened her jaws to release it back to the skies...

Woke with a start.

Juro's hand was on her shoulder. He had been shaking her. "It's getting late," he apologized, "and I need to make sure Maruko's okay."

She pushed herself up, rubbing her eyes. "How long was I asleep?"

"Not too long," he said, pulling her to her feet. "You can nap on the way back if you want."

"No," she said, too quickly, hugging her suddenly-chilled arms, "I'll be fine."

"Either way." He shrugged and boosted her onto the horse's back, then jumped up behind her. "Maruko would kill me if I let you fall twice," he said, reaching around her to take up the reins. He was warm and solid at her back, and before she knew it she was dozing. Dreamless.

THAT AFTERNOON, everyone was subdued. Only after supper did they each start to shake off their individual dark thoughts. They played cards, which might have been boring had they not swapped pennies for embarrassments. Upon winning a hand, the victor could make a demand of another player. Before it was over, Arten had made a whole host of animal noises, including running outside once to howl at the moon like a wolf, made various humorous contortions of her face and body, and had to read some poetry and awful passages aloud. The reading had been, by far, the most trying for her. Juro, she decided, could be particularly evil at times.

When they retired for the evening, Arten remembered the book and tried to return it to Maruko.

"I wouldn't give you such trash to read!" Maruko snorted. "Why would you think that?"

"Juro said you thought I'd like it."

"Juro!" Maruko snapped. He had just whisked out of the room. Maruko's eyes narrowed, and she glanced sidelong at Arten. "What *did* you think of it?"

"It was frightening, with the mummies and tombs and spiders and things. But also confusing. They'd be fighting, then there was kissing and it didn't any make sense."

Maruko snorted again, this time to swallow a laugh, and she pronounced some words that Arten had misread or not known, and the confusion was quickly cleared up. Arten found herself suddenly hot and uncomfortable.

"Why...would he...?" she fumbled.

"Why does Jerko do anything? He's probably outside pissing himself laughing, thinking he's so funny." Maruko was scowling. "Best thing to do, Arten, is not give him the satisfaction."

When he came back in, Maruko was primly waxing on the literary merits of the novel while Arten nodded gravely and tried to keep a straight face. The second his back turned, though, the well-aimed book crashed into his head from Maruko's expert arm. That set them off bantering with each other and all seemed right between the three of them again. By the time Arten was sprawled out on the low bed in their guest bedroom, the breeze tickling over her from the open window, cool and butterfly-bush scented, the terror of the previous night seemed a distant memory.

THE SHARP HISS of her name woke her. She thrashed awake, confused, tangled in soft sheets on a too-large bed, and the moonlight bathed a room where the proportions were all wrong.

"Shh!" the hiss came again. "It's just me."

"Juro?" she said, her voice thick and her mouth dry. She was clammy with sweat. Had she been dreaming? She struggled to free herself from the confines of the sheet.

"Yeah. Be quiet," he warned, "or you'll wake her up."

"What?" she asked, pushing herself upright and taking steadying breaths. *I didn't dream*, she told herself. *There was no danger.*

"Here," he whispered, thrusting a bundle at her chest, "put these on."

"But what—?"

"Shh!" he hissed, then made a motion for her to hurry up, let himself out of the room, and closed the door silently behind him.

She shrugged into the cast-off clothing he'd thrust upon her, stuffed her feet into her boots and, rubbing her eyes clear of grit, went out into the hall after him. He held his finger to his lips, beckoned her to follow. She crept close on his heels down the hall, down the stairs, through the kitchen, and out the back door. Once outside, she demanded, quietly, to know what was going on.

"I want to show you something," he said but would offer no further details other than that it was in the woods.

"I'm tired, I don't want to go traipsing around the woods in the middle of the night," she grumbled.

"I'll carry you on my back," he offered.

"I don't need you to carry me," she snapped, keeping her voice low, but she relented. "Fine, lead the way."

He led her deep into the woods, to a different meadow, this one surrounding a small pool, bisected by a shallow stream. He boosted her up into a tree and climbed up after. She sat, straddling a sturdy branch, back against the trunk, while he sat on a lower branch. She kicked his shoulder and glared at him. He made a gesture imploring patience. She sighed through her nose and leaned back to wait.

Knuckles tapping her calf startled her from her doze back to alertness. She followed the line of his arm to its terminus. To the mother deer, her muzzle extended out of the underbrush, her perked ears swiveling, her legs emerging in elegant steps. To the two shapes that followed her to the pool. Twin fawns. Albino fawns.

The full moon caught in their coats and they shone. Arten hardly dared to breathe. The tree frogs and night birds sang, it seemed, just for them. Her heart filled and broke to see the small family drink from the pond, to see the twins frolic around one another in the thigh-high grass. Innocent of the turmoil their existence was causing in the girl who beheld them. A noise turned all three into statues, ears scanning. They moved on, swallowed by the shadows of the trees.

Juro's tapping caught her attention again, and she followed as he descended to the ground. The noise of their descent, of their crossing into the meadow, sounded ominous in her ears. The woods near them had quieted as they trespassed into the clearing. Juro stopped, staring down at a few glinting hairs shed by one of the fawns in their play. He bent, collected them into his handkerchief, folded them reverently away.

He stood and his voice was ancient as he said, "I'm glad they came tonight."

"Are you going to hunt them?" she asked, dreading the answer.

He was silent a long time, looking at the square of cotton in his hands. Then he tucked it deep into a pocket and said, "No."

"They're twins," she protested dully.

"Do you actually believe that?" he turned on her, his face cold and remote in the bright moonlight. "That it's better to have half a soul in one body than a whole soul split between two? Who are you, who am I, to decide what is best for this pair? To decide which one dies, and which one must exist knowing that half of their soul is gone forever."

"It must be done," she said, saw him go rigid with anger.

"Why?" he snarled, "Because the temple tells us so? Because the saviors have decreed it? To protect us from demons?" he sneered.

"Yes."

"And what is a demon, hmm? Anything the venerated decide is threatening to them! Have you ever known anyone to be possessed by a demon? To become the embodiment of evil, to sow corruption and destruction in their wake, to undermine the foundations of society?"

"No," she admitted, and he plowed on before she could say more.

"That's because it doesn't happen! The venerated, the dedicates, frighten us with demons, threaten us with exposure, to keep us in line. To keep us trusting them. Our land is governed by fear, our rulers twisted by hatred and self-deception."

"Just because we haven't seen a demon doesn't mean they don't exist," she said, trying to sort through the confusing flurry of his words. "So, for all you know, that's evidence that the temple is doing a great job."

"I have seen a demon," he said softly, almost to himself. He turned his face to the moon, angling away from her.

"Not the fawns," she said dismissively.

"No," he agreed. She wanted to challenge him, but something in his stance, in his face, stilled her tongue, stilled the churning deep inside her that had not quite calmed since seeing the temple cells prepared. For a flash, she imagined she was one of the albino fawns, shining and exposed, frozen and tensed, alerted to Juro, waiting for him to reveal himself as friend or foe.

"This year," he said mildly, still looking at the moon, "is the tenth anniversary of my mom's death." His eyes moved to hers. She couldn't look away, couldn't move. "You've never asked why I was crying when you found me in the woods that day." He smiled, mocking and sad. "I've always wanted you to."

"Why were you?"

"My dad had just told Maruko and I that we were forbidden to speak about our mom. That as far as this village would know, his new wife was our natural parent. You see," he looked back at the moon, and Arten felt a small, shameful, instinctual relaxing in her muscles, "Maruko and I had been setting up our family shrine, gathering fresh flowers for it, to honor the memory of her." He continued on, face glazed with memory, "Dad moved the shrine after that, hid it away in his bedroom. He didn't want people asking questions about us, about where we'd come from.

Much farther than anyone suspects. The stigma around my mom's death was difficult to flee."

"What was she like?" Arten dared to ask when he fell silent.

"She was a wonderful person. What I most remember is how brightly she sang. How her singing filled me up, deep inside, with contentment, no matter how terrible I felt before.

"And she was strong. My dad offered for her the day she was eligible. His family was wealthy, and even though he was nearly twice her age, he was entranced by her spirit, certain she would produce him lively heirs. I think it surprised him when he found himself in love with her. He'd gotten her with child early into their marriage, but she was still too young to have them easily. I was not easy for her to bear nor to raise, considering she was still nearly a child herself. But Dad did care, by that point, and they only had Maruko when she was ready for another." He fell silent, his fingers twitching agitatedly at his sides.

"What happened?" she asked.

His head snapped to her, like he'd forgotten she was there. "You haven't put it together?" She shook her head. "And here Maruko was worried we'd given ourselves away today." His smile was mirthless. He reached out and squeezed her hand, softening the sting of his words. "I brought you here tonight to tell you. I guess I should do it properly," he said.

"You don't have to," she offered.

"I want to," he said. His fingers touched her cheek, soft and light, and something equally soft passed across his face, something she couldn't identify. *Pity?* He led her to a little knoll, far enough from the stream that the biter flies wouldn't bother them. Then he stamped down the high grass so they could sprawl out on their backs, hands behind their heads as they looked up at the faint stars and dazzling moon. His elbow knocked against hers.

"Maruko," he began, "didn't want me to tell you this." She remembered hearing the hissed exchange in Juro's room through her adjacent wall. It had been too quiet to make out. "She's still afraid. Of our dad, of what people will think if they find out. But I know we can trust you. I've always trusted you."

"I won't tell anyone," she promised.

"I know," he said, then told his mother's story.

She had been married at thirteen, a mother at sixteen. A mother again at twenty. Toward the end of her last pregnancy, she'd begun having chills. The healers had been concerned, but when Maruko was born, healthy and whole, everyone dismissed it as a strange humor of pregnancy. It was easy to do, since the first one had been so rough on her.

He'd been told later that there had been a progression of symptoms: she'd begun to have nightmares, she'd spilled scalding water on her hand once and not been burned, she could never quite get warm over the winter, the herbs she'd clipped early in the spring had died from frost while everything else bloomed. But he only remembered the one time.

He woke in the night, during the first hot days of summer, chilled. Confused, he went to his parents' room. There was frost crackling out from under their door and filming the metal latch. He slid the door open, saw the frost thick upon the bedroom floor, climbing up the walls in fracturing bursts, the bed was steaming with cold. He went to wake his dad, but the man wouldn't rouse. Then he went to his mom. Her skin was warm, she was smiling and more serene than he'd ever seen her. He didn't want to wake her, but his feet were cold and the ice had moved up to the ceiling, so he shook her.

As soon as she opened her eyes, the ice stopped its progression and started melting. The air became balmy again. Then his dad woke, took in the damp state of the room, and both his parents sent him back to his room. He would have thought it was a dream, except a few weeks later, a man came, and young Juro overheard the offer to get his mom to safety. When he asked why she wasn't safe, she didn't answer, except to say she wasn't leaving him or his sister. It wasn't until two years later that his question was answered. When the dedicate came and took her away. When she was pronounced as Tainted. When they jailed her and paraded her at temple services to decry her as demon-possessed to the town. When they drugged her and chained her to a metal stake and burned her at the Midsummer mass, to burn away the demon and ascend her soul.

"I remember her screaming," he said, his voice thick. "The way her voice broke before the end. Her beautiful voice that had brought only comfort and peace. And the smell..." He took a few deep breaths. "But the worst was afterward, when the venerated and the dedicate told us how fortunate she was, how lucky," the word was bitter and hard, "that she was blessed with ascension." His tone was dark as he said, "I wanted to believe it, too. Wanted to believe she hadn't been tormented and killed for nothing. I tried for years. But I don't.

"She told me, just before they burned her, that she'd never been happier than since she'd become possessed, and that was why she deserved to burn. Said it felt like she'd been missing some piece of her all her life and finally found it, and if that piece was evil and she couldn't tell the difference, she needed to be taken from us for our own good. But whatever power lived in her, whatever it was that had come into her soul, it wasn't evil, it wasn't Tainted or dark. She burned because the temple was afraid of her power, nothing else."

As Arten listened, a force was growing in her, pushing against her ribs. Not the Words, but an urgent need to confide in Juro, to reveal her secret to him. She rolled onto her side to face him. But she wasn't brave enough to say the things screaming through her mind. He wasn't done, and his next words derailed her.

"So, when the venerated spoke today...of sacrifice and rejoicing. Celebrating the murder of people like my mom... It was a punch in the gut. Ten years, that's what's been sacrificed. The last ten years of our lives without her, and the next ten years. And yet we can say nothing, we can't even mourn her. Because if people knew, they'd shun us. Maruko would have no prospects, people would be leery of doing business with me. The offspring of a Tainted woman is as good as half-demon.

"We've...heard it all, seen it all. Lived and moved on. Put it behind us. Put her behind us." Anger and pain sparked in his voice. "A new mom, a new village, a new life. A new name." She saw a glisten of moisture trailing into the hair above his ear.

"I'm sorry, Juro," she said, then hesitated, "Is...is Juro your name?"

"Yeah," he said. She saw the muscles of his jaw clench. "But my family name isn't Swain." He looked over at her, his eyes dark but limned with silver. "If you want to know, I'll tell you." He shifted onto his side, mirroring her, their elbows pressed together.

"I want to know, if you want to tell me," she said.

He studied her, searching her face. She wondered what

he saw there. "Tsyaro," he finally said. "But my many-grand-father changed our name to Tsyaro from T'shya'onath." Her eyes went wide, and his acknowledging smile was bitter. "I see you recognize the name."

"Why...why are you telling me all this?" she asked, a quaver of fear in her voice. T'shya'onath, an ancient noble house that had been possessed by demons and extinguished by the saviors. A corrupted bloodline that had brought their land to ruin before the temple had taken it from them. Or so she'd been taught.

That smile acquired a glimmer of malice. "Do you think I'm a demon, Arten? That I've brought you here in order to consume your soul and usurp your body for my brethren?"

It was, in fact, what had flashed through her mind. But the wetness still glimmered on his temples, and she saw in the man before her the distraught boy she had befriended in the woods. The one who had cried over the memory of his mother, who had known her better than anyone and been known in return.

"No," she said honestly.

He loosed a shuddering breath, closed his eyes. She watched a tension drain from his shoulders. When he opened his eyes again, they swam with silver. "Good," he said.

"Why tell me, though? Isn't it risky to reveal your secrets?"

"Of course it is. But it's you, Arten. I've hated keeping this from you, all of it, for years. The deception became intolerable, and I drove you away to save myself the pain of it. That...was wrong of me," he admitted, "and I'm sorry." He reached out and smoothed her hair back, left his hand on her neck. "I wanted to tell you for so long... I need you to understand." She felt a flicker along her jaw, light enough to be the breeze.

"I understand."

"No, not that. Not my past." He frowned, searched for words. "When my mom... I was so lonely when you found me, Arten. You changed that, helped me in ways you will never know. I have always been grateful for your friendship, even when I threw it away. And I have always admired the fierceness of your spirit." She shifted, preparing to protest, to turn the conversation to lighter topics. It was his thumb that brushed her cheek and stilled her. "As much as I admire and care for you," he continued, pleadingly, "I need you to understand why I can't offer for you."

She felt her brows travel upwards. She didn't know what she'd expected him to say but that was certainly not it. "I never expected you to," she blurted, unthinking.

He stopped, stopped breathing. "Oh," was all he said. He drew his hand away. Somehow drew him*self* away, so that the space between them yawned emptily, though they had not moved apart.

She rushed to fill the void. "I do understand, though. You're...well, noble. And I'm nobody. And you're in hiding, so I suppose you don't want to be tied down in case you need to leave again."

"You sound like my dad." He sighed and shook his head. "That's not... It was so hard, losing my mom. I don't know if I could go through that again. That's why I won't marry anyone under twenty."

"What does being twenty have to do with it?" she asked.

"The power, the Taint, whatever you want to call it," he explained, "manifests in people around my age, usually. But it can start as young as sixteen and go as late as twenty. It doesn't," he swallowed again, "run in families, so Maruko and I are safe."

"As young as sixteen," she repeated to herself, a kernel of hope flickering in her. "But no younger?" she pressed him.

"Not that I've ever heard." Then, "Why?"

"I never knew that," she evaded.

He didn't say anything for a time, didn't look at her. "We should get back," he declared, rolling onto his back, then up to his feet in a smooth motion. He held out a hand to help her up, but she had already done the same. He turned, shoulders sloped, and took a step back the way they'd come.

"Wait," she said, stopping him with a hand on his arm. He waited, his back to her, while she reached for what it was she felt she needed to say. "I'm sorry. About your mother," she said. It wasn't the thing she wanted to say. "I'm glad you told me. Everything." That wasn't it, either.

"Thank you," he said. They walked back to his home in silence, accompanied by the sound of their feet on old leaves and shoulders against fresh ones.

Why tell me you won't offer for me, why do I need to understand that? she thought at his blank back. *Are you saying you would offer for me if I were older? Would you wait for me, for seven years?* No, that was absurd. Seven years may as well be an eternity. *Why tell me you're descended from the remnants of the ruling families, before the saviors liberated the continent? Is that even true? Why would you lie to me?* And, most importantly, *how are things going to change between us? I just got you back. Why do I feel like you're about to leave again?*

The thoughts remained in her head, silent. At the door to the guest room, he stopped her, hugged her fiercely, kissed her temple, then disappeared into his own room. She lay in bed, puzzled, listening to him pace through the adjacent wall. There was a sharp creak, like he'd thrown himself onto the bed. Cursing. *He never curses by the demons, or pyres,* she recalled, nor did his sister.

Her last thought before she fell asleep was, *Is it possible that I'm safe until I'm sixteen?*

S HE GOT her answer four days later.

The week started well. Though Leif did not appear as promised, he kept up their correspondence, which Juro couriered for her. Juro had given her a new book on Firstday but hadn't apologized for the poor taste of the first one. This new book was an adventure story with no embracing, and Arten's reading was improving, which was, Juro had said snobbishly, the point. He also read out any words she didn't know, explaining them as needed. All in all, he was very accommodating. He acted as though their midnight conversation had never happened. And things settled into a new type of normal between them.

It took her three days to get the shop tidied to her satisfaction. She'd put Juro to work anytime he dropped in, but he didn't complain. By the end of the third day, everything was dust-free and in its proper place. To her eyes, the place looked better than it ever had under Deric's care. She let herself imagine his grudging approval. The grin fell from her face when she realized they would have arrived at the fair by now.

She stuck her head in the book that evening, read it to the end, then lay on her pallet, trying not to think about all the excitement she was missing out on. *Deric probably doesn't appreciate it*, she grumbled to herself. He was at that age where, in her vast experience, boys became moody and stupid. He was probably only interested in complaining and catching some shop-boy's eye. She didn't envy Leif his attraction.

Leif...why hasn't that demon-scat come back? she wondered, turning onto her other side with a grunt. *Is he regretting his decision to teach me things? Am I too demanding?* That didn't explain, though, why he hadn't come back after visiting her that first evening. If both their parents were set on their match, he should be coming over to *woo* her, if nothing else. He'd said as much before.

She resolved to get answers tomorrow, even if Juro had to pummel them out of him, and promptly fell asleep.

THE MORNING DRAGGED, even though there was a near-constant stream of customers. Juro came in mid-morning, responded to her glare with a smirk, and lounged against the counter, examining the items under the glass. When it was, at last, just the two of them, she stalked over and thrust a note at him.

"Good morning to you, too, Arten," he said dryly.

"Read it," she demanded.

He raised a brow, opened the note, "'Why haven't you come you promised.' Hmm, you've misspell—Ow!" He rubbed his arm where she'd hit him. "What was that for?"

"Don't leave until you have a proper answer." She scowled at him.

"And if he's not inclined to answer?" Juro tucked the note into his pocket.

"I don't know, you figure it out. Punch him, kiss him for all I care."

"As you wish, my lady," he said with dramatic formality, ending in a flourishing bow. She was reminded forcibly of who he really was. How arrogant of her to use him as her personal courier, to make demands of him. Her face heated. "And when I return," he called back over his shoulder, pausing in the doorway, "I hope you'll have figured out how to get that stick out of your ass." She was still sputtering as the door slid closed behind him.

The stick, however, was firmly wedged. She decided to grind her frustration out on her slate, copying lines out of the novel to practice stringing words together. Her writing was much improved at the individual letter level but the spacing between letters still made it all but illegible. The shop was stuffy and hot, and it was a mindless task. Her thoughts wandered. To Juro and Leif, to Deric and her father, to her mother and her uncharacteristic silence since Saviorsday, to the dedicate and the cleared-away cells.

The Words began to slither upwards. She froze, her thoughts usurped by terror. *Not now, not now!* As they scrabbled up her throat, she knew she couldn't stop them. They were on the back of her tongue, clawing forwards...

Panic tightened her chest. Some part of her screamed in the corner of her mind. There was a sharp sting on her cheek. She looked down, bewildered, at the hand that had slapped her. It stung with the impact as much as her face. Her breath was coming in short bursts, her thoughts careening in circles of fear, but the Words had retreated.

The bell rang, grating against her raw nerves. She started to her feet like she'd been burned and, repressing her shudders, rushed to greet the customer.

It wasn't a customer, just Juro. He gave her Leif's reply, but she didn't hear his banter. He was grinning, asking her what was wrong.

"Now's not a good time, Juro," she said, headed back behind the counter.

"Want me to read it to you?" he offered, following her.

"No. Please just go."

"Ah, I know. You don't want me to see the love notes you're writing!" He snatched her slate off the counter and held it up out of her reach. "Dearest Juro," he pretended to read, then said in mock surprise, "Why Arten, I had no..." He faltered. Confusion, then something more intense, passed over his face, wiping away the smiles. "...idea," he finished. "Arten," he continued in a rush, breathless and wide-eyed, "what is this?" He turned the slate to her, jabbed a finger at the symbols written at the end of the line she'd been copying.

Strange, fluid symbols she had never seen before. Symbols she had certainly written.

"It's nothing," she lied.

"Why did you make these symbols?" Juro demanded, advancing on her. He looked intense, his eyes wild.

"I," she faltered, falling back a step, mind working quickly, "There was a customer. A man," the lie tumbled out. "He had...a belt. With these symbols. And I...thought they were pretty"—that lie stuck a bit—"so he let me copy them down."

Juro's face paled, and she saw him draw back into himself. He set the slate on the counter. "Did you know the man?"

"No."

"Would you remember him if you saw him again?"

"Maybe."

"If you do, tell him to come see me, that we have a mutual interest. And, Arten, you must tell no one else. Get rid of those symbols. If anyone asks, the man doesn't exist."

Well, that's easy enough, considering he actually doesn't exist. "Okay, but why?" *You've seen them before, what do they mean? Why do they scare you so much?* She suspected she knew.

He was still staring at the slate, unable to look away. "I'll tell you later," he said absently.

"When?" she pressed.

He looked at her then. Considered. "Tonight," he said finally. "Meet me at the old-man tree, after your mom's gone to sleep." And left.

Somehow, she made it through the afternoon, through the evening with her mother, where they exchanged not a single word. No lectures, no disappointment, no nagging about forgotten chores or how she wasn't taking care of her appearance. The silence scared her more than the Words had. When she was certain her mother slept, she rose from her pallet and crept out of the house, down through the woods to the tree near the creek with a gnarled protrusion that looked like a sneering man with a bald pate. Juro sat amongst the roots, leaning back against the trunk. He looked up as she approached, didn't say anything.

She sat next to him, their shoulders and crossed-knees touching. Also said nothing.

"This was my mom's," he said, and she noticed the small book in his lap. He opened it, turned to a page as he said, "My dad doesn't know I saved it." He cleared his throat and continued, "This is closer to the end, when she couldn't tell the difference. We had to keep reminding her to stay hidden." He passed her the book.

The moon was waning, but still nearly full. Its light dappled the pages, and she couldn't quite make them out. She stood and found a shaft of light between the trees to illuminate the page. And froze. It was no wonder she hadn't been able to read it, the page was full of symbols, so much like the ones she'd written earlier, interspersed with actual words. She turned the page carefully, saw the mixing of symbol-words and normal-words continue. For pages. Her mouth was dry, heart hammering.

Juro appeared at her back, his hands closing on her shoulders. She jumped and yelped. He reached around her and took the book out of her trembling hands before she could drop or crush it.

"Sorry," she muttered.

"It's alright," he said but didn't put his hand back on her shoulder.

"What do they mean?" she asked.

"I don't know. The dedicate wanted to burn it, said it was full of demonic spells. I don't believe that, though. I think...I think she got confused and forgot what language to write in. Sometimes she would say words that didn't make sense, and when we didn't understand, she would close her eyes like she was concentrating and try again until it came out normally." He sounded old and tired. "When people noticed, we told them she had a brain fever. I...forget that part, sometimes. Today, those symbols on your slate...they're the same. That's why I need to talk to that man."

Her breath caught, she asked, "What would you say to him?"

"I would ask him who made his belt, nothing more. And then I would find the belt-maker, because that person or someone they care deeply about is drawing symbols that will draw the temple's gaze. Whoever is making these symbols is in real and immediate danger of discovery."

"So, you'll tell them to stop making the symbols?"

"No. I'll tell them to flee before their life is taken from them."

She shivered at his dire tone. "Where could they go?" she asked.

He looked at her, then away. "There are places, I'm sure, and people who would help them."

People like you? She didn't dare ask. Instead, she said, "If the temple is looking for them, is it realistic to think they could find somewhere outside its reach?"

"We must hope so," he said, "because without that hope...we consign them all to burn."

She shivered again. *'Whoever is making those symbols is in real and immediate danger,'* he had said. *Am I? This is the first time...he said his mother went years without discovery. But her family helped her hide it. My family, can I trust them with this?* No, she knew, deeply, instinctively. Her family would not help her hide.

I can't leave! she thought, desperately, her chest tightening, panic clawing at her.

Then Juro's arms were around her, pulling her close. "I'm sorry," she heard over the steady rhythm of his heart, "I didn't mean to overwhelm you. It's too much, I'm sorry." She leaned against him and, slowly, her paralysis seeped away. "If you," his voice faltered, "if you feel that you need to turn me over to the temple, I understand." She felt him swallow.

"No," she forced out. "I won't." Her hands were leaden, but she managed to hook them around his waist.

His arms tightened around her shoulders, he laid his cheek against her head. "Thank you," he whispered.

I am too young to be Tainted, she thought, *maybe that will be enough to hide me for a few years, buy me enough time to figure this out.* "I should get back," she said, straightening.

"Stay," he urged, not letting her go. "Come swim with me."

"Why?"

"Because it's a beautiful night. And because" he added unhappily, "soon enough, we won't have the option."

Because I'll be married. And I won't be able to sneak out of the house. And I won't be free to be friends with him. Her gut wrenched. "Okay," she agreed.

Afterward, he held her hand as he walked her home, even though they both knew the terrain, and kissed her cheek when they said goodnight. Her hand felt cold and empty as she lay on her pallet. She curled around it and cried silently.

4

A DELAY

STEKIN

He had been careless. The years in the canyon city had dulled him. They had ambushed him at the stream, these bandits. Three of them, two wielding longswords, the third a bow. The archer had him pinned down, or thought she did, while the other two rifled through his meager possessions. There was an appreciative whistle when they finished counting his coin. As there should have been.

"We're going to be relieving you of the burden of your gold, mister," one said. The leader? No, he looked to the other for approval.

"If you follow us," ah yes, that was the voice of a leader, "we'll kill you. Eventually. Joff here likes to play first." Joff, the gold-reliever, grinned, exposing his decrepit teeth.

"I do not wish to harm you," Stekin said. He was going to say more. But a flash of the power he had been chasing flared. He snapped alert, his eyes fixing on a distant point only he could see, his nostrils flaring as though he could scent it. Every particle of him focused on that vanishing point, every muscle, every sense attuned to it. It faded, was gone.

"That's funny, you harming us." Joff laughed, "Oh that's rich. I'll have to tell my kids that one."

"I am out of time," Stekin murmured to himself.

"I'm afraid you are," the leader agreed, his weapon drawn. "We were going to let you live, you know," he added, an insincere apology.

Stekin's eyes snapped to the man. He drew back his lips, revealing all of his considerable teeth. "I was about to say the same," he said. And lunged.

The bow string twanged, as he had known it would. He twisted in his flight to knock the arrow away. He had meant to catch it, but his reflexes were not what they should have been because of his inconsistent diet, and the arrow spun away. The archer was good, she had three more in her fist, had already fired the second, and he was in range of the leader's sword. It was cleaving upwards, to catch him and let the weight of his body help tear him apart. He batted the tip aside, rammed his other fist into the man's chest. It gave with a crunchy squelch. He grabbed the man's body as they both fell, putting it between him and the archer. The man was dead but still dying. His eyes widened as the arrow thudded into his back, then they lost focus.

Stekin did not want to give the archer time to thread two fresh arrows into her fist. He pushed the dead man away and coiled himself. Another arrow released as he jumped towards Joff, coming under the overhanded cut. The fletching of the arrow grazed his back. His fist sent Joff flying towards the archer, neck broken. He ran low, using Joff as a screen for the seconds it provided. The archer's eyes were wide with shock when she found him again. She released her last arrow, straight at him, it flew less than a palm's width before he snatched it out of the air. Two steps later, it was embedded in her eye. She had not tried to run.

"A shame," he said to her corpse. "You were too good for them." He closed her remaining eye and relieved her of her bow and quiver. It was a matter of minutes to find the leader's knife, to retrieve his own scant possessions. He took one of their packs, the least repugnant one, stuffed his coin and the dagger in the bottom, along with their reserve of dried meat save a portion which he chewed as he set out. It was old and hard, but his stomach worked around those small inconveniences.

He needed to hunt. Now, he had the tools to do so.

His face stretched in what he knew was a mirthless smile. The source lived, he had the position. *Three days, maybe four*, he thought. *And I will eat well tonight.* Events were turning in his favor.

5

THE TRUTH REVEALED

ARTEN

"Any love notes for me today," Juro asked the next morning. He was far more chipper than she, though his eyes were smudged underneath with dark. She had completely forgotten about Leif's reply and said as much. Juro pretended to be put out, then offered to read it to her. It was quite long, so she accepted.

Besides, I need a laugh.

"My dearest Arten," he began, grinning, as he skimmed the letter.

"It doesn't say that, it just says Arten," she groused, because she always did, because that was part of the game.

"I —" he started. His mouth hardened into a line.

"What is it?"

"I," he continued, but the simpering tone was gone, "am a complete rabbit turd. Like a rabbit turd, I am small and smelly and not fit for anything but wiping from the bottom of your shoe."

"What did it really say?" she asked when it was clear he was done.

"That his mommy and daddy told him not to play with

you anymore," he mocked in distaste. "Seems they think you're trying to seduce their son into giving away their precious family business secrets. So, he's not to see you again, and they'll be reevaluating their understanding with your dad once he returns. So much for the merchant dynasty," he scoffed. He added more gently, "You don't need him, anyway."

"I guess not," she said glumly, thinking about the Words and Juro's dire warning yesterday. What did learning to run the shop matter when she would be leaving in a few years?

"I *mean* I can teach you about keeping accounts. If you want."

"You can?" It surprised her. Juro seemed to her to have grown into a bit of a wastrel. His family had money, he only attended to the business interests when his father was away, and he spent most of his time with his horse or, this summer at least, lounging about her father's shop.

"I'm more than just a pretty face." He grinned. She rolled her eyes. "More importantly," he leaned in conspiratorially, "I will."

"You will?" she asked, suspicious.

"Sure," he said with feigned casualness, "if you do something for me in return."

"Uh huh. What do you want?"

"I don't know yet. Let's call it a deferred claim."

"No," she said firmly, "you could turn that into anything. You could have me...eat a worm or something."

"If I recall," he studied his nails, "you've eaten a worm before."

"That's not the point."

"I can think of much more interesting things to have you do than eat a worm." He grinned wickedly. Before she could protest, he breezed on, "I respect your business sense, though. Never enter into a contract with unknown terms. Well done. I will have an answer for you when I return."

"Where are you going?" she asked a little too quickly. She scowled when he smirked at her.

"Can't bear to be without me? Well, I'm sorry to cause you distress, but I have a very urgent appointment with my horse. He doesn't ride himself, you know."

The shard of chalk caught him in the back of the head as he left but didn't silence his laughter.

AFTER DINNER, Arten answered a knock at their back door. It was the Mikneilsons. She let them up and whisked herself away before her mother could notice her and demand she stay. She knew what they were going to talk about, knew she'd rather be doing anything else than hearing their accusations and the bartering over her price. She trudged through the woods to Juro's. *Funny,* she thought, *how I think of it as Juro's house now, not Maruko's.*

Maruko answered the door.

"This isn't a good time, Arten," she said through the sliver of open door, glancing back over her shoulder.

"I came by to talk to Juro," she said.

Maruko eyed her sharply. "You two have been cozy lately," she said. Was that bitterness?

"He comes by the shop," she protested. "You could come by, too."

"Hmm." Maruko looked back over her shoulder again. "Let me see if he's free." She shut the door, leaving Arten on the step.

She didn't have long to puzzle over the odd behavior.

Juro cracked the door open and slid through, closing it quickly behind him.

"This isn't a good time," he echoed his sister. He looked a little harried. "What's wrong?"

"Nothing," she said, "I just came by to...accept your offer."

"Did you now?" a slice of mischief twitched across his face. "I'm glad to hear it. Wait here." He slithered back into the house.

She toed some gravel in the flower bed back onto the drive while she waited. Raised voices rushed out when he emerged once again.

"Here," he thrust two books at her chest, "The assignment is inside the front cover. I really must get back." He glanced at the door. "I'm sorry we can't have you in tonight. Please, don't tell anyone you were here, or anything of what you've seen or heard."

"I won't," she said automatically.

"Good. Thank you." He kissed her forehead. It felt patronizing, left her bristling. "Goodnight. Leave through the woods," he said and dove back inside.

She trudged through the woods, crunching leaves and underbrush loudly under her sturdy boots. *Another one of their secrets, I guess. They're supposed to be my best friends, but I wonder if I even know them.* The small part of her mind protested that she was keeping her own secrets, and she told it to shut up.

She went into the small office below the stairs, taking the lantern with her. The murmur of voices overhead filtered in, and she tried to ignore them. Inside the thinner book was a thick packet of paper, folded in thirds. She took it out and read:

MY DEAREST ARTEN,

Per our agreement, you must complete all written assignments pertaining to our agreed upon course of instruction in return for receiving the benefit of said instruction. All other assignments, written or verbal, that fall outside the agreed upon course of instruction are non-compulsory.

Attached, you will find the complete schedule of assignments.

Yours sincerely,

Juro Swain

SHE HAD to look up some words in the dictionary he'd loaned her a few days ago, but the lettering was clear and precise, making it easy for her to read. She turned to the assignments. There was a day-by-day breakdown of what she was expected to read and a numbered activity to complete. The activity sheets were carefully drawn to look like ledger pages. Some were mostly filled in with empty spaces, some were missing entire columns and rows, and toward the end, they were mostly blank with just grids of varying sizes drawn. Most of the activities she didn't understand, but the day four activity made her smile: *Congratulations, you've done well so far. Today you may either: a) take the day off, or b) tell me how much you appreciate me.*

She put the papers back in order carefully. *He must have spent all day preparing this,* she thought, awed. Not just that he could create the plan and activities for her with so little notice, but that he had invested the time not knowing if she would agree to his terms. She felt strangely solemn as she opened the book to begin reading the assigned pages.

When the stairs creaked, she snuffed the lantern and waited in the dark for the Mikneilsons to leave, for her mother to tire of shouting for her to come in, for the frustrated stomping to ascend the stairs and settle into sounds of domestic industry. She then crept out to find a match, lit the lantern again, and went back to her task. It was past midnight when she heard the yowling of a cat outside. A very particular yowl.

She doused the lantern again, stowed it and her books under the counter in the shop, and let herself outside. She kept to the shadows as she skulked to the edge of the woods, just in case her mother was still awake and looking out a window. Once she was under the trees, she circled back in the direction of the yowler. He met her halfway.

"In heat again, Juro?" she chided. He just grinned in response, and she was glad that the dark covered her flush. *Why are you so flustered around him lately? Stop it!* "Your secret meeting ended, I take it?" she said quickly before he could make a comment she would regret.

"I'm sorry about that," he said, earnestly. "Are you...angry?"

"No. You can't tell me everything, I get it." *Everyone has secrets.*

"Have you started the lessons?" he asked, clearing away a place for them to sit at the base of a tree.

"Yeah," she said. They talked a little about what she'd read, and he explained some of the bits she hadn't quite understood.

"Don't be so hard on yourself," he said, "it's a dense text, and you've understood far more than you give yourself credit for."

"That's nice of you to say." She sighed unhappily.

"It's true," he insisted. "And I think you know it. So, what's eating at you, really?"

She sighed and slumped against him, propping her cheek against his shoulder. She told him about the Mikneilsons' visit, the comment about *a good bargain* she'd overhead as they left.

"So, the rabbit turd's offer has been salvaged," he spat.

"Sounds like it."

"You deserve better than him," he said angrily.

"He's not so bad," Arten protested. "As far as rabbit turds go, he's not that smelly. And, being realistic, only rabbit turds are going to offer for me." She didn't mean for it to come out as glumly as it did.

Juro's fingers found hers, laced with them. "I'm sorry," he said. She didn't know what for, didn't want to ask.

Just kept thinking, *It doesn't matter, I'll be burned or on the run in a few years. Leif is temporary.*

She said, "We'll still be friends, right?"

He growled, actually growled, startling her. "Let him try and keep me away." She squeezed his hand, and he squeezed back, rested his cheek against her head. The tree frogs sang. A deer crashed through the woods far away. She wondered if it had twin fawns in its wake.

Much later, she said, "I think Maruko is mad at me." He made a languid noise of inquiry. She wondered if he had been asleep. "When she answered the door, she seemed upset that we're spending time together."

"Not mad at you," he mumbled, "but at me."

"Why?"

"Because...I'm being stupid. Playing with fire. Going to get burned."

She stilled, searched for the scrabble of Words inside

her, but they were quiet. "What do you mean?" she asked carefully.

"Don't worry about it," he said through a yawn. He relaxed against her sleepily.

"Ugh, you're heavy, get off," she complained, pushing away from him. "I feel sorry for your horse."

"You *wish* you were my horse," he muttered, "because then you'd be betw—wait, that's not right."

"Whatever hilarious thing you think you were about to say," she stood up, "I can promise you it wasn't funny. Now come on, get up." She grabbed his arm and hauled on it. He complained, but managed to get to his feet, with the aid of the tree at his back.

"You can be so mean," he sulked, then yawned again.

"Yeah, I don't want you to sleep in the woods, I'm a terrible person."

"That's not what I meant," he protested. Then, "It *was* funny, I'm sure of it."

"Sure, Juro." She rolled her eyes. "Sure it was."

"I'm glad you agree," he said, catching her arm and pulling her into a hug. She protested and pushed at him, but he hugged her tighter, saying into her hair, "I'll go, I'll go, just give me a minute."

"When did you become so clingy in your sleep?" she groused. "You used to kick and elbow me if I accidentally rolled into you."

"You didn't use to smell this good," he muttered, nuzzling her hair.

"Ugh, spare me. Is that supposed to be your oft-bragged-about charm?"

He groaned. "You wound me." She jabbed him in the ribs. "Ow, and again. Alright, alight, I'm going." He released her and pushed away from the trunk. "See you tomorrow," he said through a yawn and lumbered away.

"Be careful," she hissed after him. He waved off her concern. She waited to turn her own steps towards home until she was certain he wasn't going to run into anything or fall down.

ARTEN LEARNED RAPIDLY under Juro's tutelage. He alternatively coaxed, harangued, taunted, and scolded her when she was ready to give up. She alternatively wanted to hug, punch, and scream at him. He was demanding, but never unkind. When she got something right, he was generous with his praise, and when she was wrong, he expected her to try again. He came by in the morning to review what she had learned the previous day; then again at noon, usually with a sandwich he would split with her, to check on her progress and answer any questions; and before close to go over her assignments and have her recite what she had learned. In the evenings, after supper, after her mother had retired, she would sneak into the woods to meet him where the butterfly bush had grown up that one summer, before his stepmother had found it and moved it into her garden. They talked about many things, in the quiet hollow, sometimes about the accounts and ledgers and how they fit together, sometimes about their families, sometimes about old adventures. Never about the future.

On the fourth day of their academic partnership, the day before Saviorsday, Arten's life began to slip sideways.

It was afternoon, the half-sandwich a distant memory, the *Principles of Accounts and Accounting* open on the long counter, Juro's assignment sheet laid out underneath it.

Arten was leaning over both, alternatively reading from the book and making notes on the work sheet with a string-wrapped graphite stick. A shadow passed over her, blocking the light. She jumped, sending the stool clattering against the back cabinets, the graphite stick clattering to the counter. She'd been concentrating so hard she hadn't heard the bell.

"Good afternoon," she said, a little too brightly to the man, trying to hide her jangled nerves. He didn't return her forced smile. He was tall—at least a head taller than Juro, she guessed—and thin, like he'd never had to put on muscle. *He must be very wealthy,* she thought, *or very ill.* His clothes offered no indicator. He wore a strange robe, a fashion she had never before seen, made of an unknown fiber. It looked a little worse for the wear, though the embroidery on the lapels looked like it had once been fine, and the color had surely been a startling blue at some point. His skin was darkened, like a field laborer's, but somehow it lacked the sun's warmth. Her smile faltered as the silence stretched uncomfortably.

"How can I help you?" she asked. He merely stared down at her, assessing. Sweat prickled on her spine under the intensity of his regard. It tried to pull her in, to claim her. She took an unknowing step back, pressing herself against the far wall.

"Sir, are you well?" she asked, her thoughts churning, trying to decide if he was dangerous, and how she could get away. His emerald eyes were too bright, hard to meet and impossible to look away from. Her own eyes darted around, looking for an escape, but kept getting pulled back to his. They burned into her, saw into her depths. She could feel him looking down, down, seeking—what?

Then, a stirring inside her chest, a churning, the

clenched knot in her stomach loosened. The Words drifted towards wakening. The voice attached to the stranger's eyes chanted to them, enticed them out. Sweating now in earnest, Arten knew two things—she couldn't look away, and she wouldn't be able to stop the Words this time. Her heart floundered in her chest. She heard the rushing of it erratically in her ears beside the rasping of her breath. The Words were climbing out of her throat, skittering across the back of her tongue.

As though he could sense how close she was to losing, he leaned in, palms resting on the counter. There was a thud as something hit the floor. His tall, thin form loomed over her. His lips parted in an angular smile, full of sharp, white incisors. The Words swarmed over her tongue, seizing control. She felt her own traitorous lips stretch as the Words strained against them. The man leaned even closer, his fingers curled into claws on the glass, his eyes glimmering with the power that held her transfixed; that and something else, something hungry.

Her lungs drew breath, to exhale the Words at long last.

There had been a noise, a shriek of defiance building in her mind that irritated, then distracted, then a sharp pain in her thigh, and the shriek was borne away from her throat, drowning out the Words. She wrested her eyes away from his with a physical jolt.

Out of her periphery, she saw him draw himself back up to his full height. She forced herself to rise from her cowered position and felt a needle of pain. Looking down, she saw a nail clenched in her hand, trembling, and a spot of blood on her thigh. She felt a hysterical laugh bud and with great effort forced it down. But it was enough to snap the paralysis of the fear, and she straightened to face the stranger.

"Please leave," she said, her voice wavering but emphatic. She stared at the broad sash around his waist, afraid to look higher, to risk being pulled back in by those uncanny eyes. He made no move to do so, merely stood there. "Leave!" she screamed at him, anger cresting, washing away the fragments of terror and helplessness, bringing strength in its wake. She raised her eyes to his face, glaring with the full force of that emotion. It burned hotter at the inscrutable expression he now wore. His dangerous eyes were hooded, the sharp planes of his face once more blank.

She was trembling now, the anger agitating her limbs, and opened her mouth to scream at him once more, when at last he spoke.

"I know what you hold inside you," he said. His words were like icepicks, driven into the walls of hope and denial she had wrapped herself in. Her rage froze. He knew. He *knew*. She was brittle, fragile, exposed. He was going to shatter her. His eyes blazed for a moment, an emerald fire, and she cringed, waiting for the blow to be struck.

But he did not strike.

"I have been waiting for you." His voice was almost gentle, so soft she wondered if she had even heard it. "You have an enemy here. I will draw him away. I will return for you in five days." His tone turned sharp, "You will come with me, or your family will suffer." The words struck her like a physical blow. Before she could respond, he reached into an inner pocket of his robe and brought out a silk purse. His long, thin fingers extracted five gold coins, which he clinked into a precise stack one at a time.

Arten had never seen so much money at once. It was enough to buy a fine horse, more than her family made in a year. She looked up at him, dazed. The purse had disappeared.

"Five days," he said. "When you come with me, this," he indicated the gold pile with a sweep of his hand, "is what I will pay your family each year until you are of legal adult age."

"You...you want to buy me?" she sputtered, indignation loosening her tongue at last.

"I *have* bought you," he corrected, and his mouth twisted up at the corners while his eyes smoldered.

She looked away. She looked back at the piles of coins. Gold that would put her in chains. She wondered if the Mikneilsons had offered as much for her. Knew they never would.

"I'm not eligible for offers until the fall," she said, trying to hide her alarm.

He looked intent, puzzled, then seemed to understand. "Your barbaric customs," he said, "are of no interest to me. I am not proposing to marry you." He leaned in again, "Nevertheless, you *will* come with me."

She tried to hold his gaze, to glare at him, but lost her nerve after a few seconds.

He turned and walked to the door, his footsteps silent. When he opened it, the bell chimed. He paused on the threshold. "Five days," he intoned. Then he was gone.

THE WORDS WRITHED INSIDE HER. All at once, the pain in her thigh announced itself. Her head spun in a wave of dizziness. His words echoed in her mind long after he left.

'I have bought you.' 'Your family will suffer.' 'I know...'

She moved through the rest of the day mechanically. Several times customers had to prevent her from giving them soap instead of salt and honey instead of pipe tobacco.

Juro tried to get her to shake off the strange mood but left unsatisfied. When the shop finally closed, she trudged after her mother, the five gold pieces clutched in her fist, inside her pocket.

She ascended the stairs, her mind full of those ominous words. Each step felt final, like a wedge being forced between her and her family, her home, her friends, her life. By the time she got to the top, she was an island. She saw her mother moving about, watched herself eat her dinner of soup and bread as though from the ceiling. She saw herself, heard her voice, but she was on the island, alone.

Her mother was speaking to her from across the sea.

"I know you've been seeing that Swain boy," she was saying, "and I won't have it. The Mikneilsons are going to renew their offer once your father returns. Their son is solid and steady, but he won't accept you if you keep on like this. That Swain boy has no interest in you, and you think quite highly of yourself if you believe otherwise."

"I know he doesn't," her voice said.

"What was that?" her mother demanded.

"He's my friend," she said, her voice was placid. "He's not going to offer for me."

"Know that, do you?"

"Yes. He told me."

Her mother made an irritated noise, attacked a smear of grease on the stove top vigorously. "I expect you not to see him again."

"I can't help it if he comes into the shop," she heard herself say, was impressed by her audacity.

The irritated noise emerged from her mother again. "We'll see about that," she muttered to herself.

ARTEN WENT TO BED EARLY, bone-weary, but sleep eluded her. '*I* have *bought you*', she heard over and over again. The Words turned around in her chest, circling slowly as she lay there. She tried to ignore them, tried not to relive their awakening. When Juro's yowl reached her, she went to meet him, not caring about her mother's wrath for once.

I can't tell him, she thought as she rested her cheek on his shoulder, her leg leaning against his. *He'll find out soon enough. But I can't...I can't...* She didn't want to see the betrayal on his face again. But she was crying, and he was worried. So, she told him the other, what her mother had said.

He put his arms around her and pulled her against his chest in an awkward sitting hug, hands smoothing back her hair. His kindness broke something in her, and she was sobbing like she hadn't since Tizzy, since what she'd overheard her mother say to her father afterward. And if Juro knew, if he knew he would cast her aside as they had done. The secret that wasn't the Taint, the one she buried so, so deep. Her curse had brought the stranger here, her curse was taking Juro away so she would face the pyres or the stranger alone. She cried out her bitterness and anger and fear. And Juro held her and rocked her and wiped her tears away.

He is a good friend. I will be sad to lose him. The thought brought no more tears, only resignation. She quieted. "I'm okay," she said at last.

"Are you?" he asked. She nodded, pushed away from him to sit curled around her knees. He offered her his handkerchief, moved to sit beside her. "I'll fix this," he promised.

"How?" she whispered hopelessly.

"I'll think of something." His hand reached up and stroked her head, came to rest at her neck. "I'll think of something," he said again. For once, she didn't believe him.

THE NEXT MORNING, she dressed for the temple in a thoughtless haze. Her dreams had been chaotic but purposeless. She donned her dress, noting absently the miracle Maruko had performed in getting out the grass and horse-sweat stains, and waited in resigned silence for her mother to be ready. Followed her docilely into the lane. Where Maruko and Juro were waiting.

Juro was, Arten realized, actually capable of charm. His jovial conversation coaxed her mother out of her disapproving reticence. Once they were talking, Maruko whispered, "We have a plan. Don't leave my side today."

Arten didn't have much choice, Maruko stuck to her like a burr, even though Arten's mother tried to separate from the Swains when they entered the temple. Arten clutched Maruko's hand under the fold of her skirt and tried not to focus on the manacles hanging over her head.

About a quarter of the way through the service, Maruko clutched her stomach. "Juro," she panted, sweat shining on her brow, "Juro, I don't feel well."

"Shh!" he hissed. "Tough it out."

"No, really," she winced, "I think I'm going to be sick. Right now!"

"No you're not." He sighed with the disdain only an elder brother can muster.

"Maruko? What's wrong?" Arten asked, turning to really look at her friend. Maruko was sweaty and shaking, her face pale, eyes glazed.

"Oh!" Maruko exclaimed, her eyes went large, and that

was the only warning Arten had before Maruko vomited into her lap. "Oh no," she moaned, "I'm so sorry!"

But her words were lost in the small horror of those around them. It attracted the venerated's attention, and he insisted Juro take his sister home. Arten trailed after because Maruko had begged piteously not to be left alone in her state, and because no one wanted her to stay, reeking as she was. Juro commandeered a horse and cart and drove them home, Arten sitting off the back with Maruko, rubbing her back and keeping her hair away from her face when she vomited over the side.

The two miles went by rapidly and, soon, Maruko was stumbling into their house, leaning heavily on Arten. Once the door closed behind them, she groaned, "Juro, you are five types of swine. Give me the damn antidote."

He pulled out a small flask. "Two sips only," he cautioned her. "When the healer comes by, you have to still be sick."

"Next time, you get to be sick," she complained after following his instruction.

"Arten's mom wouldn't have let her come back with us if I were the sick one," he pointed out.

"Oh, shut up and help me to my room."

"Just let me carry you, you're wobbling all over the place."

It was a mark of how awful she must have genuinely felt that Maruko said, "Fine."

Juro scooped her up and carried her up the stairs. "Arten," she called over his shoulder, "go take a bath, there's some clean clothing in there for you." Arten just stared after them. "Ugh, you walk like an ox," she heard Maruko complain as they went into her room. Juro emerged a few moments later and frowned to see Arten still standing in the hall.

"What's wrong?" he said, coming down the stairs.

"What...what happened? Is Maruko going to be okay?"

He grinned, "She'll be fine. We just poisoned her a little."

"What? Are you crazy?"

"It was her idea." He shrugged. "I wanted to go with migraine, but she said it wouldn't be persuasive enough. And she's right. If you're going to try and fool the temple, it needs to be damn convincing."

"You *are* crazy," she muttered. "Maruko...you're sure she's going to be okay?"

"This isn't our first fake-poisoning." He grinned again. "She'll be fine. But you, I'm afraid, stink. Go on, get cleaned up. I've got to take the wagon back." He propelled her down the hall, into the bathing/laundry room.

She washed her dress, then herself, dressed in Juro's castoff clothes she'd worn once before, then dashed upstairs to check on Maruko. She was sleeping, curled around a ceramic pot which, for the moment, was empty. Arten leaned her back against the bedpost and settled herself to wait.

THAT EVENING, Maruko was up and about. She'd taken the rest of the antidote after the healer had left. He had scratched his head and said, "It looks like moxglove poisoning, but that can't be right..." Based on the stricken glance that shot between the Swain siblings, he was correct. Arten doubted they would use this particular trick again anytime soon. He'd given them some general stomach soother and promised to send around a small bottle of the moxglove antidote later, just in case.

Maruko and Juro chatted and bickered throughout the evening as though nothing unusual had happened. Arten couldn't join in. She felt like an interloper, like a demon they had unknowingly invited in. *Four days*, she kept thinking. *He's coming for me in four days. I have to...flee, hide, something.* Then one of her hosts would laugh, and she would be struck with horror that Maruko had poisoned herself and Juro had gone along with it.

Something Juro had just said cleaved through the fog. "What did you just say?" she asked, her voice pinched.

"Dedicate Brecarian was not at service today," he said.

"Why not?"

"How am I supposed to know that?" He snorted but exchanged a guarded glance with his sister.

"You know something," she insisted. "Tell me."

"We know that he was...called away. To a nearby village. Venerated Vachel isn't happy about it."

"Thinks his glory is going to be stolen," Maruko said, her disdain plain.

"What do you mean?"

"There hasn't been a...sacrifice," Maruko spat the word, "in this part of the country in more than ten years. Vachel wanted it to be from our village so he gets the credit, so his name goes down in a roster back in the high temples. He wants to retire to a busy temple in a city instead of this backwater."

"How...how does the dedicate find them?"

"We don't know," Juro growled. He started pacing. "He had his eye on me for a few days. I caught him skulking in the barn one night last week. He was looking at Katre Bryne before he left. She's a bit old for it, so I think he's lost whatever trail they follow. Unfortunately for him, he's running out of time."

Aren't we all? she thought, but asked, "What do you mean?"

"Midsummer mass. That's when they'll do it, if they can. A holy day, a day aligned with fire. It makes a memorable sacrifice," Juro ground out. *Their mother was burned at Midsummer*, she remembered.

"Is it only at Midsummer?" Arten vaguely remembered the buzz around a sacrifice from when she had been too small to understand what was going on, and much too small to attend it. She only remembered it because she and Deric had been allowed to stay home that Decaday while everyone else went to the temple. She didn't remember anything else except that it had seemed like a special treat to skip the service and play.

"No. They'll sacrifice whenever they need to, but they try to align it with a solstice or equinox if they can." His face twisted in distaste, "To get the largest audience."

Maruko interrupted to berate Juro for not telling her that the dedicate had been investigating him. Arten kept thinking, *He was right next door. Searching for me. If the Words had escaped that night...* She would have been in the cell today, not in the temple.

It was then that she knew. When the stranger came back, she would go with him. *Four days.* She didn't want to burn. And he had spoken to the Words inside her. He knew what they were, he had controlled them, called them forth. *Maybe he can take them away entirely.*

'I have bought you.'

A slave. But alive. Better than the alternative. Isn't it?

SHE COULDN'T SLEEP. The Words were stirring.

They had seen the path to release, had been drawn from their torpor, and she felt them waiting, circling slowly in her chest, sliding through her lungs, scenting fresh air. They no longer clawed for release. She now realized they had been a dream of themselves before. Incoherent and thrashing. They were more dangerous than ever. Biding their time.

Four days. No, three. She had wasted today being afraid. She had not shown her friends how much she cared, had not savored these last days with them. She got up and went to Maruko's room, crawled into bed with her. She held her friend's hand, soothed her when the stomach cramps spasmed. Recounted her favorite memories of their adventures together to distract her until she slept again.

The next morning, when she and Juro were alone in the shop, she said, "I never did my day four assignment." And then told him how much she appreciated him. Not just his tutelage but his friendship. She told him of those moments that were most cherished to her. Not all of them, but she hoped enough. How he had helped her when she got stuck in that tree and hadn't laughed at her for it. The time he'd given Deric a black eye to match the one her brother had given her the day before. All the times he'd taken the blame for something she did to spare her from her parents' punishment.

He cleared his throat, blinking, and joked, "It sounds like you're breaking up with me."

"No," she said, "but I can't smile today."

"Will you tell me why?" He looked troubled.

"Not yet."

He reached out to touch her hand. The bell rang, and he pulled his hand back. "I'll be back around lunch to check on your progress," he said, businesslike, then bade her a quick farewell.

"I'm learning to keep accounts," she explained, gesturing to the books and activity sheets in front of her, in response to the inquisitive look of the customer.

"Aren't you a bit young for that?" the woman asked.

"Am I?" Arten deferred. She had learned a thing or two about censuring herself to the customers in the last weeks. Two weeks ago, she would have said, *Clearly not, since I'm doing it.* Now, she was able to pack that thought away and shove it down into the miasma at her core. She imagined she felt the Words pause and investigate it.

ARTEN GAVE the three days her all. Poured herself into her studies, so she could see Juro beam with pride, see the happiness her efforts brought him. Worked after close to clean the shop, not for her mother's approval, but her father's. She would have been gone five days by the time he returned. She wouldn't get to say goodbye.

That last night, she told Juro and Maruko over supper, "My mother won't let me stay any longer." A lie. She wanted to say goodbye on her own terms. "So, this will be my last night here." *In the village.* She thanked them for the effort and distress they had gone to in giving her this respite. For being such fast friends. She tried to force herself to be light-hearted and have fun. To enjoy these last moments.

She went to Juro's room later. He answered her soft tap, half-undressed, preparing for bed. She had intended to invite him out for a last walk through the woods under the stars, to tell him goodbye. Seeing him standing there, she saw at last what she had been avoiding seeing. He was grown up. And she wasn't, not enough. He had been trying to fit himself back into her world, to be close the way they once had been. But he wasn't that person, anymore. And whatever they were trying to recapture had been doomed from the start. Even if the stranger weren't taking her away, she would be married. They could never go back. The lost years could never be regained. They might have been friends of a different sort, once she was married off, but that wouldn't happen now.

So, instead, she said, "Thank you. For these last days, few weeks, really. It means more than you know. But promise me that you and Maruko will never do something so stupid again."

"It was worth it," he said, looking at her intensely.

"No, it wasn't," she said, unyielding. "Something could have gone wrong. If Maruko had been harmed by all this, do you think I would not have felt the guilt of that for the rest of my life?"

"Nothing went wrong. We've done this before, you know," he crossed his arms and glowered.

"That doesn't mean it can't happen. Something can always go wrong, no matter how hard you try. People always get hurt." She scrubbed traitorous tears away with her fist.

"Arten?" Juro reached for her, touched her shoulder. "What's wrong?"

"Nothing," she lied. "Promise me you won't do something like this again."

"Okay," he said quietly, "I promise." His hand on her shoulder had tightened, was pulling her towards him. She wanted to let him, wanted to lean against his chest and cry, wanted to tell him everything, to lay down the weight that had been crushing her day by day. And was terrified that she would. *He'll know soon enough,* she thought, brushing his hand away.

"Don't come by the shop tomorrow," she said, already halfway to her door. She ignored his protests, ignored the soft knocking several times in the night, was gone before breakfast.

6

LEARNING HER NAME

STEKIN

He had laid a false trail, called the dedicate away. Three days out on foot, two days to entice and confuse the man, and one night back in a hired coach. He arrived at dawn, at the next village over. He caught a ride on the back of a wagon to get to her village. Then walked through the woods, a more direct and less traceable route, to get to her shop.

She is so young. He had to be careful. Anything but a legal agreement would open him to reprisal from the temple. When she left, there must be no excuse for the temple to follow them. They would not send dedicates after an adult who fled, but a child? A man's property? The whole temple would be after them if he absconded with her. No, he needed her bound to him until she was sixteen and attained her legal freedom.

It was late afternoon. She was alone in the shop. It would be so simple to go in... His eyes flashed eagerly. No, no, best not. He had waited this long, he could wait a little longer. He *would* wait a little longer. His fingers curled into the tree bark at his back, cutting slivers free.

It grew late. One of the parents had returned. He left the shadows of the woods.

He knocked on the back door. He felt her coming down the stairs to answer it. Braced himself.

"You came," she sounded a little surprised. She looked so small, so very young.

"You fear me," he said, smelling it on her.

His eyes tracked her throat as she swallowed. "Yes," she whispered.

"Yet, you are relieved." It was a question. He waited.

"I fear the pyres more," she said, trying to square her shoulders.

He smiled sharply. "You are wise." She would not beg then, not cry and plead not to be taken. She was marvelous...

"Wait, please!" she cried, throwing a hand out towards him, as if to push him away. The other clutched her chest. He stepped back, unaware that he had moved, unaware that he had been drawing at her. He could see her power, a tumult inside her, chaos and fangs and hidden, somehow. She was concentrating, panting. The power sputtered out.

Interesting. How did you manage that? He had never seen another's power so visibly.

"I think," she said shakily, "it's best if you keep back."

"Very well," he agreed and turned his power in tight, controlled bands to leash it.

He followed her, at a distance, up the stairs.

"Who was it?" a woman's voice snapped.

"A man," his source answered vaguely.

"What did he want?"

Stekin moved to the open doorway. "To transact business with you," he said before the girl could answer.

The woman stood up, eying him warily. "What sort of

business?" Her eyes jumped to a knife on the table. She moved her hand casually closer to it.

"That is not necessary," he said, "but pick it up if it comforts you."

The woman's fingers twitched like a dying spider, and she closed them into a tight fist at her side. *Interesting.*

"What sort of business," she repeated.

"Are you the guardian of that child?" he gestured in the girl's direction.

"Yes. Why? What's she done?" The mother's hard gaze darted to the girl but quickly came back to him.

She chose not to tell her parents about my offer. He invited himself in and sat on the bench opposite the woman. "I wish to indenture her to me until she turns sixteen."

The mother scoffed. "Well, then I can tell you your business is concluded. We have been promised an offer when she turns thirteen. She will be married."

His source had come up behind her mother. "This is his offer," she said quietly and unwrapped the five gold coins, placed them on the table. The mother looked down at them, sat slowly.

"Her bride price is three times that," the woman lied, the bite gone from her words. "Not to mention the financial care she will provide for us in our old age."

Stekin revised his plan as he drew out his purse. If this woman was motivated by gold... He counted out fifteen more gold pieces. Enough to buy a house with some land. Then he counted out forty more, stacking them neatly into columns of ten. "I am willing to offer twenty gold at signing. With ten gold paid per annum at each anniversary," he gestured to each of three of the columns, "and the last payment to be made when she turns sixteen."

Sixty gold was enough that they would never have to

work again. If they invested it wisely, they could live in a grand house with servants for the rest of their lives. The woman would be a fool to turn it down. And a bigger fool to take it. He had not specified what the servitude would entail. He already knew which type of fool she was.

"I see," the woman said, staring at the coins. Her eyes flicked up to him, "You understand, my husband must formalize the contract with you."

"I understand. I insist upon it."

She was nervous. "He is, unfortunately, away at the moment."

"I see." A delay. His eyes narrowed. He felt a flicker of power from his source, looked to see anxiety on her features. *She does not want the delay either.*

"We expect him back," the mother reassured urgently, "in only five or six days!"

He did some quick calculation. *Too close to Midsummer. The dedicate will be a problem.* He swept the money back into his purse, leaving the original five gold on the table. The woman stiffened. "Very well. I will return in five days. You may keep that," he nodded to the coins, "as a gesture of my good faith."

He stood, she echoed his motion. "I look forward to seeing you then. I didn't get your name," she asked.

"Nor I yours," he smiled coldly. *Take that as you will,* he thought maliciously. "I will be using your barn tonight," he added, and placed another gold coin on the table as though it were an afterthought.

"You are welcome to it," she said, but it sounded forced. He was already out the door and down the stairs.

Small feet padded after him. He stopped at the exit, turned to face her. She looked scared and overwhelmed. *They always are. But not this young.*

She asked him, her knuckles white on the railing, "What's your name?"

"Stekin," he said. "And yours?"

"Arten."

"Arten." He fixed the name inside himself.

"The dedication is after me, isn't he?" she asked, her voice small.

"Yes. If he comes for you, run. Get somewhere safe and hide. I will find you. Do you understand? I *will* find you."

She nodded, "Yes. Did...did you draw him away?"

"Yes."

"Are you going to do so again?"

"Yes."

She said nothing else, so he left. After the door slid closed behind him, he heard her small whisper of, "Be careful."

She is so young, he thought again, as he tried to find the least reeking place in the barn to sleep. *What am I going to do with a juvenile?* He frowned up at the rafters in the hayloft. *She is alive, I have found her, this is what is important. Juvenescence is transient*, he reminded himself.

HOURS LATER, a prowler came into the woods. Stekin left the hayloft and intercepted him. *This scent is familiar...*

"Halt," Stekin called. His voice carried through the trees.

"Who's there?" the prowler hissed. "Identify yourself."

"One could make the same demand of you."

"You first," the prowler invited.

"I have paid for accommodations at this house for the evening. And you?"

"I am a neighbor," he said just as vaguely.

"Ah. The son of Harun Swain," Stekin guessed. He had been intrigued when his inquiries about the area revealed that Harun Swain, a valued member of the network, lived next door to his source.

"How do you know my father?" the prowler growled.

"He provides services for me, after a fashion." *That scent...it does not belong here. How do I know you?*

"What services?" the son demanded warily.

"Discretion, amongst others." *Honeysuckle,* the memory finally triggered, *and pyreberry. You were the reason she died.* He felt a growl rising in him. "Go home, *Tsyaro*. Do not come this way again." He did not bother to mask the threat.

There was panic in the boy's voice when he said, "How do you know my father?"

Stekin loosed the growl. The young Tsyaro-Swain ran.

Swain is Tsyaro, he mused as he trekked back to the barn, *Unexpected. Harun will be displeased to see me. And the boy...*

I wonder what he remembers.

7

FLIGHT

ARTEN

The days that followed were terrifying. Arten had been prepared to leave with the stranger—Stekin, she reminded herself—that night. She was resolved, resigned, ready. But they hadn't left, and the peace she'd found inside herself evaporated.

She would see her father again, and brother, just when she'd accepted that it would be best to leave quietly. And... Juro and Maruko. She didn't want to see them, didn't want to say goodbye again.

And the Words were agitated. The stranger's—Stekin's—presence had roused them. They pricked tiny claws at the base of her throat, eager for his return. She was afraid to talk, afraid to sleep, afraid to feel any of the emotions demanding her attention, lest the Words escape.

The morning after her sale had been postponed, Juro had come by, looking tired and agitated. Had said he was going to be busy for a few days. She hadn't asked, hadn't wanted to care. She did the study work anyway, to distract herself from the waiting, from the fear that each chime of the bell would reveal the dedicate at the door. The accounts and numbers seemed to soothe the Words, or at least distract her from their churning. She read and worked problems every minute she could, even late into the night.

She was measuring cloth for a customer on the third day when the jangle of harness reached in from the lane. Hooves turned onto their drive, crunching the gravel heavily. A wagon creaked and groaned down the incline. It was too early, her father wasn't due back until Decaday, Saviorsday at the earliest—two days from now. She looked anyway.

Her gut jumped and fell at the same time, wrenching horribly.

"Father," she breathed. Her hands started shaking. She ran out of the shop, ignoring the entitled exclamation of her customer, and into the lane behind the house. It was an eternity for him to park the wagon, to climb down from its high seat, but as soon as his feet touched the ground, she had her arms wrapped around his waist, her face buried in his shirt. She couldn't stop the tears.

"Hey now, hey now," he soothed. Some part of her heard him order Deric inside to help the lady, but most of her was wholly occupied with clinging to him, absorbing the safety he had always represented that now seemed so paltry. He couldn't protect her. He couldn't make everything alright. The temple would come or the stranger would come, and he could not stop them. He was just one man. As small and powerless as the rest of them.

She pushed away, tears dried out. There was no point in crying, no point in mourning. She had three options: wait for the dedicate and burn, run away with no plan and the Words scratching to be free, or go with the stranger. She had decided, didn't regret her decision. She couldn't afford regret or wishfulness. Juro's mother had lived only a few years before they found her. And the dedicate was already here, looking.

"I'm glad you're okay, little goose," her father said, smiling down at her.

"You're back early," she said.

"We pushed hard to get back. You were pretty sick when we left, we were worried." He petted her hair and hugged her, then said, "These ladies deserve a rest. Help me get them settled."

The sun was hot overhead and she was sweating by the time they had the horses unhooked from the wagon. She stood on a stool, currying away sweat and grime, the particles sticking to her, clogging her nose. But her father was on the other side, just as sticky and grimy, his hair bobbing as he groomed with vigorous strokes. *This is the last time we'll do this*, she thought. She wondered why she was so certain of that. *The stranger—Stekin—said I'd be free after I was sixteen.* But she doubted she would be. *I might be dead by then, or he might just keep me enslaved. I don't know anything about him.*

They finished with the horses, turned them out. Rinsed off under the pump. Her father settled an arm around her shoulders and said, "Let's go in."

The moment she'd been anticipating for three weeks. The moment where she would unveil all her efforts, where he would exclaim over how organized and clean the shop was, at how orderly and precise the accounts were, at how much she had learned, at how much better she had run things than Deric. And he did. But the praise and delight drained her, each word emptying out the piece of her that belonged here, the piece that needed him. Until she was hollow.

She tended the shop while he and Deric unloaded the wagon. She didn't ask what they'd bought, wasn't tantalized by her father's hints. When they were done, he asked, "What's wrong, Arten? I thought you'd be excited by all this."

She felt old and gray. And said, "I have something to tell you."

ARTEN TOLD HIM, in the small office under the stairs, about Stekin's offer and how she wanted him to take it. He protested. "I'd rather work for him and come out my own person than be married off," she said, not quite a lie. She didn't tell him about the Taint. Couldn't. Couldn't disappoint him that way. Didn't want him to go through what their neighbors had.

"Leif's solid, dependable," her father protested. "His offer is fair."

"This is slavery for a few years," she said, "Leif is slavery for a lifetime." He was simply staring at her, bewildered. "Please, Father."

"I'll think about it," he promised miserably. She thanked him, kissed his forehead, left him alone.

Deric was at his usual post, peering at her books and the assignment papers. "What's all this?" he demanded. Pushy. Defensive. Nothing had changed.

"I was learning to keep accounts," she said, putting the papers away neatly, stacking the tomes alongside the few novels Juro had loaned her.

"Why?" he asked suspiciously.

"It doesn't matter," she said. "Look, be nice to Leif, alright? It's not his fault our parents are idiots."

"What are you talking about?"

"It doesn't matter." She sighed. "Just remember, it's not

his fault. And if you can manage to stop thinking about yourself for more than a minute, you might notice he's keen on you." She tucked the books under her arm. "I'll be back for supper," she said.

"What? Wait, where are you going?"

"To say goodbye," she said to herself, sliding the door open.

"You're not making any sense. Did the fever affect your brain?" Deric groused. She ignored him, let the door slide closed behind her.

IT WAS HARD. Easier than the first time, because now she had something to tell them. The stranger—*Stekin*—had given her a plausible reason for leaving, one that could be made sense of.

"Arten, don't do this," Maruko pleaded. "What does this man even want you to do? It's not safe."

"It's the best option," she said neutrally.

"Marriage isn't bad enough for this," Maruko protested. "This man could kill you, or worse. I can't let you do this. Juro, say something!"

Juro had been silent, staring at her, his face as blank as a stone. Arten had been actively avoiding his gaze.

"Juro!" Maruko shouted, "Tell her this is madness!"

His voice was low and tight as he said, "Maruko, get out."

His sister jerked as if struck. "No, Juro, wait. Think about this... Dad—"

"I have," he said in that same restrained voice. "I have thought of nothing else for months. Maruko, please."

Maruko left. They were alone. He was standing very close. Too close. His fingers were touching her cheek. "Look

at me, Arten," he said. She didn't. She couldn't. "Please."
She did.

His eyes were warm and bright, urgent. Needful. She
dropped her gaze. He had shaved. When? Weeks ago, she
realized. She hadn't noticed. He was talking, his teeth flashing. Asking her to stay, to let him offer for her. To marry
him. He took a deep, shuddering breath, was going to say
more. To say things she didn't want to hear, to say things he
couldn't unsay.

"I can't," she said, placing a hand on his chest to halt his
words. He stopped breathing. "It's not about you, it's not
anything like that. I...have to go. There's more going on than
you know."

"Tell me," he pleaded.

"I'm in danger," she said, meeting his eyes, wondering if
he would understand, "if I stay." He didn't. He was full of
pain and loss. There was no flicker of recognition, no flash
of horror.

"I will protect you," he said.

"No." She smiled sadly. "You can't. This man, he may be
able to." She felt so old. Dried out.

"You'll come back? To me?" he whispered.

"I don't know," she admitted. Would promise nothing.
He said her name, over and over, each time a plea, a declara-
tion, a wound. She didn't know she was going to kiss him
until she did. Hadn't known she wanted to. Hadn't thought
there was anything left in her to feel with. Until it shattered
and the shards sliced her apart with each soft touch of his
lips.

SHE DIDN'T THINK she'd sleep that night. Didn't think she'd

ever sleep again. She thought of Juro, of Maruko. Wondered where Dedicate Brecarian was, if he was outside in the woods right now waiting to take her. Wondered where Stekin was. Wondered if she would survive the next two days. Saviorsday and the temple was in two days. Midsummer the day after. Midsummer, when Dedicate Brecarian and Venerated Vachel expected to sacrifice her, not even caring who she was, just that she was Tainted. She thought of Juro again, of how much he would hate her when he found out, when it broke him. Thought about what might have been.

SOMETHING WAS WRONG. The Words knotted around one another in her abdomen, waking her. It was fully dark, the quiet time of night where small sounds were over-loud. She heard Deric's low snores through the shared wall, a sound that was jarring for its long absence. Through the other wall, she heard low voices, staccato and hissed.

She scooted over to the wall and pressed her ear to it. Her parents were arguing. Another sound she had grown accustomed to missing.

"—not letting some man, some foreigner, *buy* her, Ellen."

"It's a lot more money than the Mikneilsons are offering. *And* when she's sixteen, she can still marry."

"Do you even hear yourself? That's our daughter! Our only daughter."

"I suppose this is my fault, too, then? That's what you mean, isn't it?"

"Selfish woman! This isn't about you. For one minute, just one minute, can't you crack open that thrice-damned heart of yours and think of her as your child? Have you no feeling left in you?"

"She is a curse. Always has been—"

"Stop right there. I don't want to hear it."

"She killed my baby girl, Jahn!"

"Lords, she's a child! She didn't—"

"And this Taint just proves what I knew all along. Proves she's cursed. A blight to this family."

"She doesn't have the Taint and she's not—"

"Oh yes she does! I've seen it."

"Bulls—"

"Charred marks on the rug. All this sneaking out at night? And she's too keen—Suddenly she wants learning when before I had to tie her down? No, it's the demons inside."

"That's not—"

"And that fever? It was unnatural. Out of nowhere? That burn just happened to appear the same day? No. Even the healer couldn't explain it. Said he'd never seen anything like it, her as healthy as obscene and yet scalding to the touch."

"But I—"

"She's got the Taint, Jahn. Stop whimpering about it and face the facts. I know that that's hard for you."

"Even if she does—*if!*—I'm not selling her to some man. Into slavery!"

"You're right, you're right...we can't send her away."

"I'm glad to hear you say that," his voice was slow, cautious. "So, we're agreed, we're going to keep her here, hide her away until we can get help—"

"Absolutely not!"

"You just said—"

"We're going to alert the temple so she can be purified and this curse lifted from our family. Dedicate Brecarian returned today. I am *certain* he is here for her. It is our moral duty to turn her over. Although it will be a shame to lose all that money."

"Hold on now."

"If you won't do it, I will! For the good of this family. We only have one child left. I won't let her ruin his life, too."

"You heartless—This is our daughter! I won't let you—"

"Wait! No, shush! What is that?"

There were heavy footsteps, the door crashed open, rattling on its rails. Her father, dressed for sleep, stood in a halo of candlelight. He froze, his face a rictus of horror and disbelief. He covered it quickly, but the sight was already burned into her mind, her memory. She couldn't unsee it.

"Come away, Arten," he said, holding his hand out to her. "Come away..." He caught up her hand and pulled her to her feet, wiping away the hot tears on her face. Why was she crying? He winced as though burned and put one arm around her, the other holding the candle to shield its light. She caught a glimpse of her mother's face—alight with vindication—before he turned her and took her out to the common room.

They sat at the bench. Arten buried her face in her arms on the table, head ringing with all she had just heard. Her father stroked her hair, stiffly at first, then settled into the familiar motion.

"I love you," was all he said. They sat there, together, until she fell asleep. She woke briefly when he picked her up, like he used to when she was little, and carried her back to bed.

ARTEN WOKE with lead in her heart and limbs. Even her

eyelids were heavy, resisting the call to wakefulness. Two more days. She just had to make it two more days. Then she would become a slave to a man who might save her from the Taint inside. With her father and Deric back, she wasn't needed in the shop. She had no demands on her today, no reason to get out of bed. Except to wait. To hope her father would sign the contract. To hope her mother wouldn't... wouldn't what?

The house was too quiet. There was no morning bustle, no creak of floorboards or careless banging of Deric around the shop. Alarmed, she roused herself.

When she sat up, she remembered with stark clarity her parent's argument the night before and the look on her father's face. And she knew why. The light was still dim and gray with pre-dawn, but it clearly showed the floor where she had been crouched was scorched to char. It ran up the wall and pooled on the ceiling.

There was no question now. No hiding it. No wondering if she was too young. No denying what the stranger had awoken. She had the Taint. The Words circled inside her.

She dressed quickly and, passing through Deric's room, noticed his empty bed. The common room was also empty. She tread lightly down the stairs, every creak jangling her nerves, filling her with a horrible certainty. There was no one in the shop.

She heard raised voices outside. Had to know, had to look. She ran to the window, grabbing up her boots and stuffing her feet in on the way. Two backs blocked her view —her father and brother—as they shifted she caught sight of the people shouting at them.

Dedicate Brecarian. And her mother.

Her mother had brought the dedicate here—to burn her. She had really done it. Arten had been certain, last night, that the gold the stranger offered would have convinced her otherwise. *Stupid, stupid!*

The stranger's words came back to her, *'Get somewhere safe. I will find you.'*

She bolted from the house, terror lending her speed. She dashed behind her father and brother, arrowing for the woods.

"Arten, go back inside!" her father cried out, fear in his voice. She ran faster. Just a few more yards—the trees reached out, welcoming her. The dedicate was hard on her heels, huffing. She broke through, flew over rocks and roots she knew by heart, heard him stumbling, thrashing behind her. This was her domain. She led him north, north towards the swimming hole, away from her real destination. When she could no longer hear his pursuit, she made her way back south, slogging through the creek, boots in hand, and jumping rock-to-rock where she could. Fear must have been driving her hard because she was pounding on the Swain door before the sun had even risen. She pounded even harder when no one answered.

This is the first place they'll look for me, she thought. *I need to get away from here.* She was thinking furiously about where else she could go when the door opened. Arten shoved her way inside and threw the door closed.

"Arten, what—?"

"Juro! Juro, you have to help me. They're after me. They've found me!"

He was alarmed by her panic. "Who's found you?"

"Dedicate Brecarian. The temple. They've *found* me!"

"What are you—" he started, then understood. "It's...*you.* They've been searching for...you? It can't be."

"It is. Juro, I'm sorry. Will you help me?"

The look, the one she never wanted to see, was right

there. Staring at her from her friend's face. Horror, disbelief, betrayal.

"Please, Juro... You said...you said there were people who helped the...the...the people like me. I need to find them. *Please!* They'll be here, soon. They know we're friends." She didn't have time to waste, didn't have time for him to process this.

He mastered himself, his face went blank. "Come with me," he said. He grabbed her hand and pulled her with him as he darted not outside, but deeper into the house, into the laundry area.

"Help me," he hissed, grabbing one side of a cabinet that leaned against a wall, straining to move it. She threw her weight against it at the base, and it jerked and shuddered along the floor a few feet. He stuck his fingernails in a tiny crack and pulled, a door slid open near the floor, only a few feet square.

"Get in," he said, pushing her through the small hole. "Go down, stay down there." He pulled a folded knife from his pocket and thrust it into her hand, "If anyone but me comes through, use this." The door was already closing. She heard him heaving the cabinet back in place. She crept down the short flight of stone stairs by feel, found a small room at the bottom, stone on all sides. It smelled of damp and soil. She felt around, wishing for a light.

There was a narrow pallet that took up most of the floor, only slightly mildewed, blankets folded atop it. It was long enough for her to stretch out on, but a grown person would have had to curl up. Her palm was sweaty around the knife. She snicked it open. She crouched at the base of the stairs, to the side where the room flared out. Listened. Waited.

For the first hour or so, the crackling of fear in her limbs kept her alert, kept her senses attuned to the upstairs. She heard when the dedicate came by. It was too far away to hear the exact exchange, but by the protests and noises echoing from all directions, she thought he had demanded to search the house for her. Juro's angry voice reverberated through the stone.

After the dedicate left, the house settled. She heard the occasional thump or scrape as Juro, Maruko, and presumably their part-time servants moved about the house. Her heart hammered again when someone came into the laundry room and fumbled about in the cabinet for something, but then they left. Time stretched away, unremarkable, unknowable.

Fingers touched her wrist. She awoke all at once, sprang back with a cry, tried to brandish the knife, but that wrist was gripped firmly. "Easy, Arten. Easy." A familiar voice. "I brought you some food." Lantern-lit features resolved into Juro's face.

"What—" she started, but he stopped her.

"Eat," he said, "and I'll talk." Juro sat on the pallet while she crouched next to the door, shoveling the food in her mouth. She hadn't realized she was quite so hungry. "The dedicate came by. I told him that I had heard knocking, but by the time I got to the door, no one was there. He insisted on searching the house. From there, we've gathered, he went to all the neighboring houses. By now, everyone knows he's looking for you. It's not safe for you here. We need to get you away."

"We?" she couldn't help but ask.

"Maruko and I are part of a network to help people... like you," he stumbled over the words. "To help you get to safety. I can give you directions to the next safe house and tell you the pass phrase. From there, they will send you to the next, and then the next. Each place will give you food, water, and shelter for the night. If you need clothing, they may or may not be able to provide that, but you should ask."

"Where...where will I end up?"

"I don't know, exactly. Northeast, I think. I wish I knew...I wish I had assurances to offer you."

"It's okay," she lied. "If I...make it," she swallowed, "I'll try and let you know. When do I go?"

"Soon," he said, "but we have a little time." His voice was that of a stranger.

She wished it was now. Because as much as she dreaded the conversation they were about to have, she needed to have it. "I'm sorry," she said.

"You weren't going to tell me, were you?" he was staring at the floor.

"No," she said. "Not after all you said about your mother, about why you wouldn't marry anyone at risk. Not after you offered anyway. I didn't want to hurt you like that. You or Maruko."

"It's not your fault," he said, "It's not demonic." She didn't say anything. "This man...the one you were going to leave with...he knows?"

"Yes. He found me. Like the dedicate."

"And you trust him?"

"I don't know. He doesn't want to burn me alive. So far, that's better than the temple." She didn't want to tell him about the way he had looked into her, riled up the Words, the hunger on his face. One man wanted her dead. The other alive. That's all she could focus on.

He was still staring at the floor. She didn't know what to say but couldn't leave him like this. She moved from her crouch at the door to sit by his side. Picked up his hand, laced her fingers in his. "You're a good man, Juro. And the...

the best friend...the best." Her throat closed up, and she couldn't continue.

"I'm going to miss you," he said, his hand tight on hers.

"Promise that you won't...forget me," she managed past the giant lump, blinking to stop the rush of tears.

"Never," he promised. "I could never..." He looked at her, then his fingers traced her face, as though he was trying to memorize it. He kissed her forehead, her cheek, her lips. Pressed his forehead to hers, breathed her name.

Too soon, he pulled away. "It's time," he said. "Follow me." He led her back up the stairs, through the small door, his hand clutching hers tightly. He let it go when they pushed the cabinet back in place. Clasped it again when that was done. "Stay close," he urged.

They went out into the house, though the kitchen to the back door. Maruko was waiting just inside it, shrugging out of a dark cloak.

"Haven't seen him," she said. "He left just after dusk. Went back to her house." Arten felt like she was in some strange dream.

"Let's go," Juro said grimly, squeezing her hand. They ran, crouched low, to the barn where they stopped in a deep shadow. "Listen carefully," he said, "follow the creek north for about five miles. At the swimming bend, there are some supplies stashed between the two flat rocks. You know the ones. Don't stop there, keep going—five miles until it doubles back. Keep heading north for another two miles, then at the meadow, skirt around east. You'll hit another creek. Follow that until you see a white rock in an S-bend, then cross. There is a house just up the hill. Knock on the back door after dark. Tell them your aunt and uncle, that's us, sent you for a smidgen of salt. Smidgen, you must say that. Repeat it back to me." She did, twice at his insistence.

"You must go, Arten. Be swift. Be safe. Go now. Go!" He released her hand, gave her a little shove.

She broke and sprinted for the trees, slowed into a jog once she was under cover, didn't pause until she reached the swimming bend. She scrabbled around, found the pack of supplies wedged between the two rocks. They were cold under her fingers, damp. She thought of the long hours stretched out across the smaller one, letting the sun bake her dry, Juro bantering with her, smirking up from its neighbor. Of the time she had sliced her foot open on something sharp in the sandy bottom, and how a ten-year-old Juro had bound the cut up with his shirt and half-carried her home. How the next time they'd come to swim, there was a pile of rocks on the bank and the sand was uniform. Every rock and tree and span of water sparked a memory. They closed in on her, demanding her attention, demanding to be experienced again. One last time. Before they died.

Her chest tightened, and she instinctively clamped down on whatever was building there. Silenced it, silenced the memories. She shouldered the pack and left. They didn't belong to her, that place, those memories. They belonged to someone un-Tainted, someone relatively innocent, someone she could never be again. She was a fugitive now. She had refused her sentence, fled from the authority of the temple, *Even if this stranger can take away the Taint, I can never come back.* Assuming Dedicate Brecarian didn't find her before the stranger did.

She wondered, as she trekked through the dark woods, slower now that she was beyond her normal haunts, why she didn't doubt the stranger would come for her. *I don't know anything about him. Except that he said he would find me.* Except that he had riled the Words inside her. Except that he had offered her parents sixty gold pieces to own her. Just remembering the gold glinting on the table made her gulp. What use could she possibly be that would justify such a sum? *Unless he intended to renege on the deal once he'd left with me. But, clearly, he had the money to honor it. Had it on him while traveling. Who is he?*

And why was she important? She wasn't beautiful or talented, and he had explicitly said he had no interest in marrying her. So, what possible use could he possibly have with a Tainted girl? *Unless it is the Taint he wants.* He had had a strong effect on the Words that lived in her. And he had been aware of them, she was certain.

She had reached the meadow and found a copse of trees near the center where she could observe the open expanses in most directions. She hunkered down in a recess where the ground had slipped away, leaving exposed tree roots that made a thin screen between her and the world, huddled back against the hard-packed dirt, and chewed a hard square of travel-bread as she thought. The pack also contained some dried meat strips, but she would save those until she needed them. Bread would be easier to replace.

I know that the temple wants to destroy people with the Taint because they're possessed by demons. No, that wasn't quite right, she remembered, frowning. *The Wisdoms* said that it *summons forth the demons, which are drawn inexorably and without surcease, until the Tainted One's soul has been completely consumed.* She'd heard it often enough in service but had never before noticed how there was no mention of possession in the text. She had always been told that the demons weren't visible, that they entered into the soul and corrupted from within, which is what made them so dangerous.

She curled up in the small space, pillowed her head on the pack and wrapped her arms around her knees. Fortunately, it was summer, so the night was balmy. A small part of her mind started thinking about what she would need in order to survive like this through the winter. Another small part wondered if the stranger would find her before then, and if she should leave a trail. The bulk of her thoughts were thinking about what the stranger had said.

'I know what you hold inside you.'

'I have been waiting for you.'

'I will come for you. I will find you.'

What if demons were tangible? What if they were tall and lean, with piercing green eyes?

If he is a demon, if he wants to consume my soul, she thought just before sleep stopped the world, *why did he try to buy me?*

8

SNARING A DEDICATE

STEKIN

S tekin had lost his quarry two nights ago. The dedicate had been following his carefully laid trail, the remnants of power drawing the man farther and farther from his true prey. Stekin had led him west and a little south, circling back at night to check his progress. Sometime two nights ago, the man had turned back. Stekin found the camp, the remnants of a fire and burnt leavings of his meal, but the man was gone. It had taken him most of the next day to pick up the dedicate's trail, to find the farm where he had commandeered a horse to speed his return. Stekin had no such authority, nor would he risk drawing the attention. He wanted no one to remember his face.

So he ran. His body shrieked in protest, hating the unfamiliar gate, hating the jarring up his spine that could not be softened, hating the diminished lung capacity. It was too risky to take to the skies, the area too populated. So he continued to run. Through the night, stopping more often than he wanted when the body demanded rest and nutrients. He avoided the roads, cut directly through the woods and hills, shaving miles off the distance. Through the next day, though the stops became a little longer each time, his breath a little harder.

At the apex of the day, he was only a few miles from *her* house. But he had to stop, had to eat something. He used the dregs of his energy to snatch two fish out of a stream and eat them on the spot, then put his back to a tree and fell immediately asleep. He awoke abruptly a few hours later. The heat had not broken and, as he was headed to meet Arten's father and finalize the contract for her, he washed up in the stream and walked the remaining distance. It would not do to arrive mussed, to present any weakness.

The sun was dipping below the tree-line when he arrived at the house. He stopped, observed. There were horses in the paddock, a wagon sat, covered, at the rear of the house. *The father is home.* His eyes narrowed. He could not sense her in the house. *Perhaps her power hides from me again.* The thought sat ill with him, and he kept his senses sharpened as he approached the door. As soon as the door opened to him, he knew something was wrong. The youth behind the door, on the near cusp of adolescence, was pale. Stekin could hear the fearful intake of breath though they had never met.

He had become accustomed to the potency of humanity long ago. *Even so, I thought the stench in the Forgotten City would kill me.* The canyon walls had kept the world out almost as well as they had kept the smell in. In his time there, he had come to distinguish some nuances to human odor. So, when the scents that roiled out of the house assaulted him, he could identify more than just the waft of fear. Anger, distress. A loamy bitterness that had nothing to do with humanity—the scent of charred wood.

But not death. He was intimately familiar with the smell of people burning. *She lives, but something has happened.*

"I think you had better come up," the youth said, his voice in a pinched stage. Stekin controlled his features, schooling his face into blank superiority, careful to turn his power so that his eyes did not betray his agitation. Stekin followed the youth inside. He saw through to the shop. It was closed and dark. *'Saviorsday,'* he recalled, and a bitter snarl flitted across his face before he caught and erased it.

Upstairs, a man sat in a chair, looking out the one window. He tensed as Stekin entered the room. He glared at Stekin, suspicious and angry. *The father.*

"Where is she?" Stekin demanded, not bothering to be polite.

"She's gone. Who are you?" The man stood.

Stekin narrowed his eyes to the merest slits to conceal the anger that flashed through them. "Where has she gone? Tell me," he commanded.

"Arten ran away this morning," the man evaded, still glaring. "And *you* tell *me*, who are you?"

"Why," Stekin asked, curbing his impatience, ignoring the question, reminding himself that he still needed this man, "would she do that?" The man looked away, jaw set, unwilling to say more. *He does not wish to reveal her secret.* "I know what afflicts her," Stekin said, "I am the only one who can help her. Tell me."

"My wife," the man choked on the word, though whether in grief or rage, Stekin could not tell, "brought Dedicate Brecarian here this morning. Arten ran into the woods to get away from him." He seemed reluctant to say more, kept spearing glances at the sliding door that led to the sleeping chambers.

"Where is the dedicate now?" Stekin's teeth bared.

"Looking for her. He said he knows how to find her and he would be back for supper."

"What else did he say?" Stekin pressed.

"Nothing that made sense to me. But I got the impression he expects to go out tonight, and he'll find her then."

Well, Stekin thought with grim satisfaction, *I will just have to ruin his plans.* He relaxed a little. He had some time.

"Show me the burn," Stekin said abruptly.

"How—how did you know about that?" The man's eyes were wide, his aggression watered down with fear. Stekin did not answer and, nervously, the man showed him through into the middle sleeping chamber.

Stekin crouched at the wall, examined the burn. Her scent clung to the center, where the fire had not blackened the boards. It took him only a moment to piece together what had happened.

"What did she hear?" he asked.

"I don't know what—" the man began.

"Do not," Stekin cut him off, "lie to me. Your daughter is in danger. From herself no less than your pyres. I cannot help her if you deceive me."

"Help her?" The man barely breathed, his voice little more than a whisper. "How could you possibly help her?" he rasped, equally bitter and hopeful.

Stekin straightened and faced him squarely, recognizing the moment as his best opportunity to get what he had come for. "If you indenture her to me, I will guarantee her safety."

"I can't sign her into slavery," the man balked, the anger returning. "My wife told me what you're offering for her, and that you refused to tell her what work Arten would be performing for you. Even if she weren't..." his voice snagged. He mastered himself and continued, "...I wouldn't sell her to you."

"That is incorrect," Stekin said, "the woman never asked what the work would be."

"You expect me to believe you will just tell me?"

"I will tell you, regardless," Stekin said frankly. "She will, if she agrees, assist me in a professional capacity."

"What does that mean?" the man asked narrowly. Stekin chose not to answer. The silence stretched then snapped as the man asked, "And if she chooses not to *assist* you?"

"As I said, it will be her choice," Stekin bit the words out of the air, careful not to let his irritation seep out. "Whatever she chooses, she will be well-housed, well-fed, and well-cared for." Before he could stop himself, the disdainful boast slipped out, "Better than she has been here, I can assure you."

The man's face went red, veins standing out. He managed to sound civil as he said, "I won't do it. You should leave."

"You will, and I will tell you why." Stekin was already tired of the game, of mincing around this man's feelings. *He does seem to care, unlike the mother.* Stekin banished the thought. "First, because I am the only one who is interested in ensuring she survives the next few days, not to mention years. Second, because I am going to make you rich. And third, because if you do not, if anything happens to her before she is in my custody, I will come back and slaughter all three of you." He knew his teeth were bared, knew that his pretense of humanity was paper-thin. Knew and cared not at all. Whether the man signed out of love, greed, or fear did not matter, only that he signed.

Stekin pulled the parchment tube from the breast pocket in his robe. Saw the man flinch away at the sliver of skin that flashed. He shook out the twin documents and held them out.

"How do I know you will keep your word," the man asked, scanning the papers, "that you will take care of her?"

"The same way I know you will not reveal this agreement to the temple," Stekin said with a sharp smile. "We both want the same thing: your daughter's safety."

He looked up at that. The look he gave Stekin was one few men were brave enough to wield. "Why her? Why *my* daughter?"

"That answer," Stekin said quietly, "I owe to Arten," the name sent ripples through his power, "not to you."

The man wavered for a few minutes more, while Stekin studied her room, giving him the time. It was relatively barren; a pallet, a small clothes chest. He nudged the chest open with a toe, peered inside. The father bristled, but when Stekin made no move to paw through her things, he stood down. The few dresses still had the remains of tidy folding but had clearly been handled with haste, rumpling them. *No, with that mother, she would not put anything important somewhere so public.* Stekin tread silently around the room, scenting the air, *Ah, clever girl.* He crouched, facing the wall between her room and the outer bedroom, scanning. Found the small line in the paneling, traced it with his fingers until he found the tiny indentations made from hundreds of little fingernails. He pried away the section of panel.

The youth and the man both protested at the same time. He ignored them, slipping his hand into the gap between the walls, just behind where the sliding door tracked. Groping fingers brushed wood. He grasped the item and carefully pulled it out, stowing it in one of the outer pockets of his robe. He fitted the panel back and stood. There had been another item there, a leather pouch that had the hard edges of coin inside. By the anxiety on the youth's face,

Stekin knew it was as secret and precious to him as this box was to her.

"Shall we?" Stekin said smoothly, gesturing for them to proceed him out the door. "Or have you decided to let her burn?"

The father gulped but nodded. Went out into the main room. The youth hung back, no doubt to check that his cache was intact. As Stekin passed, he said quietly, "I will not reveal your secret. I suggest you make your exit soon. Your family is about to crack apart."

"You don't have to tell me that," the boy muttered darkly. "That woman," he hissed and cut an angry glance to the door that had remained closed, "has hated Arten since Tizzy, our sister, died. And once Arten's gone, that blackness will turn on me."

Stekin moved through the adjoining bedroom, his eyes flicking to the secret panel he now knew was there, and out into the common area. The father was seated at the table, frowning.

"This says I am indenturing her and relinquishing guardianship to *Bearer* not you," the man said. "Why?"

"You find it nefarious?"

"I do. What honest man wouldn't put his name on a contract? This is a set up for you to sell her."

"Yes," he said, "it would give me the freedom to do so. And you are correct in suspecting my motivation to relinquish the contract to another. However," he added, interrupting the man's angry outburst, "the person to which I will give it, at an appropriate time, is your daughter."

"You expect me to believe that?" he scoffed.

"I have only one expectation of you, sir," Stekin said precisely, teeth slicing through the air. "For you to sign. Now."

Then it was done, the father's signature soaking into the duplicate copies of the contract, Stekin's mark glistening below.

"You won't even sign your name," the father scowled. Stekin knew he would be stewing in guilt for years over this moment.

"My mark identifies me sufficiently," Stekin said, stacking the owed coins from his purse on the table. They glowed cheerfully in the lantern light, mockingly. He felt a modicum of empathy for the man. "Because you have asked, as your wife did not, and because you seem to genuinely care about her, I will tell you that I am called Kaz," he paused and looked down at the contract to read the man's name, "Jahn." Stekin pushed his copy of the contract, tightly rolled, into the document tube. The other lay, curled at the ends, on the table.

"Kaz," the man said slowly, menace and hatred in the sound, committing it to memory.

Stekin left without another word. Dusk was upon him, and he had much to do before the night was done.

As soon as the trees swallowed his shadow, Stekin stumbled. He steadied himself with a sapling. *I have no time for this,* he snarled. His body was tired, imbalanced from the emotions and chemicals running through it. It needed a rest, but he denied it. *I must stop Brecarian before he goes out tonight. Then I must find her.* He set his mind to working out how to stop the dedicate. He did not wish to kill the man, at least not tonight.

Tomorrow is Midsummer. It will be bad enough if their expected sacrifice is not present, but if the dedicate is also missing, the temple will flock here to investigate. That would endanger the Tsyaro family and, if word got out that Arten was a source, it would be difficult to replace them. No, he had to stop the dedicate tonight, but not harm him.

BRECARIAN SURFACED NOT long after the light had completely faded. Stekin heard the sound of another, deep in the trees. *Following a dedicate? That is foolhardy or perhaps brave.* He would circle around to that part of the woods later, after Brecarian was taken care of, and see if he could make a trail out in the dark. *An interesting person,* he thought, *and perhaps willing to help us. But if not, I cannot risk them seeing me take him.* So, he let Brecarian round the house and knock, watched as the door slid open and the house swallowed him. When the door slid shut, before the lock threw, Stekin chanted, his words low and precise, of no tongue known to these people. His power flared out, spearing for the house in an invisible rush. He strained his ears. Heard the soft thump of three people collapsing, but no more. He had missed one.

I hope it was not Brecarian, he thought as he sat heavily. His power was now wan and sluggish, his fingers trembled slightly. He watched the house and waited. Half an hour later, someone inside stirred, passed by a window. *The mother,* he sneered. *The fool.* His targeted lance hit her square in the chest and she, too, collapsed to the floor. The house was quiet. He had to wait another hour for the spy on the other side of the woods to leave.

Alone, Stekin went to the house and let himself in. The youth was slumped at the top of the steps, a lit lantern leaning precariously against his leg. Stekin extinguished it with a word. Brecarian lay in a tangle at the base, as though he had tumbled down a few stairs. The dedicate had an abrasion on his arm and blood crusting one nostril but slept quietly. Stekin stared down at the man, wondering what to do with him. He toyed with the idea of dumping him in the temple's cells, locking him up and letting *him* be humiliated with the stares and whispers come morning when the village flocked to the Midsummer mass. But he might cast the blame on Arten's family. *No, I need—Ah, yes. That will do nicely.* He felt his mouth stretch in a toothy grin as he climbed the stairs.

Close to midnight, he gained admittance to a small, prosperous home. Brecarian, dressed in some of Jahn's clothing, slid from Stekin's shoulder onto the bed. He sank down several inches. Stekin passed some coin to a businesslike woman saying, "He will sleep for a while, but when he starts to stir, he will be able to perform."

"Don't worry, dear, we'll make sure he wakes up the right way. I've got just the girls in mind."

He slipped her some more coins, "When he asks, remember me as tall and green-eyed."

"You *are* tall and green-eyed, dear," she said, then tapped her chin, "I suppose you want us to misremember, for instance, that you are wearing someone else's clothes and to forget that distinctive footwear?" Neither the youth's nor the father's shoes had fit him, so he still wore his desert sandals.

"Exactly," he said. He turned to leave and felt a pang of conscience. When Brecarian awoke in the manner he had arranged, he would not only be livid but may also be a danger. Even the small modicum of power he had could be unbalanced by amorous activity, especially if he was undisciplined as most dedicates were. "Madam," Stekin said, "I must warn you—"

"Oh, don't worry about that," the woman waved off his concern. "We know who he is."

"Do you?"

"He came through about five years back. Hounded after our Tammi for months. Claimed she was Tainted just because she liked to have fun and didn't want to get married. She passed his test, though. And she'll enjoy repaying him for the attention he gave her."

"I see," Stekin said, his distaste for the man and his profession rising. "He may become," Stekin paused delicately, "odd. During the act. If so, you must warn your girls to get away from him directly."

"Oh, we know about that, too," she smiled tightly. "This isn't our first dedicate. We know how to shut down the overspill."

"Overspill? An interesting word for it." Stekin was intrigued by this woman.

"You have a better one?" she eyed him up and down.

He inclined his head but did not specify. "It is not a trivial matter." She just shrugged prettily. "How do you stop it?"

"Tell you what, honey," she smiled, "you stay the night and let me show you a good time, and I'll tell you."

"I will gladly pay you, madam, but I cannot avail myself of your services. How much is your time worth?" She gave him a number and a location that might be more to his tastes. He paid the coin and ignored the tip. A bucket of water was her expedient method of shutting down the flareout, thrown in the face. And, if there was still sputtering, he was assured that a firm pinch in a particularly sensitive area would finish the job. He declined her offer to demonstrate.

He was tempted to stay for a moment, not for the services offered, but for the expansive, soft beds. He was bone-tired, his considerable strength drained from dragging an unconscious Brecarian three miles through the woods, so as not to be spotted on the road, after having run all the previous night. But he had to find Arten. He had bought them some time, he could not waste it. So, he forced himself back into the woods, back to the house whose occupants would soon be waking. He shuddered out of the borrowed clothing, skin crawling now that the end was near, and scrubbed down under the pump outside before donning his robe once more. The dedicate's robe he bundled up and tucked under his arm. He would dispose of it away from here.

It was nearly dawn. He reached his senses out for Arten, but she was dark to him. Whatever mechanism she had learned to shut down her power was in full effect. No matter. He would find her. He knew just where to start: with that Tsyaro boy who had been skulking around.

THE BOY ANSWERED his insistent knock, too quickly for him to have been asleep. He was heavy and dull as he asked, "What is so important it couldn't wait until morning?"

"Invite me in, Tsyaro," Stekin said, wielding the name to good effect. He was admitted with alacrity.

"It's you," the boy exhaled, his face haggard.

"Where is she?" Stekin demanded.

"Who?"

"Arten," he hissed. "Where is *Arten*." A sound upstairs. His eyes snapped to the noise. A female, the right age, but not her. He dismissed the girl and grasped the boy's shirt. "Where. Is. She?" *Calm down, they are not your enemy*, he reminded himself. He released the boy, who was sputtering denials, forced his hands to his side. Felt eyes on him. The girl watched him. He remembered round cheeks and staring eyes, a fist plugged into a small mouth, tiny fingers reaching for his hair, a woman's laughed apology.

"It's you," she whispered, frozen halfway down the stairs. "It's *you*." The candle in her hand was shaking, the light stuttering, small wax droplets arced to the floor. Stekin stared at her frankly. *How can she possibly remember me?* "You're here?"

"I am," he said, turning to her, putting the boy from his mind.

"You've come for Arten?"

"I have."

"Juro...Juro, it's *him*," she said again.

"You keep saying that, who is he?" the boy sounded disgruntled.

"Don't you remember?" she sounded dazed, her voice wavered. "He came for Mom."

Stekin must have been more exhausted than he thought. He heard Juro's noise of rage, he turned towards it, bringing his arms up to block the swing, but he was too slow. A fist connected with his temple, he felt himself dropping to the floor, blackness blanketing his vision.

9

CONFLAGRATION

ARTEN

A rten slept fitfully. She woke, heart spasming at the forest sounds. The crash of deer through under-growth. The squeak of rodents as they were carried away in owl claws. The scuffle of tree rats in the canopy. The raucous pleas of a nearby toad for a mate. When dawn finally arrived, she gave up trying to sleep.

Creek on the east side, follow it to the S-bend with the white rock. She stretched cramped muscles and chewed on another small hunk of bread while she surveyed the meadow. It was exposed, daunting. It had seemed a good idea to stop here last night, but now she cursed herself for her lack of foresight.

She should cross now, before it got too light. Yet she hesitated. The dedicate could be out there, waiting for her to break her cover. She chided herself. *It doesn't matter, you need to go anyway. Go. Now!* She sprinted across the meadow, spooking a covey of quail and some small animals near the water that disappeared with splashes and rustles.

The dedicate had not been watching. Lungs and legs burning, she leaned over her knees to catch her breath. The air was humid, tasted fresh. Her hair curled with sweat and dew. She gulped a little water from the stream, filled and stoppered the gourd, repacked the items that had been jarred by her run.

Most of what was in the pack was food. Dense bread, thick-crusted and tightly-wrapped to stave the bugs away. Bite-sized strips of dried meat, wrapped in small bundles, tied with too much twine. A small coil of thin, sturdy rope. There was also a small compass that she had not noted in the dark, and a thin packet of paper with a tiny stylus and dry-ink all bound in an oblong of stiff, oily leather, small enough to slip into a pocket. *I wonder if he's as generous with all the people like me*, she thought, touching them reverently. Somehow, she knew he wasn't.

These small extravagances had been his prayer for her safety. The needles, two for clothing and one for leather, picked into the inside seam of the bag, the small pouch of linen and sponge-cloth, those were Maruko's prayer. The bag itself was fine—much finer than she had noticed the previous night—sturdy, water resistant, adjustable to her frame.

There was one other item. She had mistaken it for a box of some sort last night, but in the morning light it proved to be a book. The cover and spine were blank, as were all the pages save the first. Maruko's handwriting was there: *Dearest friend, write your adventures so that when we meet again we can relive them with you. —M.* Juro's handwriting followed. In the clear lettering he had used in all her lessons were only the words: *I love you.*

She clamped down hard on the feelings. Tucked the book safely away in the bottom of the bag. Tucked the compass into her dress pocket. Moved on.

The creek was entirely pleasant. It gurgled along beside

her, not wide enough to break the shade of the trees and cause the underbrush to grow up at the edges. She leapt from rock-to-rock down its center, not minding if the water splashed onto her boots or legs as the sun baked the air around her by degrees. She hated every step. Hated every pretty sight she wanted to share with Maruko, every lounging tree and good hiding spot she wanted to share with Juro. Hated the perfect temperature of the water and the way it tasted fresher than what had been her creek.

Hated that, in midsummer, the temperature in these woods was almost pleasant when her own would be scorching. *Not in midsummer,* on *Midsummer,* she realized with a shudder. *Or near enough; tomorrow, I should have burned.* She was so distracted by imagining the other ways today could have gone—cowering in a cell as the villagers streamed past gaping and talking about her as they went to services, the house and shop ashes because she had burned up two nights ago and killed herself and her family—that she missed the S-curve and almost missed the white rock.

Almost, because it was actually impossible to miss it. The rock was taller than she was and listed out over the creek drunkenly. She was wondering how it stayed upright when she realized what it was she was seeing. She scrambled up the hill, searching for the house. It wasn't difficult to find. At the top of the hill was a small clearing. A squat, square house sat in the middle. It was a cabin more than anything. There was no glass in the windows, just shutters, and the woodpile took up the full length of one side of the house. A door at the front, with a dirt lane leading down and away to where a path had been cleared in the woods, presumably to connect with a larger road. Another, narrower, door at the rear, close to the wood pile. She moved through the woods and took up a post near the back door.

After dark, Juro had said. She had to wait until after dark. After dark on nearly the longest day of the year. It was barely past midday. She found a place to sit, where she could keep an eye on the door and see a short section of the lane. Right now, the house was quiet. *The family is probably at their services.* It seemed impossible that it was only Saviorsday, that she had only yesterday awoken in her own bed. *I wonder if this village will have a sacrifice tomorrow... I wonder if the temple would tell us if they did.* She knew people were sacrificed, but it always seemed to happen far away. Even the last sacrifice in their village had been from the west side of town and no one her family had known. None of her friends or age-mates had been actually afraid of the Taint. Until the Words had come, and she had been.

She chewed a crisp of meat and chased it with some water. It was hotter up here, away from the creek. While she waited, she thought about Maruko and Juro, wondered what they were doing. Wondered how Venerated Vachel was reacting to her escape. Wondered if the stranger was talking to her parents right now, how he would react to the news. The heat and the steady droning of insects and distant trickle of the creek were loud in her ears, every rustle of leaf or creak of twig sent her heart racing, her eyes darting around. She wrapped her arms around her knees to stop the twitching of her limbs that wanted to flee. But she was exhausted and, even as her shoulders knotted with tension, when after each scare no threat appeared, her eyelids began to droop.

She snapped alert with a yelp. A tiny hand was shaking her shoulder and a small voice was saying with insistent politeness, "Miss? Miss?"

"Miss," the little girl said, "Mama says you should come in out of the heat." The girl, who couldn't have been more than eight, grasped Arten's hand and pulled on it. "Come along now," she said, smiling. Arten clamped down on the thing that welled in her and pushed herself up. She held the girl's hand like it was spun glass and followed her up to the cabin.

The woman who drew her inside with a falsely welcoming smile was petite and wiry. The glare she turned on Arten once the door closed might have been formidable if the woman didn't look so concerned, and if Arten hadn't seen worse from her mother before breakfast.

"Why are you sitting outside my house?" the woman asked, suspicious, keeping her daughter behind her.

"I was told to wait for dark and come to the door only then," Arten said, hoping she sounded sufficiently polite and harmless.

"Who sent you?" she asked, narrowly.

"My aunt and uncle," Arten recited. "They sent me for a smidgen of salt."

The woman visibly relaxed. Her worry came to the fore, and her face changed into intense concern. "Oh, you poor thing," she said, sending her daughter to fetch a cup of water for Arten. She pressed Arten down onto a wooden stool and drew up another in front of her. "You must be new to this, not to know. Did they not explain to you?"

"I left in a hurry," she shifted on her stool. "Explain what?" The water was pressed into her hand and she sipped at it politely.

"After dark, dear girl, means after dark. You can't be lurking around in the daytime or people might see you. My daughter, for instance, or a neighbor. It's very risky for us, you know, to shelter you. We can't have you drawing attention by loitering around and being spotted. I'm so sorry, but you do understand?"

"Yes," Arten said, abashed. "I'm sorry if I have caused you problems."

"No, no, it's fine dear. We're relatively secluded out here, we like it that way. But do, please, keep it in mind." Arten assured her she would and apologized again. "Now, now, that's enough of that. Tell me, do you need anything? Your aunt and uncle generally keep people stocked up, but every now and then something slips through."

"I," she hesitated, wondering how much to tell this woman, "I haven't been ...doing this very long. I think I'm okay, at least until it gets colder, or I run out of food."

"Well, since you're new to this, I'll remind you: don't hesitate to ask if you need something. Especially as it gets cold. We may not be able to give it, but it's part of our oath to do our best by you all."

"Your oath?" Arten asked. *To whom?*

"That's neither us nor them," the woman said quickly. "Just remember it."

"I will," she said.

"As far as food," the woman pressed on, her face creased into thoughtful lines, "that's easy if you know how to set a snare. Can you set a snare?" Arten admitted she could not, and then spent the next few hours learning from the little girl how to do so. They were back in the woods, the small hands patiently correcting her work, showing her how to trigger the traps, why her mistakes would cause it to fail. Once she had mastered it, the girl grew bored and asked if she knew any fun games. Arten taught her snake and tree-rat and took the part of tree-rat, which was more challenging. It was strange to play with this young girl, as though she were not Tainted and pursued. As though everything were normal and they were the best of friends.

"It's nice that you're my age," the girl said happily, as

they rested after she had successfully *eaten* Arten. "Everyone else that comes through is older and serious. I'm glad you came."

I suppose if the people she's used to seeing are Juro's age, I do seem like I'm her age. "I'm glad, too," Arten said, and was rewarded with a smile. "What's your name?"

"We're not supposed to use names," the girl said, straightening and looking serious. Her father's words and demeanor, perhaps.

"I'm sorry," Arten said quickly, "I didn't know. It's all ...so strange. A few days ago, I was normal." *Well, not entirely true, but near enough.* "What can you tell me about the others like me?"

Not much, it turned out. Only one or two a year came through, and the girl only remembered about a handful of them. Arten learned only that they were mostly women and, save her, grown up. *That supports Juro's theory. And, if his family has been running a stopping-house like this, that would explain where he got the data for it.*

It was getting dark. The little girl jumped up, saying, "You need to stay out here until it's fully dark. I have to go eat now." She scampered off. Arten waited. When darkness was complete, she performed her expected ritual. A man opened the door this time.

"Follow me," he said, and led her back into the woods, far from the house, to a little stone cellar built into a hillside. It looked like it had once been for food storage of some sort, but roots and time had pushed through the walls in some places and the damp leaked in. "I'll come back to let you out in the morning," the man said and closed her inside without another word, deaf to her protests. The door was made of thick, tough wood, banded with iron. She heard the click of a lock outside.

He locked me in, he locked me in! she fought the rising panic. *What if he doesn't come back? I'm trapped! I can't get out. I'm going to die in here.* Her stomach churned, the Words surged with it. She was sweating, trembling, clutching her stomach with low moans.

You're fine, you're fine, she told herself, concentrating only on forcing the Words down. *You're fine, you're fine. You have enough food for several weeks. And there's plenty of water in here, if you get desperate enough to need it.* A line of sweat rolled down from each temple, leaving a refreshing trail. *Juro wouldn't send you here if it weren't safe, if they weren't like him*, a small voice objected, and she pushed it down, pushed it deep, buried it as she shoved the Words and the terror back, back.

Finally, she remembered the stranger. *I will find you.* That quieted the Words at last. They coiled tightly, deep in her abdomen, waiting.

She curled up, pillowed her head on her pack, expected her deep fatigue to pull her under. But it didn't. She kept thinking about Vachel and Brecarian, wondering where the dedicate was, wondering if the Swains were right now being interrogated by the venerated. Tomorrow would be Midsummer. Tonight she was locked in a cellar. She wondered who would open the door in the morning—the man who had locked her in? Brecarian? The venerated from this village?

Juro wouldn't send me to someone who planned to hand me to the temple, she told herself again. *How well does he know them, though? And how well do they know the place I'm to go next? Even if these people keep whatever oath they have taken, who's to say they all will?* She shivered and hugged herself more tightly.

But she couldn't stop thinking about the festival, about

what could still come to pass. She imagined being chained to the Midsummer pole, standing atop oil-soaked wood, waiting to burn. Her friends—Juro, Maruko, Leif—and her family all lined up in front of her, forced to watch. Her father's hand tossing the starter onto the kindling at her feet, his face set, determined not to give in to her pleas. Her mother's look of righteous condemnation. Deric...would he even care? The screen of flames and smoke that would cloud them from her sight. She wondered what it would feel like, whether she would die before her skin melted away or if she would experience the pain of it. If her lungs would fill with smoke and choke her before the pain was unbearable.

She was so focused on the horror of being burnt alive, she didn't notice the Words. Spiraling up. Stealthy and sinuous. Gliding past the constriction in her throat, filling her mouth like smoke. Only then did they blaze, shredding her tongue and cheeks and throat as they thrashed to escape the teeth she clenched only just in time. She was taut, every muscle braced against their escape, her breath heavy and fast through her nose. The cellar was too warm, the damp turned to steam. She pushed back into a corner, wedging herself against the cool stone. The blocks warmed under her touch, black streaks trailing behind her frantic fingers. Her burning hand slapped her cheek. She bit back the scream of pain, knew there would be a palm-sized burn there. Her dress began to smolder. She tore it off and threw it away from her.

I can't stop them. She looked at her hands, shaking with fear, her skin slick with sweat. *This is it. The gods or the saviors are punishing me for trying to escape my fate. I'm going to burn anyway.* She would have cried if she had any moisture left in her. The Words leapt from her tongue to freedom, launching themselves up, scorching, flaring into the world.

She burned as the Words poured out in a ceaseless torrent. Years of Words erupted from the deepest parts of her. She was screaming, but the Words consumed the sound, transmuted it into their own inferno. Everything would be ash and she could do nothing to stop it.

10

JUST IN TIME

STEKIN

He was somewhere soft, comfortable. Luxurious.

Stekin sighed and stretched. For a moment, he thought he was home. It had been so many years, but he had found it, found the source. A wrongness niggled at him, and when he stretched and his ankles extended beyond the bed, he knew. He was not home. She was not safe. He had to find her.

He sat up, more slowly than expected. His head throbbed with the movement, the world tilted briefly.

"Who are you?" a voice demanded. Male, full of hostility, tinged with petulance.

"Juro, is it?" he said neutrally, forcing himself to look at the youth, to hide the discomfort of his physical state. "Juro Tsyaro."

"You know my name." The boy scowled, arms crossed as he leaned by the door to this bedroom. *Guarding a prisoner?* Stekin wondered, amused. "You will do me the courtesy of telling me yours."

Ah yes, courtesy. Properly valued in that part of the world. How did they end up here? "My title should be sufficient for

you," Stekin said. Watched the boy swell with indignation.
Said, before he was interrupted, "I am the kaz."

The youth contorted with a mixture of feelings Stekin
did not care to guess at. While he was occupied with this
small revelation, Stekin stood, smoothed his robes, noted
the missing items.

"You will return my possessions to me. I will give you
half an hour of my time, then I will retrieve the girl," Stekin
pronounced. He crossed to stand in front of the boy, who
needed to look up only a hand-span to meet his eyes.
Quietly, he added, letting his teeth show, "As one who is
sworn to my service, I expect your complete cooperation. Do
I have it?"

The boy glared at him, unflinchingly, mutinously, but
hissed, "Yes." He physically swallowed his distaste and
added with poisoned courtesy, "If you would follow me."

Stekin followed him out into the upstairs hallway, down
the staircase, and into a room that looked like some poor
version of a library. Stekin selected a chair and lowered
himself into it while the boy muttered something about
retrieving Stekin's belongings. He stifled a sigh. He was not
in the mood to sooth this youth's ruffled temper, but he
could not afford to lose their assistance. If nothing else, the
past twelve years had taught him just how precious people
like Harun and his children were.

The houses that had gone dark had become nearly
impossible to replace, leaving dangerous gaps in the escape
routes. He had talked to many of the safe-houses while he
had wandered this part of the world, inquired about the
numbers of refugees they had helped, verified their needs
were being met financially for the services provided. The
data he had gathered indicated that the number of people
passing though the network in this part of the world was

significantly higher than the number that exited it. Once Arten was in his custody, once she was safe, he would worry about investigating further.

So, when Juro returned with his sister, who was bearing a plate heaping with bite-sized sandwiches, he resolved to make an effort with the boy.

"Appreciated," he said, inclining his head to the girl respectfully as he took a sandwich. "You have questions for me." He held her gaze, ignoring the boy for the moment. She was the one practically vibrating with the need to speak.

"You came for our mom," she said.

"I did."

"And now you've come for Arten."

"I have."

"Why?"

Stekin asked for her name and she supplied it. "Maruko," he said with patience he did not feel, "your father is part of a network of safe-houses for people who are afflicted with what the temple terms the Taint, is he not? And you, yourself, are an active participant in aiding said people?"

"Yes," she said slowly.

"Why do you aid those people when it risks bringing both the law and wrath of the temple down upon you and your family?"

"I think it's wrong to burn them. It's wrong for the temple to hunt them down." *She is very good at concealing the pain of her mother's death.*

"I, also, think it is wrong." He would not tell her every-thing, but she deserved to know more. "I have the ability, like the dedicates, to detect those with power. I found your mother—she was very strong—and tried to get her to come with me to a safe place. She chose not to. I taught her what I could to help her keep her power hidden. By the time I became aware she was losing control, I was too far away. The dedicates found her. I arrived too late for anything but to watch her ashes cool." He felt a specter of rage and grief pass over him at the memory. It was a partial truth. He had arrived in time to hear her screams, to hear little Maruko's bewildered cries, small Juro's alarmed shouts, to watch Harun crumble. "I carry her with me, even now," he added grimly.

Juro snarled from his defensive position at the door, "It's your fault she's dead." He advanced on Stekin, fists balled and raising unconsciously. His sister jumped up and grabbed his arm, holding him back. "You could have saved her, but you left! You left her to die!" There were tears on his face, even as his veins stood out.

Stekin bared his teeth and let the edge of his own anger show. "No," he said with soft menace, "the fault is your own. I wanted to save her, but she refused to come with me. Because of you, Juro Tsyaro. She forfeited her life because *you* needed her."

"You're lying!" Juro growled, broke from his sister's grasp, lunged for Stekin.

Stekin stood and intercepted the swing, closed his fingers around the fist aimed at his temple once again. He caught the other fist that followed. The boy tried to tug his hands free, confused by the strength of the grip. Stekin's eyes flashed and his fingers tightened. The girl gasped, the boy winced. The expression on the girl's face leashed his temper. He released her brother with a shove that sent him staggering.

"I have wasted enough time here. You will return my possessions," he said coldly, "then you will fulfill the oath your father swore, the oath that binds you both, and help me locate Arten." His eyes flashed again as they lit on the boy, "You will pray to the demons you worship that she is still alive. If she is not, if she is even harmed, you will not live to regret striking me last night." The boy had the presence of mind to be frightened.

"Juro, get his things," the girl suggested, helping him up and pushing him from the room. *She is the true protector,* Stekin saw. *The boy plays at it, but he is ineffectual.* He realized she was speaking to him, tore his eyes away from the door through which the boy had exited. "Juro says you are the kaz," she was saying.

"I am."

"I apologize for my brother. We are honored that you, personally, took an interest in our mom. And honored again that you are taking an interest in our friend."

Not just a neighbor, but a friend. "She ran away last night," Stekin said, "you must help me locate her."

"I will tell you what we know," Maruko said, then told him how Arten had come to their door, how they had hidden her from the dedicate, how they had followed the man to her house, then sent Arten into the night to find the next safe-house.

"Ah, it was you I heard in the woods last night," he said approvingly.

"*You* were there?" she looked shocked. He ignored the question. Juro returned with the document tube, his purse, the box he had taken from Arten's room, and his pack and weapons.

"Tell me," he said, checking his property, ignoring the indignant posturing from the boy, "was Dedicate Brecarian at services this morning?" Everything was in order. He stowed Arten's box in his pack, arranged everything to his liking on his person.

"No," Maruko sounded worried. "We think he's tailing Arten. Tomorrow is Midsummer," she said ominously.

"Very good." Stekin wrapped the rest of the sandwiches in a linen napkin and tucked them in his pocket, ignoring the girl's quickly-suppressed horror and the boy's blatant disgust. "Give me the directions you gave her." Maruko gave them, Juro had given up any pretense of civility, and without anything further, Stekin left. His keen ears picked up their argument just as he entered the woods.

I will write Harun a letter, he felt his irritation rising again. *And I will not fail to stress how his child's attack cost me the lead I went to great lengths to arrange.* The boy would be a problem when Harun died. The girl...an unknown. He thought about her as he trotted through the woods, following the creek. Wondered if she would be following this same path before long. Even after all these years, there was no way to predict who had the potential. He hoped she would. She was formidable, strong. She would make a good source.

He was alert, his senses cast wide, searching for Arten or the dedicate. Near dusk, he found where she had slept. Continued east, following Maruko's directions, found the bend. Was on his way up to the house when she flared to light. He staggered and nearly lost his balance. This was no brief flash.

His body was running towards her, automatically, unerringly. The beacon of her power was growing, blinding. He threw a hand up to block it so he could see the ground as he loped over it. There was the thin scent of char trickling out from behind an ancient, sprawling shrub. He pushed it away, saw the door. Saw the lock.

Ripped both away with a snarl. A tongue of smoke boiled into the night.

He plunged into the opening.

Arten was cowered in the far corner, her power so blinding he could not look at her. He could smell the heat, the burnt stone, the tang of burning hair. He had mere moments before he lost her, before the power consumed her. He was kneeling in front of her in two bounds, his fingers digging into her shoulders. He felt the skin of his palms searing, the scent of it mingled with hers.

"You must release it!" he shouted to her over the hiss of water sublimating, the crackle of heat fracturing through rock. She was staring at him, unseeing, beyond hearing, focused completely within.

"You *must*!" he croaked, a hint of panic and something else in his words.

She did not respond. Was unable, he suspected.

He released her shoulder, dug his fingers into her cheeks. He could break her jaw if he was not careful. Gently, he forced her teeth apart, forced them wider, ignoring the pain in his hand. He broke through her resistance. The chanting started, rough and hoarse, but it built into a screaming torrent as the power poured out of her.

He caught it, drew it to him. It writhed, wild and scalding as he thwarted it. It bent to his will.

When she finally slumped over, passed out and empty, he laid her dress over top her and lifted her head to place her pack underneath. Then he went back to the creek, took off his robe and laid down in the shallow bed. The water washed away the sweat and smoke, flowed over his myriad small burns. He turned his head to the side and let it flow through his mouth, rinsing the ash, soothing the rawness.

His hands were a throbbing mess, the skin bubbled and

blistering. He felt her power turning inside him, flowing to the direction of his own. He knew his eyes were glowing as he directed the combined power to his hands, setting a healing.

By dawn, his hands and throat were healed. His body had cooled. He stood and rubbed the water off his skin, donned his robe. He went to check on Arten, steps lighter than they had been for more than twelve years.

11

CAPTURED

ARTEN

W hat she noticed first was how much her jaw hurt. The pain was unrelenting and intense enough to wake her from her dreamless sleep. Her teeth had clenched against it, and it took her several minutes to force them apart. A wisp of wind snaked in from the open doorway sending a shiver through her. Why was she so cold? She pushed herself upright and the blankness in her mind began to refill with snatches of memory, sluggish and fuzzy.

She recalled the fear, the searing inside. A cracking of wood and snapping of iron. Icy fingers piercing her shoulders—she could still feel those fingers, like puncture wounds. She remembered them prising apart her jaw. The Words escaping, lurching forth in a rasping lump, tearing at her throat, scalding her mouth. Her tongue touched the slick surfaces where tender new skin was growing. Her fingers touched a cheek where the outline of her hand ached below the skin. She remembered the feel of the last Word, long and barbed, scraping a sharp trail up her throat and clicking against her teeth as it left. The feeling of absence as pressure disgorged.

The flash of green in the darkness.

He took them away, she thought, stunned. *How did he do that? Was that what he was trying to do in the shop?* A hundred questions chased through her head. If he could take the Words away, why had he offered to buy her? Were they gone forever? *Can I go home?* Hope swelled and immediately burst. *How would I explain this?* She had never heard of anyone being cured of the Taint before. What if they didn't believe her? Would they burn her just to be certain?

She wriggled back into her dress, grateful for the thin layer of cloth. *Why am I so cold?* she wondered as she chaffed her arms and hugged her legs. *And what do I do now?* She prodded at the still place where the Words had swarmed, head buzzing. She saw the remembered flash of green again, wondered, *Will he come back?* He had found her. Had somehow stopped the inferno of the Words. Had touched her cheek and hair afterwards. A parting?

It doesn't matter, she decided, *I need to continue on.* It was tempting to go home, to see if she could convince the temple it had all been a mistake. But it wasn't worth the risk. *Once I know how to prove I don't have the Taint, then I can go home.* The thought decided her.

Dawn was upon her. As it filled the room like a slow spring, she saw the damage she had wrought. Everything was covered in a haze of char, the walls in the corner had crumbled away chunks of their stone. The scent of ash and skin became intensely apparent, and she gathered her pack and darted outside before she retched on it. The door was listing, still attached by a single hinge, a huge crack splitting it near the handle. She crouched in the bush that embraced it and waited for the man to come back as he had promised.

She'd only just settled when an abrupt voice from the other side of the bush said, "Come with me."

"Who's there?" she demanded, startled, jumping to her feet. She had heard no one approach.

"Keep your voice down," the words were frosted, impatient. She pushed branches aside to reveal a tall, gaunt form.

"You came back," she whispered to herself.

"As you see," he snapped. "Now, come." The command was also a warning. He didn't like repeating himself. She tugged her pack on and emerged to face him. He pivoted on the spot and strode away, leaving her to trot after. His robe rustled against the underbrush, dry twigs snapped under his sandals.

"How did you find me?" she asked his back, ducking under a low-hanging branch. "Where are we going? How did you take the Words away?"

He stopped, and she pulled up sharply to avoid crashing into him. "Enough," he said, his voice quiet-edged. "It is not safe here. I will answer you when we are not in danger of being observed."

"But where are we going?" she pressed.

He frowned at her over his shoulder, didn't answer, kept walking.

They walked in silence. Around midday, she realized she had been following him blindly, trusting him to lead her, and that she would be wise to start paying attention in case he left her out here. Part of her was alert, wary of him, but a larger part trusted him after last night. Why would he save her just to harm her out here? Why come back for her this morning if she wasn't useful to him? Why offer her family so much money?

She pulled out her compass and started paying closer attention.

In the late afternoon, they stopped in a rough circle of old trees, shady and cool, the thinnest trickles of water bumping out over the mossy rock-face that sloped up just beyond the southern edge of the ring. Arten wedged her gourd under the trickle to let it slowly fill while they rested and ate. He parceled out some of the jerky in his pack to her, after he saw her nibbling at the travel bread to make it last.

"We are going somewhere safe," he said. The trees and rocks muted his words.

"Where?" she asked warily.

"To the place I live." She found the wording odd. "You will have a home there."

Her head jerked up at that. "And if I don't want to go?" she dared, hating how small her voice sounded.

"You will, regardless. I am, as of now, your legal guardian and in possession of your indenture contract."

"They signed it?" She wasn't sure if she was relieved or disappointed.

"Yes."

So, her parents were now wealthy. Her mother, who had tried to turn her over to the temple, had the gold she had been so reluctant to relinquish. She wondered what they would do with it. Wondered if they would move to a new city, like the Swains had, to escape the shame, to hide their newfound fortune. She wondered if the temple would confiscate the gold if it was discovered. Wondered if her father would be punished for her escape.

"Why did you buy me?" she asked, unhappily.

He was cold, factual, in his answer, "There are many reasons. What I will tell you now is this: without my assistance, you will die. I needed you to come with me. Because you are still the legal property of your father, this was the way I saw to make that happen."

"But *why*?" she insisted, gesturing formlessly. "How can I possibly be," she gulped, seeing again the coins stacked on the table, "useful to you?"

His eyes narrowed as he considered her. "Once we have arrived, I will explain. The matter is...private." He said the word with a gravity that implied a significance she didn't understand. "I cannot risk its exposure."

"You mean if I'm captured," she said, shrewd and bitter. He inclined his head in acknowledgment. "Is he still...is that likely?"

"We have embarrassed and thwarted the dedicate. It is likely he will continue his pursuit," he said dispassionately. He studied her then offered, "I will not let him harm you."

She shivered, despite the heat. "How can you prevent it? You can't stand against the law..." she said, shredding a leaf with her fingers.

"Arten, I have and will continue to stand against them, as long as I must," he said, his voice crisp and biting.

She barely heard him, her attention turned inward. When he had said her name, she had imagined skittering in her abdomen, light as a dry leaf. Her stomach tightened. Had the Words come back?

She had to ask. "Are they gone? The Words?"

He tilted his head to study her, didn't have to ask what she meant. The coldness in his voice warmed slightly as he said, "No." Was that pity or disgust?

She couldn't shake the phantom of that feeling. Didn't protest when he said no more and pressed onwards. Was happy to distract herself by noting their position and the terrain, by trying to memorize the route. *Although it's pointless since I didn't pay attention earlier.* And since she didn't know where they were going. Stekin seemed to, though.

He stopped as they crested a tall hill, when they had

walked about five miles. His fingers wrapped around her upper arm, too tightly to be comfortable, as he drew her in front of him. He pointed over her shoulder, his words angled down at her as he said, "Do you see the house there?"

She didn't at first, but then made it out, the corner of a shingled roof on the far hill. "Yes."

"Wait here until dusk then go to the house and knock. Tell them you are on your way back from visiting your uncle, who caught two large fish yesterday."

"It's another of the safe-houses?" she asked.

"Yes. I will return to you tomorrow." He released her arm, and she felt him turn to leave.

"What? Wait!" she yelped. "Where are you going?" The thought of being shut up in another cellar made her stomach turn.

"I must provide compensation for the damage done by your conflagration and ensure that there is no lasting damage to the network."

"But...what if it happens again? What if you didn't take them all?" she asked in a whisper, hoping he would assure her it couldn't, that the Words were gone.

"Tonight, you are in no danger," he said, staring through her torso. The tiny hope snuffed out at the implication in his statement.

"How do you know?" she shuddered. "What if they lock me in?"

"You will become accustomed to the locks. It is for the safety of both parties."

"But—" she protested. He cut her off.

"You will do this," he said, his eyes flashing, the green flaring with that internal light. She backed up a pace, alarmed. "I will return tomorrow." He left, not looking back, his strides long, quick, and silent.

What was that? His eyes had done that before, when he had come into the shop. *And again last night? I thought I imagined it*, her gut writhed. *How can his eyes...*

The obvious answer presented itself: *He's a demon.*

But if that's true, why is he helping me? And why doesn't that scare me?

Her head hurt, everything hurt. She found a place to settle, where the corner of the roof was still in view, and waited, probing the tender skin inside her mouth. After a time, she pulled out the journal, found a wax-and-paper-wrapped graphite stick in a tiny pocket along the spine, and wrote an abbreviated and poorly-spelled account of the last few days. It took her the rest of the afternoon. When dusk fell, she gently tucked the journal back in the bottom of her pack, shouldered it, and went down the hill.

They put her in a cellar again, though this one was under the house, accessible from an outside door. When the lock snapped closed, she felt a shudder that could only have been the Words. She nibbled on her bread, sucked on the dried meat strips until they were soft enough for her bruised jaw to manage without pain, pillowed her head on the pack. The cellar was dry, the stones around her were cool, and there was only a hint of mouse about the pallet. She fell asleep almost at once.

THE MORNING CAME TOO EARLY. She awoke with a start at the clanking of iron against iron as someone fiddled with the lock. She cowered involuntarily when the door swung up and away, silhouetting the bulky form of the homeowner.

He tromped down the stairs and lifted her to her feet with a callused hand. He was kind and earnest, gave her the next direction, wished her speed and safety on her journey. Much more talkative than the previous night, that energy firmly directed at getting her into the woods. *Probably just grateful that I didn't burn his house down,* she thought miserably as she put her back to him and trudged away.

Where is Stekin? she wondered, her mood darkening further when he did not materialize out of the woods. She thought back. *I guess he didn't say* when *he would be back today. He has to travel all the way we came yesterday and back again—that will take time. I probably won't see him today at all. What did I expect?*

She knew what she had expected, though it seemed silly now. *For him to grow wings and fly there, I suppose, since he* must *be a demon.* She rolled her eyes at herself. *Whatever happened with his eyes, it must have been a trick of the light. I was exhausted and frightened yesterday,* she told herself.

She should have been paying attention. The field she passed through was quiet, but she was busy thinking about Stekin, busy thinking about anything *but* Stekin. All she noticed was that the droning of the insects hazing the grass seemed loud. She ignored it. She should have stopped, should have realized the animals had gone quiet. Should have run away.

But she didn't. She blundered on, oblivious. Until a whistling grew in the air behind her.

Something hit in her in the back before she could turn around, wrapped thin arms around her. Ropes, weighted on the ends, lashed around her chest as she fell forwards.

She landed heavily on her shoulder. The ropes bound her arms to her sides. She struggled frantically to free them, writhing on the ground, concerned only with escape. Not with who had caught her.

The shadow fell long across her, approaching from behind. She rolled over, faced him. The robe, the long trailing belt, the swagger.

Dedicate Brecarian.

No no no no no... Paralysis threatened to seize her. She snarled, screamed at herself. *Get up!* Got her knees under her. *Run run run. I have to run.* He was close, too close, there wasn't enough time.

She gained her feet. Took two quick strides, digging her feet into the ground with desperate strength.

The dedicate was there, his longer legs closed the gap with a lunge, his hand hit her squarely in the back. She lurched forwards, went down hard, jarring her chin, rattling her teeth.

Her breath left in a whuff, empty of Words.

A weight slammed into her back. Brecarian pinned her to the ground, sitting on her spine with knees crushing along her ribcage, his panted, hot breath on her neck.

"You shouldn't have run, girl," he growled. "Just made things harder for yourself. And your family. And—Who helped you? It was the Swain girl, wasn't it?" He laughed harshly at her silence, mistaking her inability to speak for lack of breath with recalcitrance. "Ah, don't you worry," he said with false reassurance, patting her cheek with the casual roughness usually reserved for animals, "I'll get all the answers I need before I turn you over to Vachel." He leaned forwards, his chest heavy on her back, and hissed above her ear, "You *will* tell me everyone who abetted you. And then you'll burn, like a good, devout girl."

He sat up. She heard something heavy and metallic being removed from a pack. "Can't have you escaping again.

You be good and I won't let this hurt you too bad." She could hear the wicked grin. Something cold and hard slid around her neck, he lifted her head by a fistful of her hair. She felt it click closed over her throat.

"It's not so bad," he said, patting her head as he dropped it back into the grass. "You're the youngest ever caught, I'll wager. You'll make my name for me. Vachel, too, I suppose. But we can't have everything." The dedicate hauled her to her feet.

Where is Stekin? she thought desperately, futilely. But she was out of options, out of time.

If I'm going to burn, I'd rather it be on my own terms, she thought grimly, consigning herself to her fate. Wondered if there was anything left to burn with. Probed for the Words. They were there, smaller, weaker than they had been. *Maybe there are enough.* At the thought, they surged upwards, desperate, as though sensing their last chance at freedom.

And stopped.

"Thought we weren't prepared for your tricks, did you?" he chortled. "We've been burning demons like you for hundreds of years."

Something was...strange. His voice had become muffled, his face wavered as if moving through water. His mouth was working, but the sounds came later all in a rush. "Let's go." He affixed a chain to the collar around her neck and tugged her after him, through the field in a new direction. To where a horse waited. How had she not noticed the horse before? She could do nothing but scramble to follow, reeling from the warping of her senses.

THE WORLD STRETCHED and bent in her vision, sounds came

sometimes as though from under water and others with ringing sharpness. Arten stumbled along behind the dedicate, uncertain when each foot would fall, uncertain if she was even stumbling.

Then she was on the back of the horse, torso still wrapped in the ropes that had caught her. Her face was pressed against the dedicate's back, kept there by the taut chain, which glinted where it draped over his shoulder. She felt the ropes digging into her arms, the sharp curve of the collar pulled up against her lower jaw and the nape of her neck, felt the scrape of the saddle skirt and pad under her thighs.

The pain was unbearable, every fiber and edge a knife. Then, sometimes, the pain was nothing, the memory of an ache from long ago.

Her thoughts were thick and slippery, like large, startled fish. There was a tall figure, gaunt and familiar somehow, that featured into them, but the image of him slipped away into the murk before she could focus on him. There was fear. The fear was easier to hold on to. The fear of burning, of ...disappointing someone. Fear of the dedicate in front of her. Fear of wherever they were going.

Fear enough to burn some away some of whatever was holding her in thrall. Enough that her blood pounded, her limbs crackled.

She tried to jump off the horse, managed only a listing jerk which set her falling. She landed face-down in the dirt, her mouth filled with grit. She tried to stand, couldn't move at all for the weight pinning her legs down.

Through the flexing of the world, she saw that her captor had fallen on top of her. His face was livid, his mouth moving exaggeratedly, but the sound was garbled and quiet when it reached her. His eyes, his nose, were preternaturally clear, even as the rest of the world blurred and smudged. His eyes were a deep brown, the iris nearly lost. For a moment, she thought she saw the color disappear entirely from them, blotted out by darkness.

She was on her feet, his face inches from her own, flushed with anger, his brows pulled down brutally. He was shouting, she felt the flecks of spittle on her forehead, but there was no sound.

His eyes released her, snapped away to some other prey as he straightened.

The fish from her thoughts was there, in the road, a dozen paces behind them. He looked taller than memory, his eyes were blazing. Her vision narrowed to his teeth, which bit the air as he demanded something. The man who held her laughed, the sound piercing the cotton that insulated her, and called back an answer. Then the pain was back, searing through her shoulder, which had taken the brunt of her fall, lancing through her teeth and jaw.

She fell, knees weakened. The world grew even fuzzier and she had little thought to spare it, only the pain mattered.

The stranger moved, too fast, closing the distance between himself and the dedicate. She saw a fist drawn back across his body, the backhanded strike that flew. The dedicate lifted from his feet and time stretched as he arced through the air and fell a pace to the side, his face twisted too far on a broken neck.

His unseeing eyes stared at her, above the collapsed ruin of his cheek. Devoured her. She couldn't look away. Distantly, she felt the shaking start.

The stranger gripped her shoulders, turning her away. He was speaking, urgent, but she could not hear him. She flinched away—his fingers promised pain—lost her balance. She was lowering to the ground, not falling. A cold palm on her forehead, then nothing.

SHE AWOKE TO PAIN. A burning band around her neck, a lightness where the metal collar had been, a throbbing in her face that speared into her skull, an inability to move her shoulder that told her something was very wrong there. A dead man's staring eyes came back to her, and all that had come before. She pushed herself upright, folding her legs together to stabilize her. The pounding in her head subsided a little, and she managed to crack open her lashes.

It was dark. Moonlight illuminated the scant grove of trees around her, the heap of grasses that were her makeshift pallet. It reflected off an expanse of fallow field she recognized. She had been surprised over there, could still see the imprint of her fall in the grass. Saw the line of bent stalks she and the dedicate had made in passage, angling towards the far edge of the meadow. Saw another, wider line leading to where she now rested.

She noted for the first time she was wearing trousers and a thin tunic—not the dress she had been wearing. A breeze stirred, chilling her neck. She reached up, touching the bare skin there, feeling upwards. Her hair had been shorn off.

There was a stirring in the shadows to her right. A glimmer of green from slatted eyes that set her instincts skittering like prey.

"Go back to sleep," Stekin's sharp words chipped through the incessant throbbing in her head. She lay back down, curled up tightly, as far from him as possible without sacrificing her makeshift pallet. She had spent the night outside with Juro before, but this was a man, and a stranger, and his presence was in no ways comforting. Why had he brought her back here? Why had he changed her clothes, cut her hair? *He killed the dedicate...*

She tucked her knees close to her chest. Fast as a snake striking, a long arm reached over, fingers found the skin of her ankle. The shock of their cold grasp made her jump, jerk away. She heard him hiss, "Sleep," and knew no more.

A RIOT of birdsong woke her, but it was the scent of hot meat that roused her. She had slept past dawn. The sun was already slanting over the trees on the western edge of the field. The stranger sat across from her, waiting, his posture stiff and aloof. She saw the glimmer of green through his lashes as he studied her. A flick of a finger drew her attention to a bowl of porridge, then he stilled once more, hands resting lightly on his knees. She shuddered to see them, remembered his cadaverous grasp around her ankle. He gestured again, a twitch of impatience at his lip.

Her shoulder wouldn't move, she winced as she reached with the other arm to pick up the bowl.

"Wait," he commanded, before she could do more than glance at the congealed muck in the bowl. It looked revolting but smelled divine. "You are injured."

"I'm fine," she lied through her aching teeth.

There was a clattering, annoyed sound. Her eyes darted around, looking for whatever animal might have made it before she realized it had come from him.

"Lie down," he ordered, "I will do what I am able."

She leaned away, involuntarily. "Are you a healer?" The memory of his bony fingers on her ankle made her skin crawl.

"No." He stared at her expectantly, impatiently.

"What are you then?" she dared.

"Your guardian," he said, a warning. A fresh memory pushed to the fore: the arc of a backhanded blow, the arc of a body as it fell. Her mouth went dry.

She lay back on the pile of wilted grass, arms clutched tightly over her stomach. She heard him as he knelt beside her, the whisper of the strange material of his robe, his slow, deep breathing. She studied the stems of grass, the nodules of bark and dirt near her face, avoiding him, avoiding those eyes that could see through her, that had twice incited the Words. She felt his hands hovering over her shoulder, the cold radiating from them strongly enough to penetrate the fabric of the tunic she wore. He was murmuring something, her ears tried to prick it out but it was too quiet. Then there was movement inside her shoulder, deep at the bones, a little churn. *Like a Word.* It grew and spread, swiftly, embracing half her back and ribs before it stilled. She was prodding at the sensation, which had become all but unnoticeable, wondering if she had imagined it.

"Stop that," he snapped. "You will disrupt the healing."

"What healing?" she asked, "I thought you said you weren't a healer?" Healers used potions and poultices, herbs and the natural physics to promote healing. All he had done was move his hands over her, like the charlatan savior that had come through their village when she was younger, claiming to heal any ailment by channeling the power of the saviors through his hands. He had been chased out of the village by Venerated Vachel, who had threatened to summon dedicates to test him for possession, even though he was in his august years and far beyond any threat of the Taint. The few people who had been cured by him had sickened again before nightfall.

"Be still," was all he said, his hands moving, leaving trails of cold-prickled flesh behind as they skimmed over her other shoulder, down her ribs, across her hips. He paused at her right hip, which had broken her fall from the dedicate's horse, the strange sensation came and went again, much smaller than in her shoulder, then he was moving on. Down her leg, stopping briefly at the right knee, back up the left one. The progression of his hands up her leg was disconcerting, even though they did not touch her. She felt a flutter of panic as he moved higher, her eyes snapped to his face. His were closed, a frown of concentration on his features, his lips moving minutely as he shaped the quiet sounds she had already dismissed into background noise. Nothing that suggested his intentions might be wandering.

The mouth stilled, a flicker of green caught her gaze. His eyes caught her, held her. Her panic grew into horror. He was going to reach inside her again, going to overpower her. She felt the Words begin to churn, lethargic but awakening once more. *No no no no no...*

"Be still," he said once more, hands reaching for her. She pushed herself away, scooting backwards. But his reach was long. His hands caught her skull between them. His mouth moved again, his eyes hooded. Movement along his arms drew her attention. A shimmer, half-seen like of heat, seemed to be growing, pushing down his arms in tight waves. The first ridges traveled down his forearm, his wrist, his hands. She felt them impact her cheeks, nothing, then the feeling of movement along the bones of her jaw, along the circle that the metal collar had cut into her flesh, swirling at her temples. It spread and grew and stilled. Stilled the pain. She stifled a sob of relief as the agony ebbed to a dull ache.

The shimmering ripples had stopped pulsing out of

him. He pulled his hands away, releasing her. His face seemed tighter, drawn, as he removed himself to where he had been seated when she woke.

"What-what did you do?" she breathed, touching her face, rolling her shoulder. There was still pain, still aching, but she could move freely again, her teeth no longer ached, her headache had gone.

"Eat," he said, reaching for his own bowl, "then we will talk."

Somehow, he managed to eat with his fingers as elegantly as Maruko had ever managed with her family's silver utensils and fine porcelain. Arten felt slovenly as she pushed the food into her mouth but stopped caring as soon as the taste hit her. The porridge was soggy and a little charred, but there were generous chunks of fresh, warm venison and some green spears she had never tasted before in the bottom.

"Where did you get venison?" she asked, licking the rough clay clean carefully. He was staring at her, a twist of disgust on his face. She ignored it and finished cleaning the bowl. "And the bowls, and these clothes?"

"I hunted. I made them. I bought them," he said, wiping his own bowl out with grass and stowing it in his pack. He stood, handed her pack to her, said, "We must depart. Your injuries will slow us down."

She followed his example, wiping out her bowl and tucking it inside her soot-stained pack. She was shaky when she got to her feet, his hand under her forearm kept her from falling. It was gone before she could object. They were moving across the field, striking east, leaving the little grove of untenable land behind them. Her eyes kept darting south, to where the monk had laid in wait for her. She didn't realize she'd stopped until Stekin said, "He will not trouble you further."

"He's dead," she said flatly, seeing his shattered cheek, the glaze of his eyes.

"Yes." He did not seem bothered by the fact. "I buried him and sold the horse he stole. To the temple, he will appear to have gone missing. It will take them many months to send someone to look for him. They will find neither him nor the demon-metal." His voice was so cold and hard that she shivered.

"Demon-metal?"

"The collar." His eyes flicked to her neck, flared, then away. Sweat prickled out along her forehead and spine at the fury in that look.

She steeled herself and asked, "Are you a demon?"

She didn't know what answer she expected, but it wasn't the tired, "Does it matter?"

"What?" was all she could think to say.

He was striding across the field. She jogged to catch up.

"Does it *matter*," he snapped, his perfectly-straight spine stiffened, "whether I am demon or not. I have saved your life twice now," he added, his voice bitter and wintry, "I have taken over your guardianship in order to continue to protect you. Are these the actions of a demon? Does a demon respect the law, does a demon act equitably, does a demon seek to minimize suffering?"

"You haven't said what you want from me," she answered hotly. "How I am supposed to repay all this *kindness*." The last word was as biting as any of his.

Tension rolled through his shoulders, as though he were making a great effort to contain himself. He said, "I want only what you willingly give."

"My life?" she guessed, mockingly to hide the fear in the question.

"No." He paused in his step, looked over his shoulder, stared through her. The Words churned. His eyes followed them with a falcon's intensity. He continued, the pause had lasted only a heartbeat. "Something infinitely more precious," he said quietly, chin angled so that his words drifted back to her.

"The Words," she whispered, shuddering, as they coiled in agitation.

She realized he had excellent hearing when he responded, "Is that how you refer to the power you carry? Why?"

She was shocked at how casually he said it. Found she couldn't answer. The fear of the Words, the fear of discovery, still bound her tightly. *You have already been discovered,* she told herself, *He knows about them, the temple knows about them. What harm could come?* Her head collided with his back, forcing her out of the internal place to which she had retreated; she hadn't noticed him stop.

A hand descended to her shoulder. It squeezed, strong, still cool even in the summer day's heat. It took her a moment to realize the gesture was meant to be comforting. "You are wise not to speak of it openly while we are still in danger." He'd mistaken her inability for caution. She didn't correct him.

"Are we?" she croaked, her mouth and throat dry. "Still in danger?"

He drew out a flattened metal container from his pack, removed the cap with a twist of his wrist, ignored its rasping complaint. He offered it to her. She sniffed at it, realized it was water. "I will not be offended if you elect to drink from your own canteen," he said as she paused. He sounded amused. She shot him a quick glare, careful not to look at his eyes, and took the vessel. The water was cool and only slightly metallic-tasting.

"Thanks," she said, handing it back.

"We are," he said, confusing her, until he added, "still in danger." The canteen disappeared into his pack once more. "We will be until we reach our destination."

"The place you live that isn't your home?" she said, surprised at her own daring.

He inclined his head in acknowledgment. "We must press on, if we are to reach the house by nightfall," he said. And they did.

She followed him, letting him set the pace, withdrawn into her thoughts. He seemed to know where he was going, found all the markers, made the right turns.

Does it matter if he's a demon? she repeated to herself. *What a thing to ask! Of course it does. Demons are... are... evil.*

But what he had done so far was not. He had, as he said, saved her life twice. He had healed her somehow this morning. She rolled her shoulder, felt the small twinge there. *'I want only what you willingly give,'* he had said. *He wants the Words, and I don't. Is there harm in giving them to him?*

The thought didn't sit well with her.

He called it power—like, magic? Only the saviors and the demons had the power of magic. And he's clearly in opposition to the temple.

All more evidence that he was a demon. *If he's a demon, and I give him power, he'll grow stronger. What will he do with that strength? Rescue more little girls and take them to a safe place?* She nearly snorted aloud at the ridiculousness of the thought.

No, she decided, *I will not give him anything until he answers some of my questions adequately.* And if he didn't like that, well, she would know whether he was earnest in his claim that she must be willing.

They stopped in a shady grove near midday. The ground was rougher now, more stones and brambles and close-grazed meadows than woods and crops. She perched atop a boulder, her toes only skimming the ground, while he settled on the far side of it. She turned around to face him, drawing her legs up and crossing them. The stranger pulled out another thin metal object, this one turned out to be a box.

He prised one side away and revealed a mound of shredded venison inside. *From the deer he supposedly hunted last night,* she thought, eying it. It symbolized wealth to her in an immediate way that the gold had not. He set it on the dome of rock between them, but she waited for him to eat a piece before she tried it. It was a little dry. He did not caution or limit her, so she gorged herself on it. She felt a little guilty when she realized what she had eaten was more meat than her family ate collectively in a whole day. The stranger seemed to have no such guilt and dipped his fingers into the metal box until the pile was all but gone. He offered her the last piece, ate it when she declined.

"Where did the rest of the deer go?" she asked as he packed away the box. "There was no carcass this morning."

"Would you believe me if I told you I ate it?" he said, his mouth angled in small amusement.

"No," she said, irritated at the levity. He shrugged, a motion that had his shoulders dipping in an elegant half-circle. It made her notice that the twinge in her shoulder had grown into an ache, and her jaw was starting to clench again. His eyes flickering over her sharply. "What?" she demanded, hearing the continued irritation in her voice. *I'm going to be miserable to be around for the rest of the day,* she knew.

"Your pain block is wearing off," he said, frowning. "Allow me to reapply it or you will disrupt the healing."

"I'm fine," she insisted.

"Only because it is not fully gone," he snapped. "Do you intend to make a habit of challenging my assistance?"

"Yes," she said, to annoy him.

"Very well," he said, standing swiftly. "When you are ready, you have but to say so." He strode off, stiff-legged. She trotted after, suppressing a groan at the aching it set off in her shoulder, determined not to let him know it.

As the afternoon wore on, she discovered he'd been correct in his statement. She clenched her teeth against the pain in her shoulder and hip, which only exacerbated the aching that spread through her face until even her teeth throbbed in their sockets and her eyes burned from the light. She had stopped paying attention, was focused only on the hem of the gray-blue robe in front of her as it swept along, on keeping her feet moving. She was fixated on the weft of the cloth, on the tiny embroidered patterns in it, on the many parts of the hem that had frayed.

The pattern, she puzzled out at last, *looks like scales.* She tried to remember all the scaled beasts she and Juro had come across, tried to remember what their scales looked like. The miasma of pain in her head made it difficult.

She stopped when he did. Her breath was coming in short, pained pants. She wanted to sit down but thought she might not be able to stand up again, so she hobbled over to a tree and leaned her good shoulder against it.

"You are needlessly stubborn." His brittle voice sounded in front of her. She cracked her eyes open, cringing at the pain from the light, closed them again. She felt his hands on her face, his long fingers cool and refreshing along her temples and cheeks. She felt the deep swirling, the expansion, the stillness. She actually cried when he repeated the effort at her shoulder. She scrubbed the childish tears of relief away as he worked at her hip, then her knee, but continued to sniffle.

He didn't ask for or wait for thanks or acknowledgment. When he finished, he went a few paces away and stood with his back to her. Somehow, he knew when the pain had cleared enough. Just when she was feeling distinctly awkward and guilty, he announced it was time to move on.

He set a fast pace. She didn't need to ask why, knew she had been shambling before he'd stopped and healed her. At the brushing of twilight, they were back in a forested area, though the ground was still rocky and poor and the trees were not as tall as she was accustomed to. The stranger was half-bent at the waist, crouched in the legs, as they threaded through the low branches, but still, she noted, his shoulders and spine were straight. She was distinctly conscious of her own hunched posture. At the bottom of a hill, he stopped her, gestured to the top with a long finger.

"I see it," she whispered, noting the house perched just over the ridge of the hill.

"Do you remember the rest?" he asked.

"Yes," she bristled, nearly forgot to keep her voice down.

"Good," he murmured neutrally. "I will see you tomorrow then." He turned to retreat back the way they had come. Stopped, startled.

He looked down, and she was as surprised as he to find that it was her hand, fingers twisted in his sleeve, that had halted him.

"Are you going back?" the quiet volume hid the tremor in her words, she hoped. The dedicate was dead, but Stekin had said she was still in danger. She didn't want to go up there alone, didn't want to face another night locked in a stone room.

Stone, she had pieced together, to contain her conflagration, to protect the normal people from her.

"No," he touched her shoulder, "but the sources always arrive alone."

They would be suspicious, he meant, if he arrived with her. "Can't I stay with you again?" Last night hadn't been so bad, not compared to the stone prison that awaited her up the hill.

"No. I need you to be safe," his fingers clutched at her shoulder, "I need those who come after you to be safe. Do you understand?"

She thought about it. "It's a test? To see if they, what, treat me well?"

"Yes. To ensure their loyalty to the network. To ensure they will provide you what you need, house you safely, release you in the morning, give you correct directions to the next house."

"W-why? Would they not release me?" Shivery fear seized her spine.

He was quiet, seeming to debate something with himself while her heart beat with sickly rhythm. At last, he said, "Not all who enter the network emerge. You present a unique opportunity to test this route."

"And if I'm unwilling to be your bait?" she hissed.

"It is, of course, your choice. However," his voice turned harder, "I encourage you to think of those who will come after you. Those who will not have me waiting nearby, those who will have no hope of rescue or protection."

"Will you?" she asked, staring at the hand still clutched in his robe, seeing it tremble. "Protect me?"

"Always," he promised with unnerving solemnity. "From anything that would do you harm. Including your own power." She remembered, viscerally, burning in the damp cellar, the snapping of iron as he tore the door open to get to her. *How did he manage that?* It must have been magic.

"You promise you'll be here in the morning?" she despised the plea even as she made it. "You'll make sure they let me out?"

"You have my word," he said. She didn't know why, but she believed him. Demon or not, she trusted this stranger.

He stayed with her, his hand cool and reassuring on her shoulder, until she climbed the hill to knock on the door. Even knowing he was down there, a shout away, it took all her nerve for her to enter the house, to descend to the stone room—this one hidden inside like Juro's had been. *Could he hear me call for help in here?* she wondered, curled around her knees with a guttering candle for company in the dark.

She took out her journal and wrote a letter in shaky hand to Juro. A letter she would never send, a letter he would never read. But it was comforting to think of him, almost as though he kept her company. Wrote until her hand was too badly cramped to continue and her eyes were heavy.

12

TALK OF DEMONS

STEKIN

Stekin waited through the night, as he had promised. He wanted to go back to the last house, to demand answers as to how the dedicate had known to wait for Arten in that field so close to their home. But she was afraid, more than she wanted him to know, and he needed her to trust him.

Perhaps it is unwise to use her for this purpose, he thought in the quiet hours of the night. *She is too important to lose.* But he was confident in his ability to extract her from danger.

The confidence of fools, or experience? he wondered, his ears picking up movement in the house. The tread of a man, descending the stairs. Stekin rose. The man continued past the hidden room, exited the house, reentered a little later with empty bowels. Stekin did not relax again until the man settled back into sleep.

She is young to tempt most, for all that she is considered mature enough to sell into marriage. I wonder which of these would be tempted were she five years older. His thoughts turned to her age.

How had her power manifested this early? She was

clearly not matured physiologically, would not be for several years. Why was he so attuned to her? No one else had felt the flash of her power nearly-thirteen years ago. No one else had been driven from their beds, from their lives, with an unassailable need to find her. Why him, why her? Clearly, she was special. Her age, if nothing else, proved her uniqueness. What would her power be like in five years? The thought left him shivering.

The predator in him stirred diamond wings. The one that had emerged when he caught the scent of the dedicate in that field, the one that had chased the man down and crushed his skull with an angry blow. The one that had pried the collar from Arten's neck, ignoring the searing in his hands and the shrieking of his power, until it broke in two. Then lapsed back into slumber. Leaving a mess that had to be cleaned up.

He turned his power in tighter bands, soothing that primal part of himself. The part that would never be what it had once been, that raged with its sentence. His power was wan, drained from healing Arten. But he had been unable to bear seeing her in pain. Especially when that pain was a reminder people wanted her dead. He would only be able to heal her twice more, he suspected, without disrupting the healing he had set on himself. *When I get back, I must have Kylik instruct me in more efficient methods for healing these bodies*, he thought ruefully. He suspected that, with Arten, healing skills were going to become essential in his life.

He could not hear her, encased in stone as she was. He imagined her sleeping, curled up around herself. She was afraid now, but she would move past that quickly. There was a strength in her, a defiance, that he admired. She would need it to survive where they were going. And she would— survive, thrive—he knew it as well as he knew the predator at his core. Nevertheless, he began the slow workings of a plan to ease her integration into his life.

IN THE MORNING, he skirted to the west and followed her silently until they were an acceptable distance from the house, then angled over to intercept her. She visibly relaxed to see him. He suppressed the satisfaction that gave him.

He questioned her about the accommodations, the directions she was given, the hospitality of her hosts.

"That is not the expected route," he said, felt his brow draw down.

"They said," she shuddered, "that there were dedicates trawling for a sacrifice at the next village, so I should keep west to avoid them."

The node, he decided, had been satisfactory. He noted that they had given her a hat to shield her from sun. He chanted his power into healing for her face and scalp and her shoulder. The knee and hip were well on their way, her youth speeding the process. She did not complain, managed to look only mildly embarrassed.

She said nothing as he led them along through the stunted woods that gradually grew taller, more comfortable for him to walk through. The hills grew steeper around them, and he stopped before midday when she began to flag. He was regretting not having strung his bow last night as he chewed methodically on the dried meat strips that had lost their novelty twelve years ago, when she spoke.

"It does matter," she said firmly, "if you're a demon."

His eyes jumped to her, studied her face. She was staring at his hands. "Why?" he asked, curious. He moved his hands behind him, leaned back on them. Her eyes moved to his shoulder. *She does not want to look at me.*

"If you are a demon, I can't trust you to keep your word," she said.

"If I am not, you believe you can?"

She thought about that for a bit. "No," she said, "but I know if you *are* a demon that I can't."

Her words sounded with pious conviction, his anger welled up. "What do *you* know of demons?" he snarled. "Have you met one, have you fought one, have you had one swear you an oath? No. You know only what that poisonous temple preaches to you." He was not a demon, he wanted to express his disgust that she could think he was. But what he was... That would be just as difficult for her to accept. So, he curbed his temper, held his tongue, and left her to her silence.

When they stopped again in the afternoon, his wounded pride had healed, and he had directed his thoughts far north and east to the place to which he was impatient to return. He had eschewed his responsibility there for nearly thirteen years. *Nhemith will not be pleased to see me*, he thought grimly. *If she yet lives.* He wondered how many would not greet him when he returned, how many new faces would peer up at him in awe and fear. *Too many, and too few,* he knew.

The mantle of his role was settling back on shoulders that had eagerly set it down. Arten was found. *Too long in the finding.* It had been frustrating, these years searching, and it had been boring, in the great stretches of waiting. He had tried to send the occasional letter north, through the network, but there was no guarantee any of them reached their destination. He could have tried harder. Should have.

Should not have been so blinded by his search as to forget all he had fought for and built.

"You look older," she said. He had not noticed her staring at him. That lapse alarmed him. Her eyes shifted away, avoiding his.

"I have learned," he said, calmly, allowing frost to coat his words, "that is it impolite to comment on someone's age." *But I am old and thinking old thoughts,* he acknowledged bitterly, as he led them onwards. *If they have found another kaz... Perhaps that would be better for all of us.* But he doubted they had and was unconvinced by his own speculation.

They arrived with little time for her to scramble up the steep hill to knock on the door. He watched her in the near-dark. He had assured her, once again, that he would be nearby. She had accepted his healing silently.

It was only as he saw her crossing to the door, head drooping, shoulders hunched, that he understood he had done something wrong. He thought back as the woman emerged, spoke with Arten. She looked around furtively, then she and the girl were trotting away. Stekin followed at a safe distance. They walked for about half a mile, then the woman uncovered a door built into one of the steep hills. Arten went inside. The woman bolted it after her and scampered back to her house.

A bolt, no lock for him to break. He heard Arten's rapid heartbeat inside, saw her power starting to flare. It was not yet strong enough to escape. Tomorrow, perhaps, but not tonight. Her breathing sped up. She was afraid. He unbolted the door, let himself in. She went still, like a terrified mouse, her sides heaving but the sound muffled through her mouth.

"Arten, I am here," he said. "You are safe."

She emitted a small whimper and sank to her knees,

arms clutched around her abdomen. The power still churned there. "Take them away," she pleaded, he smelled the salt of tears. "Take the Words away..."

"Soon," he promised, "but not tonight." He sat beside her. He wanted to fold her into his side but knew she was still worried that he might make physical demands of her, so he kept his hands on his knees and just sat with her.

"Why not?" she choked out.

"You are not yet strong enough." He closed his hand into a fist in his lap to keep it from reaching out. "I apologize," he said, genuinely, but also to distract her, "for being dismissive earlier. You startled me, and that is not easily done."

She shook her head, thought he would not be able to see it and said, "It wasn't that."

"Then what?"

"It was... I don't want you to be a demon," she blurted. He heard the shame in her voice, and the plea.

"Why is that?" he asked, carefully.

"Because I...trust you," she managed, "and I'm afraid that you'll turn out to be as bad as the temple."

"Do you think I will?"

She was quiet for a long time. Her power settled and dimmed to his vision while she thought. "I don't think you're a demon," she said at last, an emphasis on the last word that angled his mouth up. She turned to face him, though she would not be able to see him in the dark.

"But you think I am not human," he spoke what she had not, a thrill going through him.

"Did you know your eyes just flashed?" she said, by way of answer.

"Does that alarm you?"

"Yes. Maybe. I'm getting used to it." She seemed surprised by the admission. He waited. "You killed Dedicate

Brecarian, you broke the door the night when I... When the Words...," she fumbled to a halt.

"Yes," the word came out a low hiss. He saw her shiver at the sound but square her shoulders bravely.

"The Words didn't burn you. Why not? Why do you want them?" The tears were done, that inner steel had come out again. *She is going to be magnificent.*

He pushed her a little, a small test. "I killed a man in front of you, you have seen that your power does not harm me. You think me akin to a demon. Yet you demand answers from me. Do you think you will not be punished for your insolence?"

"Do it then," she said. A challenge, a taunt. *Prove me right, she means.*

He could not stop his hand this time as it reached out. She flinched away from his touch at first. He rested the heel of his palm on the bridge of her nose, felt the heat of her forehead under his hand. His fingers stretched and closed, curling over the soft skin of her scalp. It was strange to feel hair and skin under his fingertips, to feel the bristle of eyebrows against the heel of his hand, instead of scales. She was so fragile. If this were his real hand, the flesh of her scalp would be peeled away. *She is not my child*, he reminded himself and pulled his hand away.

"What was that?" she rasped, shivering when he stopped.

"A gesture of affection," he said automatically, off-balance. *I know she is not my child, why did I even think that?* he wondered, appalled. He stared at the offending hand, was glad she could not see his face.

"So why do you want them?" It took him a moment to pull his thoughts back from their horror to the conversation he had interrupted.

"We will talk more tomorrow," he said, standing. He did not trust himself to answer her without revealing too much. *She can still be captured. I cannot risk an unmoderated tongue.* "Goodnight, Arten."

He was at the door, closing it behind him, when she whispered, "Goodnight, Stekin." His eyes flashed, fiercely pleased with the cautious respect in her voice. He knew she saw it.

The moon would be dark tomorrow night, tonight it was a mere sliver. A risk, but one he would take. He had only spent a short time as himself in the past month, his biology was getting confused. That was the only explanation. Catching the deer had been a necessity, a tiny slice of night shifted, a proper amount and ratio of fuel consumed, to ensure his human body did not weaken. He had not flown since he left the Forgotten City, and even that had been furtive and abortive. He needed to remember himself, not just survive. He needed to *be* himself.

He walked silently through the woods until he found a small clearing where a tree had fallen, cracking open the sky. He removed his robe, folded it across the fallen tree trunk, set his pack and sandals below. Stepped up onto the tree, felt its rough, crumbling bark under his toes. His power rippled, and a few chanted words later, the tree groaned and snapped under his weight. He brought down powerful wings, pushed away with his limbs, darted into the sky. He climbed higher and higher, until the air was frigid and thin, and any humans looking up would be unlikely to see even the dark shape of him against the stars.

He stretched his wings, reveling in the feel of the sky caressing his scales. He whirled and flew, wrapped himself in the wind and night. A scent of *home* reached him, of ancient ice and stunted evergreen. A home that was lost to him. He banked, angled himself towards their destination, towards what most of his people called home. A place that seemed so small to him now that he had lived in the world again. But they could not leave, not until his work was completed.

He turned back, feeling heavy and ancient. He had gambled the last twelve years that Arten would be able to help him complete his work, that she held an answer for that which he had been searching for so long. The years were no great loss. He had been chasing his tail for decades before she flared into existence. *It is a great burden to place on an individual, though*, he knew. *All the more that she is a human juvenile.* He would have to be careful, be gentler with her.

I do not think I have many years left, and I will not see her like again.

13

THE WORKSHOP MAN

ARTEN

A rten's scalp crawled with the memory of his touch. *He as much as said he's not human*, she thought, staring into the blackness above her. *He looks human, though.* But there were little things that, now that she was thinking about it, bothered her. *He doesn't sweat*, she recalled. *And he has those odd gestures and noises, not quite like anything I've heard from other people. He could just be from far away, though,* she mused. *But that doesn't explain the sweat, or the way his back doesn't seem to bend.*

I wonder if he really ate the whole deer?

She turned onto her side, scrubbing a hand over her scalp. His hearing was keen, she remembered, and his hands...they always gripped too tightly. On her shoulder, when he had forced apart her jaw. It was strength that pulled the door open, she guessed, not magic. *Strong enough to break iron?* That seemed impossible. Her fingers touched her throat. *He somehow managed to get that collar off... What did he call it?*

Demon-metal. He hadn't seemed to care for it. She resolved to ask him about it tomorrow.

Remembered the way his eyes had flashed when she'd said his name.

Those eyes... It wasn't the way they lit up that frightened her. It was the way they focused on the Words, how they could see through her. How they could see into the core of her and how the Words responded to them. Her Words—her *power*—was what he wanted. Despite her resolve, she'd begged him to take it tonight. And he'd left when she questioned him about it. What did that mean?

She sighed and rolled onto her other side, hot and agitated. She needed to sleep. She forced herself to recall Juro's lessons, to rework the assignments in her head, distracting the Words until she fell asleep.

THEY TRAVELED with minimal conversation for the next two days. Arten observed Stekin, cataloging his behaviors, his oddities, wondering which were natural and which were alien. She tried to figure out what he could be, thought back to all the stories with magical creatures. Most of them featured demons and lesser demons, but aside from demons, none of the creatures existed. She thought she was onto something when she remembered magical twins. But a dispassionate, "I have no twin," had been his response to her careful probing, ending that line of thought.

He seemed distracted, rarely noticing her except for when they parted in the evening and met again in the morning. He kept looking northeast, and his jaw would tighten at whatever was waiting there. Sometimes he would look back at her, *through* her, and frown. That night, he assured her he would be nearby, as he always did, and she went down to the house.

A man opened the door. She didn't think anything of him except that he looked nervous. That wasn't unusual. Most people had glanced around anxiously after seeing her. She asked him for some bread or grains as he took her out to a second little building behind the house. She had run out of Juro's bread today, and Stekin had insisted that she ask, that it was expected of her to do so. He unlocked the little building, gestured her in urgently. She looked around in the lantern-light, saw she was in some sort of shop. There were metal tools peeking out from under vast leather aprons covering the workbenches and shelves.

"You willing to pay for it?" he asked, rolling back a leather rug to reveal a hatch.

"I don't have any money," she said, surprised. He grinned up at her as he hauled the hatch open. It made her skin prickle.

"You must be new to this," he said, affably. "The price for bread isn't money." He sounded kind, almost fatherly, but something was telling her to get away.

"What is it? I don't have anything."

"I'll come by a little later and tell you. Now come on, hop in," he gestured to the hole in the floor impatiently. She edged forwards and peered down. There was a ladder leaned against the wall of the stone room. He held the lantern so that she could see to the bottom.

"Nothing to worry about," he soothed, showing her the pallet and blankets, each of the corners. The room was clean, downright plush compared to some of the cells she had slept in.

She stepped to the hatch and descended the ladder, trying to keep as far away from him as possible.

"Atta girl," he crooned. *Don't do it, don't do it. You can still get out of here*, a part of her warned as she took the last few steps down. Her feet touched stone, she looked up. He was standing over the hatchway. "You just wait right there," he said.

Then he reached down, yanked the ladder out of her hands, walked it up out of the cell.

"Wait!" she cried, staring up at him. She heard the clatter as he dropped the ladder on the floor above.

"Don't worry," he said, "I'll be back for you." It was anything but comforting.

"No, wait, I changed my mind. Let me out!" she called up, but the hatch was closing, was closed. There was only a quiet thunk as the rug was put back in place, the muffled sound of his boots as he left the workshop.

The Words were rioting inside her. When had they gotten so strong? *It's okay, I'm okay,* she told herself, told the Words, *Stekin would come if I were in danger. Stekin won't let me stay trapped here.*

A traitorous doubt niggled. She only had his assurance on that. Could she depend on him? She crouched under the hatch, rocking herself, repeating a litany of trust in Stekin until the Words were no longer clawing at her throat. Only then did the smell hit her. Stale sweat and something sour and something musky like an animal. It was stronger near the pallet and on the far side of the room, so she went back to crouching under the hatch.

It'll be fine, she told herself, over and over. *This is just another house. Tomorrow, he'll let me go.*

The hatch opened some time later, startling her from a daze. A lantern-lit face appeared, grinned to see her below.

"You're not going to cause me any trouble, are you?" he asked, warningly. She shook her head and scrambled out of the way as he dropped the ladder back in. She pressed against the far wall, the stench heightening her feeling of unease.

His boots descended the ladder in measured thuds. Then he was in the stone room, setting the lantern in the corner behind him so that he was all shadows when he turned to her again. The room was too small, he filled it somehow.

He advanced on her a step. Two.

The Words churned.

Another figure descended the ladder silently. Her heart raced with relief to see the sandaled feet drop to the floor.

A familiar hand closed on her host's shoulder, in a grip Arten knew was painful. "She may not give you any trouble," Stekin all but purred, "but I will."

"What the—" the man started, half-spun, angry and shocked. His protest was cut off with a grunt, his shoulder sagged, Stekin's knuckles looked a little whiter.

"Leave us," Stekin said to her. She didn't need to be asked twice. She was up the ladder in a moment, out the door of the workshop in another. Before she reached the woods, she heard the man's screams start. She ran until she couldn't hear them anymore.

14

THE WORKSHOP MAN

STEKIN

He found her huddled in the hollow of a tree. Her power was erratic, volatile, it had led him to her with ease. It took some patient coaxing to get her out. Her hand was hot and twitchy when she at last took his. She squirmed out of the hollow, and the stench of the room assaulted him once more.

"Come," he said, carefully controlling his disgust. She followed him automatically, the strength of her grip the only testament to her unease. He led them towards the scent of water, the sound of a volume of it pushing past rocks and banks.

"Is he dead?" she asked at last. Her voice was hollow.

"No. Injured. And we had a long talk about how he will never again assault a source."

"Was he going to kill me?" She was too calm. He knew that would break soon.

"No," he said and explained what the man had intended. The most basic version, at least. He did not tell her of the other scents in the room. Pain, blood, excrement. He did not tell her that the man had confessed his intent to keep her for several days before releasing her again. How he had done so in the past—kept the sources who passed through until Saviorsday, when he could spend the entire day satisfying his various proclivities at their expense, releasing them the day after. Each with scars, not all of them visible.

Stekin also did not tell her how intimately and lingeringly he had hurt the man. There was no need to distress her more.

Her hand had tightened on his. She had gone even more pale. They said nothing else until they found the river.

"Arten," he said firmly, pulling her attention to him, "you must bathe. I will wash your clothes." She startled, pulled away. He should have anticipated that. "I will go downstream," he offered, "you may join me when you are ready." He knelt and placed his pack on the ground. A moment later, he felt the item under his fingers and drew it out. Offered it to her. "Put this on so I can wash the smell from your clothes." She took it but made no other move. "Now," he added with a hint of command. It jolted her into motion.

Moments later, she emerged from the underbrush, garbed in the single-piece female garment. The ones he had acquired to disguise her gender were balled in her hands. She thrust the clothing at him. He took them and headed downstream to find a place where he might be able to submerge. He found something suitable, disrobed, and went in. The river was warm save for the deepest part, and muddy. Less than ideal, but he abraded his skin and hair with his nails until the stain of the room washed away, held his head under the water to wash it from his nostrils. Free of it, he began the chore of removing it from their clothing.

He chaffed the cloth between his knuckles with rapid

motions, wishing it were the man's neck twisting and wringing between his hands. The creature had been careful, selective in his...activities. Nothing alarming or physically jolting enough to cause a flare-out, just enough to keep his captives compliant, to let him experiment. Out here, where the temple ruled, Stekin could little afford to dispose of the man. He was a craftsman, would be missed. Stekin had had to settle for leaving him with a wound that would reduce his enjoyment of his varied appetites.

His robe was spread to dry, and he was working on her tunic when she found him. She stayed quiet and hidden, so he did not acknowledge her. She would come out when she was comfortable. He finished with the tunic, wrung the water from it, spread it on the bush next to his robe. He was careful to keep his back to her. Humans, he had learned, were nervous about nakedness, especially the front parts. But she did not emerge, even after the trousers had been hung to dry. Even after he seated himself, legs crossed, facing the river, and waited. And waited.

"I know you know I'm here," she said eventually. *Observant*, he thought, pleased.

"Then why are you still hiding?"

"You're naked," she said, disdainfully, to which he made a dismissive noise. "People care about that, you know," she scolded him.

"I am aware," he said. "People often care about a great many unimportant things." *My people included.*

"I suppose..." she said, unconvinced.

"That man wished to harm you. You are wondering if I am the same," he guessed.

"Are you?"

"I can tell you that I am not, but you must choose whether to believe me or consider me a threat."

She said quickly, suggesting she had been thinking on it for some time, "You killed the dedicate. You could do anything you wanted with me, and I couldn't stop you."

"That is accurate." He paused, considered the lie he was about to tell, decided it was worth the risk. "The only thing I want from you is your power."

"Do you expect me to believe that?"

A phrase I wish humans had never learned.

"I expect you to now, and always, know your own mind," he said a tad more harshly than he intended. He was tired of humans challenging him, demanding proof of his veracity and intentions. *As if any proof I were to provide would not be engineered to gain their trust. Ridiculous species.*

She emerged from the bushes, cautiously, and came to sit near him. Far enough to be out of reach. Next to her clothes and pack, he noted.

"There is a dagger in my pack," he said, with feigned disinterest. "You may keep it." He was a little disappointed when she retrieved it. *Being opposite a blade makes a better friend*, he recalled a saying he had picked up... Where? Somewhere. *Do people still say that?* he wondered idly.

He stretched out on his side, his back to her. "Try and get some sleep," he said over his shoulder. "If I am not here when you wake in the morning, I have gone back to let him out."

"You trapped him down there?" she whispered, startled.

"Yes," he felt the night air on his teeth as he grinned, "gladly." Her power calmed almost immediately, and she fell asleep soon after. He turned onto his other side to look at her. So small and breakable, the thief leader's long dagger clutched over her heart. She had been in no real danger. He would not have permitted the man to touch her, but what she had experienced was real enough. That dank room, the proximity of that creature. Her anxiety was natural. He would not put her through that again.

15

THE GOOD HOUSE, THE BURNING RESOLVE

ARTEN

W hen Arten woke, Stekin was gone. She felt a moment of panicky abandonment, then noted his robe was still hanging on the bushes, his pack still where she had left it last night. *That means he's coming back.* Then she recalled what he had said the previous night, about letting the man out of his cell, and let out a tense breath. While she waited, she put on her trousers and tunic, dressing behind a bush just in case he happened to return in that moment.

She thought of the man, trapped in that stinky room, imagined him huddled below the hatch as she had been, Stekin looming over him. It was a comforting picture.

Stekin didn't let him hurt me.

She had always known there was some nebulous danger from certain men. She'd heard the stories from village girls, told in hushed whispers, like ghost tales. She'd always thought of them as exaggerations, something that *could* happen but rarely did. For herself, she had never been concerned for her safety before fleeing, and since, had only ever considered that the people who locked her in at night might not return in the morning to free her. The fear had seemed irrational yesterday. But now, she wondered what other dangers there were, waiting for her at the next safe-house or the next, that she had never considered. She had never thought someone would want to bed her. No one had ever looked appraisingly at her, the way they sometimes did Maruko. But the man last night, she was certain that had been his intention.

The world seemed so much larger and darker than before.

At least I have Stekin. Demon or no, he has been an ally. He had killed a member of the temple, he had stopped the Words from consuming her, he had punished the man who would have attacked her last night. *If he hadn't come along, I would be like any other person fleeing the temple. That man has probably hurt people before me. Maybe Stekin will prevent him from hurting people after me, but what if I had been alone?* She shuddered, recalling the smell, the sight of the ladder whipping away, the hatch descending.

Stekin came back just then. She jumped, brandishing the dagger. He flicked a look at her weapon, then away.

"Do you know how to use that?" he asked as he drew on his robe and cinched it closed with his belted sash.

"No," she admitted, flushing.

"Then keep it hidden. Your best defense will be surprise." He tied his sandals on, winding the straps around his ankles. "There is a belt for it in the bottom," he nodded at his pack, "wear it tucked under your clothes." He finished tying the sandals while she rummaged for the belt. Her hand pushed aside a box that made a familiar wooden clunking, but she forgot it immediately when her fingers brushed a coiled strap of leather. She pulled the belt out. He showed her how to wear it, spent few words insisting she practice drawing the dagger unseen while he repacked both their packs.

"What are the landmarks today?" she asked, drawing and sheathing the dagger while keeping that side turned away from him, trying to keep the long hilt from tangling in her tunic.

"There are none. We will cut northeast."

"He didn't tell you? How are we going to get to the next house?" she cried, dismayed.

His voice was chipped and icy as he said, "We are not going there. I will not subject you to someone like that again."

"No!" she said, surprising herself with her vehemence, "No, we have to go."

He stood and turned to look at her, expectant, displeased. Waiting, she realized, for her to explain.

She felt distinctly odd and somehow older as she did, "You said people are going missing. Well, we still haven't found out why." She gulped. "I'm...I'm lucky. I've got you. But those other people, they don't have anyone. They're scared and hungry. And I just learned that the people they're...we're, supposed to be able to trust might hurt them. Us. I want to find them, so you can stop them."

What she really wanted to do was vomit. Her stomach was clenched in knots despite her brave words, despite her conviction. She didn't know if she would be able to make herself enter the next cell, but she had to try.

His eyes were narrowed, his mouth a thin line. He was quiet for some time. She fidgeted under his gaze.

He's actually considering what I said, not just dismissing it.

No adult had ever done that before, not sincerely. They always knew what was best for her, told her what was in her best interests from their wealth of wisdom and experience. *He owns me, why is he even humoring me?*

"Very well," he said at length, "If I deem it too dangerous, you will stop." It was not a suggestion.

"Okay," she agreed quickly, having just realized how differently he could have reacted to her protest. The remembered sight of a pulverized cheek, the arc of a body heavy with dead weight, forced itself to the surface. *I shouldn't borrow on my luck.* "Let's go get the landmarks," she said with more confidence than she felt.

"There is no need. I know where we are going."

"You do? How?"

"I established this network. I am one of a few invested in maintaining it." He said it as though it were of no importance.

"You?" He didn't acknowledge her surprise, just handed her pack over and set out north, roughly following the creek. "Is that why you're so rich?" she pressed, "Do you make money off us somehow?"

"No," he said, disgusted. "The sale of sources is forbidden, not to mention repugnant."

"Sources?"

"Sources of power. People like you."

"People with the Taint," she murmured to herself.

"Never call it that," he snapped. She apologized quickly and his shoulders relaxed a fraction. "Sources are highly valued among my people. You are all precious. To be cherished."

"Why?"

"Because you are rare. Scare enough to begin with, but

few survive to reach us. Between the temple and its fire-thirsty dedicates, the flare-out, and people not emerging from the network, we are fortunate that any reach us." His voice was tinged with steel and bitterness. His strides were long, and she panted to keep up.

"How...how do you find us?" she managed. "How do you know we're not...normal?"

He glanced back, slowed. "These days, sources find us. They emerge from the network, and we take them in. Before that," he paused, "there were scouts," he finished carefully.

"How did that work?" she pressed.

He glanced at her again, assessing. "Much the same way dedicates operate now. They followed rumor, watched children of the right age, investigated secrets."

"Oh."

"You sound disappointed." He seemed amused.

"I thought you could see the Words—the power," she corrected.

"In general, when the power is emerging, it is still hidden from such sight. Yours, however, I can often see." He paused, glanced at her again, made a decision. Continued, "There are a very few of us who are sensitive to power moving across the world."

"Can the dedicates see it or...feel it? Is that how Dedicate Brecarian found me?"

"No. Brecarian found you because your mother told him to come. Then you ran. People who do not have the power will usually submit to the test. The ones who have reason to fear usually run." They had come across a deep, narrow ravine. Its bridge had collapsed. He tossed her across. Followed with a running leap. She was perversely pleased to see him stagger on the landing.

"What test?" she asked as they cut northwest. He glanced to the east only once. *This route is delaying him.*

"You have already taken it." She puzzled over that briefly. "The demon-metal."

Her fingers went automatically to the tender semi-circle under her jaw, probed the new scar. "What," she rasped, her mouth dry, "what is it?"

"A device of restraint, of torture to some of us." His tone was dark, scathing. "It binds our power, renders us defenseless."

"Us?" she asked unthinkingly.

"Surely," he snapped, "you have determined by now that I, also, have power." She fell back a few steps, caught off guard by his sudden temper. She added *demon-metal* to the list of topics not to bring up, alongside *demons* and *the temple*. She was beginning to sense a theme.

"I apologize," he said, interrupting her speculations on what other topics she might be wise to avoid. "I should not have spoken to you that way."

"Oh," she said, not knowing what else to say. They walked with their own thoughts until they reached their destination.

It was a farm, empty sheep paddocks and a two-stall barn, a pigsty on the far side, chickens strutting about the yard. She crouched with Stekin in the undergrowth at the edge of the cleared land. His hand gripped her shoulder. She looked at it. Looked back at the farm house.

"You need not do this," he said.

"I'm going to," she declared, more for herself than him. *I am, I am.*

"I will be nearby. Call for me, and I will come."

"Okay," she said, distracted and anxious.

"Arten, there is another thing you must know."

He sounded so grave she actually looked him in the face for a moment. "What?" she asked, looking away quickly.

"Your power may overwhelm you tonight. Know that I will not let it."

"Okay," she said again. He squeezed her shoulder, then moved away, leaving her to wait for dark, to tell herself what she needed to hear to ensure she crossed the open yard to the door. She wouldn't have had the courage if he had waited with her. But alone, she was able to remember why she wanted to do this, to imagine how frightened the others had been, crouching in the bushes waiting for dark, wondering if evil waited behind the pastoral veneer.

When the time came, she sprinted to the door. She nearly forgot the phrase Stekin had given her but remembered enough, it seemed, to gain admittance. The door closed behind her, and though her muscles tensed and sweat sprang out, she clamped down on the yelp.

"Need anything, son?" the weathered woman asked her, leading her down into the cellar, past sacks of potatoes and flour, crates of vegetables fresh and limp, a barrel of something alcoholic that reeked. She ducked bundles of herbs that hung from the ceiling.

"S-s-some bread, please," she croaked. "Ran out." She didn't know if *bread* had a universal cost, or if the last man had just said that, but she'd promised herself this morning she would always ask for it from now on.

"That all the clothes you got?" the lady said, sliding open a panel on the back wall, revealing a clean stone room that smelled of nothing worse than potatoes.

Arten nodded, clutching her pack's straps, her shoulders curved inwards.

"From here on, it's a bit farther between the houses," the

woman said sternly, "you'll need to overnight outside here and there. You done that afore?"

Arten nodded again.

"Good. It can get cold at night, even in the hells of summer. Reckon my boy's got a few things he's outgrown that will do for you," she mused, rubbing her jaw. "Wait here," she said, setting the lantern down. She stumped away, back up the stairs, leaving Arten alone with her stores.

She returned shortly, a bowl in hand. "Just some chicken stew," the woman said with a grimace that might have been intended as a smile, "but I reckon it'll do you. You're thin as a rake, son." She pushed the bowl on Arten. "Eat up now. I'll have you some clothes in the morning. No, no, you keep that," the woman waved away the lantern Arten tried to hand back to her, "I imagine it gets mighty dark. Goodnight."

Arten inhaled the stew, sitting on the pallet of straw-stuffed potato sacks. Then cried.

She's the first person, other than Stekin, who hasn't treated me like I'm contagious or dangerous, or shameful. Even though she was dangerous. Even though there was a special stone-lined room in this house because the woman knew how dangerous someone like Arten could be.

And I am *ashamed,* Arten realized, forehead on her knees, tears soaking through the cloth, *I'm defective and Tainted. People are right to look at me like they do. I don't care what Stekin says, this is part of my curse, there's nothing to cherish in it.* The Words were swarming inside her. *This power should have killed me. I should have burned on Midsummer. What am I doing, trying to escape my fate? Running from the temple is madness.*

The tears dried up in a sudden flare of anger. *Why am I listening to this demon who tells me stories about how the Words make me special. Of course he's convincing, he's probably lured hundreds of people like me to whatever end he has in mind. He's perfected the art of it. Why am I helping him?* she despaired. The stone room seemed, for the first time, like a safe harbor. Keeping her hidden, keeping Stekin away. Giving her space to actually think about what had happened since she'd fled, without his presence influencing her.

I shouldn't trust him. He's violent, has no qualms about murder, was almost gleeful about hurting the workshop man. If that's not bad enough, he's rich. He bought me. She saw again the liquid shine of the staggering number of gold pieces stacked in front of her mother.

The rules and the laws don't apply to the rich the same way. Juro's father had said that bitterly and frequently enough in her hearing (though to her, the Swains were rich so she didn't know what reason he had for complaint).

And Stekin's proven he doesn't mind killing temple officers if they threaten his property. What if I become a threat? Or he loses interest? She shuddered, and the Words prickled in the motion.

When she turned sixteen, the contract would expire, but where they were going was beyond the reach of the temple. *Who's to make him release me when the time comes if the temple has no sway? What does he want me for and why won't he tell me? It can't be good.*

A wave of homesickness crested over her. She wanted to go home, to nestle into her father's side, to sit under the old-man tree with Juro. To have them tell her what she should do, to see further and more clearly than she could. Her father would have something useful to say about Stekin, some warning to give, some *thing* for her to be watchful for and wary of. Juro would probably know what he wanted to use her for. He'd have a plan to make sure she came out to the advantage in whatever future Stekin was plotting.

Juro, who was in league with him.

She threw herself down on the pallet, creased the journal open. Wrote an angry letter to Juro, demanding answers from him. Did he know he was working for a demon? Why did he join the stupid network in the first place, when he didn't know anything about it? How many people had he sent into their clutches?

As she wrote, a new resolve settled in her. She would see this through. Not for Stekin, but for the people like her. She would work with Stekin, for now, against those who would harm her and the other Tainted. But she'd keep her eyes open around him, be wary. *And when I get to the end of this network and discover who Stekin's people are and what they do with their* sources, *well, if I don't like it, I'll burn it all down.*

The Words wriggled happily at the thought.

She slept better than she had in months, dagger clutched next to her heart.

THE WOMAN, good to her word, had a bundle ready for Arten in the morning. A warm shirt, a pair of thick canvas trousers that were a bit big but intact, a box of matches tucked in one of the pockets. She also gave her a bunch of carrots and a head of cabbage, both a little wilted but perfectly edible. Lastly, the bread.

"Can't make the travel stuff, but it's fresh. Should last you a few days," the woman said. Arten threw her arms around her and thanked her fiercely. "Now, now, it's just what I hope someone would do for my own boy," she said, giving Arten a motherly pat.

"I won't forget your kindness," Arten promised, memorizing the woman's face.

"You're a good boy," the woman said a little thickly. "Just you remember, if a Caid Larkin ever makes it your way, you remember he's mine and you take care of him."

"Caid Larkin. I will. I will," she said.

"Good," the woman gave her smile-grimace, then sobered. "Now, normally I'd send you skirting round to the east, but they've got dedicates lurking over that way. They're on the scent of some poor soul. Don't you worry, we're looking, too. But I don't want you getting caught up in that. I'm sending you west." The woman listed off directions which had Arten angling primarily west, out onto the plains. "It's a hike, since it's not in the usual line, but you might could make it by tonight if you bustle. I reckon it's worth the hassle to keep clear of those dedicates. You're a good boy, so I don't have to tell you to be...kind, when you get there." Arten didn't have time to puzzle over her meaning because the woman shooed her on, saying, "Go on now, don't want to lose the daylight."

Arten ran across the yard before she was tempted to stay. Ran west and a little north, leaving the farm behind. Ran across the grassy yard, through the thin line of trees and into the tree-pocked grazing land. She scrambled up a scrubby hill, scraping her knees and palms, paused at the top to look back, down on the farmhouse, on the toughened woman throwing scraps to her pigs. Then she plunged down the other side, running as though a demon chased her, as though she could outrun her curse and her doubts and the Words that never left her.

She ran until she was out of breath and her legs ached. Then she slowed, walked off the stitch in her side. She'd left Stekin behind, but a part of her was glad for it. She didn't want to see him right now, didn't want to hear his false words. '*I will find you*,' he had said. Well, let him find her. She wasn't going to wait.

He needs me, for the Words or whatever, but he needs me. Alive. Unharmed. More than I need to be either of those things. She was tired of being afraid, of depending on him, of trotting after him. She hated how easily she'd trusted him.

Demon or not, she reminded herself firmly, *he's hiding something from me. He's bewitching me with his words. And not just me.* How many people did he have at the end of this network, and what did he do with them? She resolved not to trust him until he answered her properly.

She munched on a carrot as she walked, found it sweet and refreshing. She thought of Juro, wondered what justifications he might have had in response to her letter if he were here. Thought about his mother, who had not been saved. About the people who, like her, had been forced into this journey. Someone's child, spouse, sibling. About all the people left behind, like Mother Larkin might one day be, wondering if their loved one made it to safety. To some promised land that probably didn't even exist.

Her ire rose, the Words rising with it. Her fingers trailed through tall grass on the rolling hills, the last pretense of woods left behind at midday. The Words were whispering dreams of fire, of sparks and wind. She tucked her hands away in her pockets, shoved the Words down.

She was a little surprised that Stekin had not come upon her yet. She hadn't even seen him in the distance. A small part of her worried that she had lost him, *or he may have given up on you.* She pushed the thought away. No, it was more likely he was trying to catch up to her. She made it all the way to the house without seeing him.

There was not much light left. She probably would not

have made the trip in a single day if anger hadn't quickened her pace. She waited behind some scrub bushes on a nearby hill, distant enough that she wouldn't be spotted from the house and ate another carrot and some dried meat strips. She was almost out of those as well. She hoped this place would be as generous as the last.

She was stowing the food in the bottom of her pack when she spied the dress. She took it out, thoughtfully. *Mother Larkin mistook me for a boy. I suppose that was Stekin's purpose in cutting off my hair and changing my clothes. If the temple is looking for a girl, they're not looking for a boy.*

If she was going to be bait, though, she would probably lure out more people like the workshop man if she looked female and helpless. She ignored the small part of her that protested that she *was* female and helpless.

Before she could talk herself out of it, she changed into the dress. Then she had to figure out how to conceal the dagger. She settled on belting it under the dress and keeping her arm clamped to her side so the bulge of it didn't show. She would work out something better for the next time.

If I'm going to appear helpless, I may as well go all in, she thought, seeing the lights wink on in the cabin in the throes of dusk. Crickets were singing all around, there was the distant bay of a wild dog pack. The wind whistled through grass. It was strange, not hearing the creak of branches and rattle of leaves, the skitter of tree rats. She felt exposed on the hill, despite the screen of brush around her, isolated. And far, far from home. She gritted her teeth, thrust her pack into the branches of the bush, then scampered down the hill as quietly as she could. *I still have the dagger,* she comforted herself. The pommel dug into her ribs under her arm.

The man who opened the door to her was young, a little

older than Juro, she guessed, but his eyes were slack, his skin papery like someone more than twice his age, his beard and hair unkempt. He led her outside and into a storm cellar below the house. When he asked her what she needed, he sounded dull. He nodded, brought her back some burnt bread that didn't smell quite cooked, a bowl of cold stew, and a shawl.

"Gets cold at night," he said absently. "She'd want you to have it. Always worried on me to wrap up..." He gulped and looked away from the knitted length. "I, uh, I don't always get up first thing. I'm just going to leave it open. You leave whenever you want." He told her the directions and passphrase woodenly, his eyes staring at nothing, then he climbed the stairs and closed the heavy door after him. True to his word, no bolt was thrown. She went up and pushed on it tentatively, heard the squeak of hinge.

When she left in the morning, there was no movement inside the house. She trotted back to the bush where she'd stashed her pack and retrieved it. After she'd changed back out of the dress, she balled it and shawl into the depths of her bag and cinched it closed. Stekin had not yet appeared. Had he even been nearby last night?

As she skirted around the house to head to her next destination, she glimpsed what she had missed the night before. The reason Mother Larkin had warned her to be kind. The two graves behind the north side of the house. One long, adult-sized, the other tiny, for an infant. The soil freshly churned. Her throat closed, and she saw a different grave. *Tizzy.* She could do nothing for that man's grief, just as she had been able to do nothing for her parents'.

Again, she ran.

She couldn't run fast enough this time. Couldn't outrun the memories, the guilt. She was panting, sobbing, couldn't breathe. Collapsed to her knees. The Words sensed her weakness, surged up. She pushed on them, but she was pushing back too many things, couldn't hold them all. The Words were a storm, pressing their way to freedom inch by inch. Her skin was too tight, itched all over. Her will was unraveling.

"Stekin," she pleaded before the Words reached her tongue, hating herself for doing so, "help me." But she had no space for Stekin nor anything else as the Words leapt from her tongue, scorched past her teeth, soared into the world.

Distantly, she felt pressure on her shoulders. A shadow knelt. Green eyes smoldered, eyes she didn't want to see. Then the sharp whiteness of teeth, a long deep breath which pulled in not air, somehow, but the Words. The ringing in her head subsided a little, the haze lessened. She saw his face, wild and ravenous as he devoured the Words, pulling them from her until they retreated back into her depths. He consumed their invisible fire and rendered them harmless.

His jaws closed with an audible snap, and his mouth angled into satisfaction. He released her shoulders and she slumped limply sideways. She felt hands catch her, lift her, then nothing.

THE SCENT of water caught her, drew her awake. The ash in her mouth and throat demanded relief. She thought she might know what it felt like to be a mummy, desiccated and empty. She cracked an eye open, then the other. Her lids rasped over them as though full of sand.

"Drink," a voice she knew said. The water was in the

same direction, she leaned towards them both. A hand was behind her back, tilting her upright, bringing her to the water. It was a balm against her lips, in her mouth. She guzzled it. "Slowly," the voice cautioned, pulling the water away. She sipped and the water stayed. Damp fingers drew a cooling line across her brow and under her eyes.

"What—?" she croaked, trying to blink moisture back into her eyes, struggling to sit up. The hand behind her back raised her, the other pressed the shape of her water gourd into her palm.

"Your power was overwhelming you," he said. She remembered similar words, a few nights ago. "I transmuted it. You will not be troubled by it for a few days."

Her eyes were focusing again. She saw him staring at her with the same too-intense expression he generally wore. No sign of teeth or glowing eyes. She looked away.

"Why?" she rasped, sipped some more water. Her arms trembled with fatigue.

"You called, I came. I was on my way, already. I could feel you losing control."

She was cross with him but couldn't quite remember why. "Tired," she muttered.

"Rest," he urged, taking the gourd away, laying her back down. She wanted to protest, she needed to keep moving, though she couldn't quite remember why. But she was asleep before she could.

IT WAS NEARLY evening before she was up and moving about. She didn't protest when Stekin informed her she should wait to continue until morning.

"I feel like I've been kicked by a horse," she complained

between careful bites of stew. Stekin had caught and cooked a rabbit with some of the cabbage and carrots and some root vegetables he had scavenged while she had slept. His usefulness was irritating.

"Your body fights the transfer," he said. "It will adapt in time."

"What if I don't want it to adapt?" she muttered mutinously into her bowl.

He stilled, said in surprise, "You wish to remain weakened after the transfer?"

"I mean, what if I don't want there to be an after," she glared at his hands, not daring to raise her eyes further. "I don't know that I want to keep doing this transfer." She knew she was angry with herself, not him. For giving in, for asking for his help. For being weak.

"If you do not, you will die." The calmness with which he stated that fact angered her further.

"Why?" she demanded.

He was quiet for a time, then said, "You mean, I suppose, that you wonder at how although I have power, I do not experience the same danger." She hadn't, but now that he brought it up, she wanted to know. "The nature of our power is different. Opposite, in most ways."

"That is completely unhelpful," she snapped.

"If you would rather wallow in your ignorance," he snapped right back, she saw a flash of green from under her brows, "I am happy to oblige you." A stuffy way of telling her to shut up and listen, she supposed. She stripped seed heads from some grass stalks, curbed her impatience.

"Your power," he continued, a frosty edge back in his words that had been missing earlier today, "is generative, it grows within you, replenishes. Like a spring. When your body can safely hold no more, your power will overflow, as a spring will overflow its confinement. Once your body becomes overwhelmed by power, it breaks down. Rapidly, permanently. Some people experience this as conflagration, like you, some as connixation, some as dissolution. The mechanics are, for now, unimportant. Suffice to say, sources flare out if their power is not removed regularly."

Great, she thought, ripping the grass into tiny segments.

"My people, conversely, can wield power, but generate only small amounts. We have learned how to transmute power from a source to supplement our own."

It was nothing she hadn't already suspected. *Except that the—what did he call it?—flare-out is unavoidable. I wonder if that's true, or if it's something he needs me to believe.* So far, he had prevented her from burning herself up twice. *But Juro's mom survived for, what, three years without flaring-out?*

"You're saying," she ground out, "if you're not around when the Words try to escape, I'll die."

"Your power is not sentient," he said with an unnecessary amount of censure, "but yes. As I am certain you have already ascertained for yourself."

She bit back an unnecessary response of her own. "How long?"

"Your power is wild. That is to say, unpredictable and beyond your control. It could be a month, it could be a day." She could feel his eyes on her, looked steadfastly at her empty bowl. "You will know best at this point. Based on what I have observed so far, I would say three days at the inside, a week at the outside."

Three to nine days. Great, thanks for that wildly helpful prediction. Another thought followed, subsuming her anger with dread: *Every nine days for the rest of my life, I'll have to go through this. I can't live like that!*

"It gets easier," he said, "and you will learn to settle your power." He was trying to be reassuring, but it felt patronizing. Her anger sparked again.

"Can't you just take it away? All of it?"

He stilled. "No," he said, his teeth cutting the air.

"But I don't want it!" she protested. "If you took it all away...I could go home."

"Do not ask me again." His eyes were glowing. With a visible effort, he controlled whatever emotion had taken him over. "It is a part of you, as critical as your heart and brain."

"Then why does it hurt me?" she pushed.

He didn't answer.

She kept pushing. "What do you do with it? You say you wield it—how?"

"Most recently, to heal you. To heal myself of the burns your power left on me. Generally, to keep those of us with power hidden and safe from the temple. Before you ask, yes, I have killed with my power, and I will assuredly do so again. I have also killed without it, as you have seen. As you judge me, consider that over the course of my life, I have killed more of my own kind than yours."

"Why?" The way he said it, the anger and sorrow, she couldn't help but be intrigued.

"I have said more than I intended," he said, and she was stoking her indignation until he ended the conversation with, "You have not yet earned the trust needed for me to share that story." He stood abruptly, took up her bowl with his own, and stalked away.

A demon with feelings and trust issues? she thought, nonplussed. *What does* he *need to trust* me *for? I'm the one who could die any day. I'm the one who needs to know* he *is trustworthy. That he's not taking me somewhere to do who-knows-what to me. Chain me up in a dungeon and drop in every few days to see if I'm ready to burst into flames yet. Or just not stop the work-shop-men in the network from doing terrible things.* All he had to do was come in a little late, or *not hear* her call, once, twice, how many times would be enough to soften her up for whatever awaited her at the end of this? She was the one in danger. It was laughable to think *she* had to earn *his* trust.

THEY DIDN'T SPEAK AGAIN that night, except when he came back to warn her that rain was coming and to put on her warmer clothes.

"I am going to find shelter," his words were icy and clipped. "You may join me if you like."

"I'm fine," she declared, still irritated.

He wrapped up his bow, packed away the few items that needed it, and stalked back into the tall grasses.

She purposefully did not look to see where or how far he went. *I shouldn't let myself become dependent on him*, she cautioned herself. *Maybe I need him to take the Words, for now, but that's all.* And while she'd never heard of demons being afraid of the rain, she felt a certain superiority in her own indifference to it.

Until it came.

Not just rain, a deluge, shot with heat lightning and growling like a territorial beast. She crouched around her pack, rain sheeting off her brows, pouring down her back, puddling on the hard-packed ground. Her boots were soaked through not long after her clothes. She didn't want to sit in the cold water, so she crouched there and prayed it would be over soon.

But unlike the rain back home, it did not abate. It poured endlessly from the skies until the water came up over the soles of her boots and she had to slosh to higher ground. She was cold down into her bones. The gusts of wind plastered her wet clothes to her skin, stripping away any semblance of warmth. She was too cold to stay put, and clearly hoping for the rain to stop was a fool's plan. But the pounding drops had obliterated any hope of following Stekin's trail. The grass was all waterlogged and windswept, to the point she couldn't find even her own trail up the hill.

A sound, masked by thunder, caused her to look up. Had she imagined it, or had someone called her name? She waited seven heartbeats. It came again, a distorted roar on the wind. This time she was certain of it.

"Stekin!" she shouted, standing up. "Stekin, where are you?" She called out for him again and again, relief fading to despair. He didn't call back. She couldn't even tell where the sound had come from, it had been so strange and echoed. Her eyes were stinging, and she knew she was probably crying. She knew her shout was a wail. *Why didn't I go after him?* she thought for the hundredth time. *Why was I so stupid and proud?*

There was a slapping sound, feet hitting water. She looked around. There. He raced up the hill behind her, his robe tucked up into his belt, as rain-drenched as she. Lighting picked out the green in his eyes. He said nothing, just took her pack and her hand and they ran. Or tried to. Her boots were water-logged and weighed her down, her legs couldn't keep up with his long strides. He stopped, thrust the pack at her, and knelt, gesturing for her to get on his back. She climbed up, locked her arms around his neck. He threaded his arms through the crook of her knees, and then he *ran*.

She had never seen a person move so fast. He was moving fast enough to pace Juro's horse.

How is this possible? she wondered, shielding her face against his back from the rain. Heat poured off him, warming her even as the wind sliced through her. She felt the pounding of his feet jarring up through his spine and into her, heard the bellows of his lungs steady and strong.

He should have slowed, should have gotten tired. How far had they come? Miles, certainly. His gait changed, his breathing shifted. She peeked over his shoulder. They were climbing. His hot hands locked her ankles around his waist, and he leaned forwards, using all four limbs to scrabble upwards as dirt crumbled away, threatening to send them back to the bottom.

They were both splattered in clay and grit when he stopped climbing. The hill was a sheer rock face in front of him. He edged along it, and she tried to make herself small and light. The rain roared but no longer fell on them. His hands untwined her ankles. She slid down his back to the ground.

They were in a fold in the rock, she could see the lightning forking and fanning overhead, but the wind swept most of the rain past and over the gap. Sprays drifted in, and the patter of large errant drops still fell from overhead, but it was far drier. He pushed her towards the back of the gap, as far in as they could go. His bow and pack were tucked there. She put hers, soggy and heavy, nearby.

There was a weighty sound as he staggered against the wall, used it to lower himself down. *Now* he gasped for breath, and she saw his limbs start to shake with fatigue.

He unclasped his belt, tucked the inner side of his robe tightly under his legs and hip, then opened the other arm and the near-side of his robe. He gestured weakly for her to sit. An invitation for warmth. She balked. His eyes flashed weakly, his teeth caught the light as he saved up breaths to snap at her.

She saved him the effort. She sat at his side, huddled under his arm, her legs tight to her chest, dirty boots smearing mud on the inside of his robe. He closed his arm around her, drew her against him as he pulled the cloth snug around them both. His skin was hot, even through her icy clothes, but dry, and he smelled more like a sun-warmed rock than anything else she could name. The air around them began to warm up, his breathing slowed.

"That," he rasped, so quietly she would not have heard had she not been pressed so close, leeching the heat from him, "is what I use it for." She started and looked up. He had already tilted his head back against the rock wall, eyes closed. The long column of his throat worked once. Then his breathing changed. His heartbeat slowed against her jaw. He was asleep.

The spates of lightning illuminated his throat. '*You have not yet earned my trust,*' she heard again. It sat uncomfortably with her. *Why* do *I need his trust?* she wondered. She didn't have an answer, just a sense of uneasiness.

Once she was certain he wouldn't wake up, she stretched her legs out beside his, leaned her back against his side, placed his arm around her middle to maximize the heat transfer. Tried not to shiver too hard lest she wake him up. She stared up at the sliver of sky, listened to the yowl of wind and assault of rain, felt the steady heart behind her.

He had been here, dry and comfortable, and had come out into the storm to find her. *But he left me out there alone in the first place*, she complained to herself. Another voice, her mother's, snapped, *Isn't that what you wanted?* She'd run away from him, been angry at him. She probably wouldn't have bothered to go back for him, if their positions were reversed.

She felt small and silly, childish. *He must really need my power to put up with me*, she thought guiltily.

But no, *he must not really need it if he's willing to waste it on running through a storm.* Why would he do that? Surely there were better uses for it. *Even if he wants to keep me safe,* she frowned, *it's just a little rain.* Well, a lot of rain. But still, it was a waste. She would tell him that tomorrow. She leaned her head back, yawning.

I never thought I would be warm again.

ARTEN LEARNED, in the morning, why Stekin had come after her and used her power to run. There was debris over the entire plain. Leaves and broken branches, from she couldn't guess where, but certainly nowhere nearby. Great sections of hillsides sloughed off, turf lying in melted ribbons at the base. Standing water bristled with tips of grasses that yesterday had waved as high as her hip. Silt was splattered generously over everything. They had gone too far west, had to angle back north, and though they didn't cross their previous path, the destruction was massive enough to convince her she wouldn't recognize it. She was horrified and amazed.

"Did you know that was going to happen?" she asked when they stopped to rest.

"It is always a risk here," he said simply.

"Thank you," she said, gulping. He inclined his head in response and went back to sorting through their packs.

In the end, they tossed away the cabbage, which had sprung up in mildew with obscene zeal, the dregs of the meat strips, and half the carrots. Her dagger had developed some rust around the hilt, and the edge needed to be honed. The leather on the sheath had come unglued, and the belt was ruined. Stekin cut it down to a size that would wrap around her thigh, and she decided she liked that better anyway. Her journal was a soggy mess, but she would not part with it. The paper and dry-ink had made it through unscathed to her delight. Stekin discarded a few items, a leather pouch, some papers that no longer bore ink, a spare bow string that had been less fortunate in its wrapping than her dry-ink folio. They tied her spare clothes from the straps of their packs to let them flap dry as they walked.

She was aching and exhausted when they reached the house, settled firmly atop a high rise where the flood waters had not reached. Her boots were still sopping and heavy, and the ground had sucked at her feet all day. But, for once, the stone room called to her, promised dryness and warmth. She didn't bother to change clothes, just trudged to the door and gave the phrase.

"Demons," the man was appalled, "You were out in that last night? You're lucky to be here."

"Yeah," she agreed, too tired to engage with him. He noticed and bade her follow. The room was through a hatch in the floor. She felt a flutter of fear until she saw the stone stairway and the room, both carved out of the rock the house sat upon. It smelled of straw and stale mouse. They left her with a heaping bowl of hot stew and a candle-end. She had the presence of mind to eat and to spread her journal out to dry, but that was all she managed. She slept poorly, dreamt of water cascading down the stone steps as she pounded ineffectually at the hatch to be released, as the room filled around her.

The next day, they climbed in elevation enough to leave

the detritus of the flood behind. It took three days to get to the next stop. She and Stekin didn't speak much, and he ranged away when she pressed him for answers he wouldn't give. But he came back at night to cook whatever he had found and share it with her.

It should have taken two days, but she was slow and sluggish. When she commented on how she hadn't been this tired after the last time the Words had escaped, Stekin remarked, "The first time you slept an entire day, so it is not a valid comparison."

"I did not!" She distinctly remembered waking up in the morning, waiting outside for the man to come. *But he didn't, Stekin came.* Stekin offered nothing but a shrug that clearly said, '*Think what you will.*'

TWO MORE DAYS, and Arten felt energetic again. Which was fortunate, because they reached the edge of the plains and entered the mountains. A small range, Stekin informed her, that bisected their route. There would be more mountains before they were done.

At the first house in the mountains proper, she was glad the Words had only started stirring. Because the stone room sent them into a frenzy. She was barely inside when she noted the smell: old char and something else. Then she noticed the corners, two of them blackened with soot, stones crazed with cracks, mortar crumbling. People had *died* in here, burnt themselves alive. And if her Words had been any stronger, the evidence of it would have set her on the same path.

She didn't realize she had been shouting his name until Stekin burst through the door. She was paralyzed, eyes wide and staring, her breath too fast. His eyes darted around, taking everything in before she could even speak. His face was hard, but his voice wasn't unkind as he held out his hand to her and commanded, "Arten, come here." She managed to reach out, touch his hand. Then it was easier, taking the steps towards him.

There were angry people, shouting and demanding something. Stekin turned her head away from them, muffled their sounds with his torso and the hand he closed around her head. His other arm was around her shoulders, holding her to him. She didn't mind. Was glad for its steadiness. It kept her from trembling apart.

His voice rumbled through his abdomen, unintelligible. It was terse. *He's angry*. She wondered what he would do. If he would lock them inside, like he had the workshop man.

His hands moved to her shoulders, he crouched in front of her. "I will not harm them," he said, looking up at her. She recognized she had been babbling aloud. Stopped. His eyes were very green, full of concern. She forgot to look away. "You have my word," he said. Waited for her acknowledgment. She nodded. "I must fix this," he said as quietly as the patter of snow. "You can go outside or stay with me as you wish."

"Stay," she said to her own shock. Something fierce and joyful passed across his face, but it was gone, and he was blank again. He stood, slipped his hand into hers. She held it tightly but didn't cower behind him. Over the shush of her pulse in her ears, she heard him command the homeowners to scour the room clean. Watched as they scrambled to obey. There were two other places she hadn't seen, one at the center of the room, one at the door. They picked up the bits of broken stone and mortar and carried them out to the trash pile, even though it was the middle of the night. Then they washed the room again. Stekin inspected it meticulously, and when he deemed their work sufficient for now, he interrogated them. When did the first person flare-out, how many had been through since then, how long had they been in the network, who was their point of contact, when had she last been by?

"You will repair the masonry damage before winter," Stekin growled.

"We can't afford that!" the woman gasped.

"Take out a loan," Stekin snarled. "I will ensure it is paid, but only if the repairs are satisfactory."

"*You* will? Who are you to demand such a thing, to promise such a thing?" the woman drew herself up angrily, past exhaustion. "You break into our home in the middle of the night, terrorize us, order us about like slaves! You should be *grateful* we're helping wretches like *that*," she glared at Arten.

"I—" Stekin's voice had gone quiet. Arten shivered from the cold of it, "—am the kaz. And I will hold you to your oath." The woman blanched, the man looked like he was going to be sick. "Make the repairs," he said, teeth biting through the words, white and gleaming in the candlelight. He squeezed Arten's hand once, then they left.

Outside, and a distance away, he growled, "Thoughtless, foolish, selfish humans!" He dropped her hand and started pacing. She'd never seen him waste movement before.

"What will you do?" she asked, crouching between two exposed, twisting tree roots, her eyes wide and fixed on him. She didn't want to hear the answer.

"Inform the council, put them under watch, neutralize them if they move one grain off the line." He was clenching and opening his hands, claw-like. She shivered at the last. "I did not say kill them," he snapped at her, "I am no barbarian." She made herself smaller, her eyes traced the line he was pacing in the pine-needle-strewn dirt.

He breathed out sharply through his nose, stopped pacing. "I apologize," he said, coming to perch on the raised root next to her. His hand, cold and bony, alighted on her head. She went still.

He sighed, and she would have said it was wistful if she had to name it.

SHE THOUGHT about that frequently as they crossed the mountains, and what he had said about trust. Another thought came to her as the days slowly shortened. *'I have bought you.'*

The mountain was not heavily populated but the route they took kept her inside consistently. That gave her a lot of time in the evenings to write and think. Stekin might own her, but he didn't treat her as a slave. He had made no demands on her, had no expectations of servitude or subservience. If anything, he acquiesced to her wishes. He cooked meals for her, hunted small game during the day and, occasionally, he would produce fresh venison or boar meat scraps. He washed her clothes every few days now that they were near regular sources of water.

The only thing he insisted on, with increasing frequency, was that she bathe. He even acquired some proper soap for her to scour herself with, and she was too relieved after freeing herself from the clinging scent of the stone rooms to be insulted.

The rooms were generally smaller up on the mountain, the families poorer, the provisions they provided were barely enough for a day. If Stekin had not been supplementing her meals, she knew she would have felt the constant pinch of hunger.

The people were a different breed. Quiet, wary, hard. Calculating with their generosity, as though wondering if this scrap of bread would mean their own family would suffer tomorrow. The rooms were often neglected, grimy, with moldered straw, and the few that weren't, she began to suspect of having been recently scoured of char. She complained to Stekin only once. He responded with a steely, "They struggle to survive. We are fortunate they help us at all."

After that, she gritted her teeth and weathered the rooms silently.

There were three incidents during the crossing. The first was when her power crested and escaped again one night. She awoke soaked with agony and sweat, Stekin already kneeling over her, his fingers digging into her shoulders. It was too dark to see anything, but she heard the deep draws of his breath, the clicking of his teeth afterwards and the satisfied sigh. She was faster to recover this time, as he had promised.

The second happened just before they crossed the ridge. They couldn't use the passes, she'd learned from Stekin, because they were watched. A dedicate monastery was situated on the main pass, and it had small outposts at each of the other, smaller passes. Ostensibly to pray for the safety of travelers and provide emergency services when necessary, but primarily to prevent sources from crossing north.

The last house, before the tree line stopped, was inhabited by a young man. He had apologized for the state of the room when he let her in, hovered near the door.

He seemed a little lonely, talked about how hard life was on the mountain, how isolated it could get. He asked what it was like for her, on the run, in the network, got her talking about it, talking about home, about her family and what she missed. He was so earnest and interested, seemed like he wanted to be her friend. Seemed like the kind of person she would *want* as a friend. She talked with him in a way she had not with anyone but Juro. Late into the night.

When she was yawning, and thanked him, talked of going to sleep, he touched her hand. They were sitting on the pallet, had been for hours while they chatted, but she hadn't thought anything of it. When he didn't leave, when he started touching her shoulders and face, telling her how much he enjoyed their time together, how beautiful she was, only then did she grow uncomfortable.

She wondered why she had let her guard down with this stranger. Tried to get him to leave again. He didn't go, kept caressing her shoulders and cheeks with light, awkward hands. When he leaned in to kiss her, her confusion vanished, supplanted by action.

The dagger was in her hand, between them, holding him, bewildered, at bay, until Stekin answered her call.

She slept outside that night, right up at the edge of the tree line. She didn't ask Stekin what he had done to the man, preferred to think he was unharmed even if she didn't quite believe it. He had returned with a blanket which they curled up under, backs pressed together for warmth against the alpine chill. Stekin wouldn't risk fire with dedicates patrolling the ridges.

They crossed the next day, had to stop for the night in a cold little valley, then finished the descent the following day.

The north side of the mountain, she discovered quickly, was very different from the south. Here, it drizzled nearly constantly. Everything felt perpetually damp: trees, rocks, their clothing. The farther north they went, the more moss and lichen crusted every surface, even the tree bark, covering the forest in a green fuzz.

The stone rooms were, like everything, damp and usually mossy. If they didn't reek of sweat when she entered, they certainly did when she left in the morning. The humidity made her more miserable with heat than the incessant sun of the plains had. Stekin wanted her to bathe daily, despaired if they didn't find enough running water for her to do more than rinse herself with handfuls of it. At least they ate well.

Before they reached foothills, the damp forest was gone, replaced with woods that were more familiar, though with a few new flora. But the heat and the journey were wearing on her, and she couldn't feel excited to see tree rats or hear the calls of the stripe-birds. The days passed in a ceaseless march, rituals marked the beginning and end, and endless walking marked the middle.

It was shortly after leaving the fuzzy forest that the third incident occurred.

HER WORDS WERE STRONG AGAIN, and she was a little worried they would escape tonight or tomorrow. She was still damp through, her skin sticky and clothes clinging, her short locks curled and wild. While the forest may have changed, the humidity was still oppressive.

An elderly woman answered her knock that evening. She looked confused, kept talking about how her son would be home in a few days, about how she couldn't remember where he had gone, but wouldn't she come in. Arten felt sorry for the lady, who muttered to herself, trying to remember where the "room for the *special* guests" was located.

At least she knows I'm not normal.

Oh, she remembered, and leaned on Arten's arm for support as she shuffled back to the kitchen. There was a door that opened into a nook with a pantry on one side and a blank wall on the other. The woman knocked at the blank wall near the bottom with a broom handle, and it reluctantly clicked open so Arten could slide it away. She knew from the weight that it was lined with stone on the reverse. And just behind it, the room.

Arten sighed and went in, skin crawling a little as it always did from the confinement she knew was coming.

"Oh dear!" the lady cried, dismayed. She looked through the doorway with such horror that Arten again felt a pang of sympathy for her. "Let me get you some food. And a candle. You *must* have a candle! Otherwise, what kind of host would I be? A poor one...yes, a poor one." She shuffled off.

Arten, knowing her role, knowing her lot, sank down onto the pallet and took in her surroundings with disinterest. *Oh, stone walls, how novel. The ceiling too, wow. Old, scratchy pallet, yep. Stinky thread-bare blanket, goody. A water jug, that's new. Oh, the night bucket, and it has a lid, I'm so fortunate.*

She sighed.

But no one burned up in here, and I doubt this old lady will be a workshop man. And she's getting me a candle. She decided it would get a *comfortable* rating when she reported to Stekin tomorrow. She felt a wistful longing for Juro's cell or Mother Larkin's. Those had been good days, and she hadn't appreciated them.

The woman came back with a small bowl of thin stew, cold with congealed fat atop, a slice of bread that clearly had the moldy spots removed, and the promised candle. Arten thanked her.

"Of course, my dear," she said with a beam. "You deserve some rest, don't you think?" She waited for Arten to agree, then nodded to herself. "Yes, good, good," she muttered, then asked Arten to please close the door, it was so heavy and her son was away, did she mention?

Arten closed herself in.

There was no lock on the stone door, but she found she was unable to open it from inside. Whatever bashing the wall with a broom did, it apparently could only be done from one direction. She shrugged and settled back onto the pallet. She wasn't worried about the woman's forgetfulness, Stekin would let her out in the morning if her hostess forgot.

The food was unpleasant, especially after the filling and satisfying meal Stekin had provided that evening. But food was food, and she also didn't want to offend the lady, even though it tasted like she'd put the wrong spice in by mistake. The bread still tasted of mold, even with the spots removed, and she gulped the broth down to wash the taste out of her mouth.

With the rare addition of a candle, she spent some time writing to Juro, complaining of how tired she was of this whole process, and wondering how long it would be until it was over. She wondered how long until her birthday, only to realize she'd lost track of the days. Eventually, she grew bored of it, laid her tunic and trousers out to dry a little, blew out the candle, and stretched out to sleep, not even bothering to touch her dagger beforehand.

She awoke, panting, from a dream of being stabbed in the gut. She got her bearings, saw that she was alone in the cell, and didn't have time to do anything more before her gut shot through with pain again, leaving her gasping. She had a moment of confusion, then it happened again and again. She curled up around her stomach as it clenched tighter and tighter until she could barely breathe from the pain, tears streaming from her eyes as she whimpered. The pain intensified. She started to moan.

Heartbeats pulsed, each an infinity of agony. She vomited. It didn't help, but her body kept doing it. She was choking from the contractions of her stomach, sobbing breaths in between. She felt like she was dying, her body was burning, though not from the Words. The pain was excruciating.

Stekin, help, she pleaded silently, unable to get any sound out.

Her vision was pulsing with light, wavering. She didn't even register him when he threw the door open and bounded to her side. Felt his hands, like ice, like blessed ice, on her forehead, her face, her shoulders. He was angry, snarling at something. Someone? Himself? Not her. All she cared about was his hands. They were miracles of relief. When he placed them over her abdomen, she sobbed, snotty tears smearing on her face.

I'm surprised he can stand being near me right now, she thought with the parts of her that weren't preoccupied with dying. She was covered in vomit, sweat, a slimy coating of fear and pain, and now snot. *I can die of embarrassment,* she decided, *if I survive this.*

She could see his face now that the pain had ebbed a fraction. It was pale and grim, his teeth bared as he bent over her, flashing as he chanted, his concentration focused solely on the skin under his hands. *Healing*, she recognized. *But I don't think it's working.* She could feel the power entering her, but it didn't feel like before, there was no feeling of rightness or relief, just a writhing, like a worm trying to burrow into a stone. She closed her eyes, focused on his voice, on the small comfort of his frigid hands. Things that told her she wouldn't die alone.

His chanting stopped, she forced her eyes open. He was looking straight at her—was that fear? No, it was gone now. He touched her forehead with the heel of his hand, then a shard-filled maw of darkness consumed her.

16

NO ANSWERS

STEKIN

Her breath came on little whimpers, even in sleep. Each one tightened the swarm of anxiety in Stekin's chest. He knew too little of healing human bodies to cure her. The poison was in her blood, pulsing through her with every beat of her pattering heart. Too frail. The only thing he could do was kick her liver and kidneys into overdrive, get them working to clean her blood faster. He did not yet know which one would counter whatever agent Arten had ingested. The woman would tell him before the night was over. He bared his teeth and channeled the anger into directing his power to shield her body from absorbing more of the toxin.

When her whimpers stopped, her panting became less frantic, her heart a little steadier, only then did he pause. He took in the room, the empty bowl, the spread of her clothes. The stench of humanity and chyme. He soaked her long-sleeved shirt in water from the jug and wiped the vomit from her. It ran onto her dress, so he removed that, wiped her skin under the stains, then dressed her in the light tunic and trousers he had originally purchased for her. *It will do for now,* he thought, gathered her against his chest, stood.

He found the woman's bedroom by simply kicking doors off their rollers until he came across it. She startled out of sleep and sat up with a cry.

"Get out," he growled.

When she did not comply, Stekin placed Arten down on the floor against the near wall and picked the woman up, bending her over his shoulder. Somewhat gently, for she was even more frail than most humans. She shouted and kicked at him.

He took her to the safe-room, set her down on the soiled pallet, picked up Arten's few belongings, and closed her in. Her cries of confusion and fear did not follow him far, swallowed by the stone.

Back in her room, he stripped all but the least noxious bedding away, tossed it in the next room. Arten was feverishly hot. He moved her to the low bed, then bent over her to bolster and protect her internal systems with his power. The defenses he had sparked in her stomach had been nearly stripped away, even though barely a quarter of an hour had passed.

It is going to be a long night, he thought grimly, his palm resting on her forehead, fingers curling closed across her scalp. The motion quieted her a little, so he allowed himself to linger for a few minutes. *I will not let her die.* He stopped the growl rising in his throat. *She is critical.* With a last curling of his fingers into a fist, he went to get answers.

The old woman seemed frightened, lost primarily, but at times shrewd and alert. She spoke of her son, asked to see him. Stekin had detected no sign of another inhabitant in the house, so her continued insistence that he should be home soon was perplexing.

He questioned her about the poison. It took several visits, for he returned to Arten's side often to pour his power into her. The bitter crone was, he believed, the woman's true nature, but after several interviews, he came to understand that the bewildered helplessness was not a false persona but a disease of the mind. And the latter was the one who had poisoned Arten. The crone had been incensed at his accusation, but the gentler one had smiled sadly and said, "It's a small kindness, all I can give."

A kindness to die quickly, rather than burn at the pyre, rather than have her soul eaten by a demon. Neither facet of her mind could tell him what agent had been used. One denied its existence, the other could not recall.

He found out around midmorning, when he heard a muffled cry from the kitchen area and went to investigate. The woman was in a curl on the pantry floor, having released herself from the room somehow. Choking on her own vomit.

Stekin watched while she died.

Then picked up the tin that was tipped on the ground at her hand. Smelled the mossy crumbles of dried leaves within. It was like soured mint and awoke an old memory of a plant the people of New Respite had spent years meticulously eradicating, claiming the root contained a deadly toxin. *Perhaps a variant grows here where the toxin is also in the leaves*, he thought, brushing it from his fingers.

Whether she had eaten it from guilt, confusion, or fear of reprisal concerned him little. He carried her body outside before he dissected it, forced it to give up its final answers.

EVERY FEW HOURS, Arten's body threw off the compulsion to

sleep and dragged her to consciousness in order to try and regurgitate the poison. He kept her clean, applied his hands to her neck and face to cool her, kept streaming his power into her in small bursts, stimulating her body's natural healing.

The woman's stomach had been perforated in several places, the lining red and blistered as though chemically burned. There had been no other damage that he could discern, aside from old age and the corruption in her brain. Her other organs seemed undamaged. The suffocation had prevented her from dying a slower, more painful way. Arten's stomach, however, was intact and her body young; he was reasonably confident she would survive. But he stayed at her side throughout the day.

That second night, she stopped vomiting and fell into an exhausted sleep. He removed her soiled clothes, washed her, cleaned all the stinking clothes and bedding. While the cloth dried, he stretched out on the floor beside the bed, pillowed his head on one arm, reached the other up to rest his fingers on the underside of her wrist. The slow, strong pulse there threaded through his sleep.

"STEKIN?" The croaked sound of his name woke him. He was awake in an instant.

"I am here," he said, sitting up, squeezing her wrist lightly. Even with his keen night vision, he could barely make out her form.

"Water?" she asked brokenly. He fetched a vessel he had filled from the exterior pump earlier, and a drinking glass from the kitchen, then pressed the filled glass into Arten's hand. Supported the bottom when her arms trembled to raise it.

She lay back, he placed the glass on the floor beside the bed. "I'm naked?" she asked, her voice sounding more strongly than before.

"I washed your clothing," he said delicately. *No need to embarrass her further.*

"I'm cold," she said, her face turned away from him.

He took off his robe and draped it over her, tucking it around her. He heard the intake of breath. *Humans are so absurd about bodies*, he frowned, stopping the irritated sigh before it escaped. "Is there anything else you require?" he asked.

"No."

"Very well. Goodnight, Arten." He moved silently to the door. She stopped him as he was crossing through it.

"Wait," she whispered.

"I will be just outside," he said, hearing the coldness in his words. *She does not intend insult,* he reminded himself and tried to make the next words kinder. "You must rest."

He propped the door closed behind him, settled himself against the wall beside it, to wait and guard. He heard her turn over, the quiet scrape of his robe as she drew it tighter about her. *How long before she trusts me?* he thought, frustrated. *Have I done something to give her cause to fear?*

The thought gave him pause. *She is juvenile, still.* He had not been around many humans at this stage, despite his long association with them. It was a time of rapidity that had always left him confused, so he had avoided it. *The sources are always older when their power comes. She has barely begun to live, is not yet ready to be her own person. When does that happen for them?* Sometime in the next five years of growth, he supposed. *I do not know what to do with a child,* he thought, not for the first time, *I did not even know what to do with my own.*

Perhaps that is why they turned out as they did. His disappointment there was nothing new, and he put it aside.

But it had turned his thoughts east and a little north. They were about three-quarters through the network now. It would still take them more than two weeks to reach its terminus. The pull to return was strengthening. Daily minutia he had not considered for years was pressing on him with increasing urgency. Who was maintaining the network at present? How much more had it deteriorated without his oversight? Who had been taken as kaz in his absence, and how would they react to his return?

They must know I am not dead, from the correspondence I have left to be sent through the network. Unless the letters never made it. And how long ago had he sent the last? Before he went to the Forgotten City. They could very well think him dead, at this point. *I wonder if they have redistributed my house and compound.* The mere thought, that his library might have been interfered with, filled him with a violent need to move, to *do* something.

He went outside and dug a grave for the old woman in the little cemetery behind her house. It was dark, the moon on the wane and not yet risen, so he risked the transformation. The rocky soil scraped between his claws as he dug a hole, tearing away the sod in two swipes, heaping dirt atop with a speed and intensity that left his pent-up muscles satisfied. He hooked a claw through the woman's ribcage, and dragged her to the grave, rolled her in with a nudge. Heaped the dirt back atop her with scrapes of his back legs, then replaced the sod. He stamped on the mound, compressing it with his weight.

I must return to the last node and give them updated instruc-

tions. At least he and Arten need not worry about the absent son coming home. There was another fresh grave in the cemetery, the stone marker carved with *Beloved Son.* It appeared to be from the spring or late winter. *She would not have lasted long on her own,* he knew.

But any sympathy for her had ebbed when he had found, earlier in the day, the two shallow, unmarked graves farther back, the scent of decay unmistakable. Arten had not been her first victim. Two of his people had been denied a source because of this woman's grief and illness. Some other mothers had lost their children and would never know. He could not even carry those people's name with him, for the woman had not bothered to carve them. *She probably did not bother to learn them.*

He would carry this woman's name with him, despite his disgust with her. *She served us many long years on nothing but faith. The murder of two does not outweigh the dozens she saw safely through.*

It sat ill with him, though. *Perhaps I am growing soft in my age.* He frowned, once again on watch outside the bedroom.

There was more than that, though. The woman had killed only two. *Arten has been physically threatened twice, but both would have let her go, eventually. That would result in a delay but does not explain the disappearances. And the incompetent fools who allowed my sources to flare-out, those numbers are too small.* Something else, something they had not yet encountered, was preventing sources from exiting the network. Which meant worse was to come.

I will *keep her safe. I must.* No one knew better than he how vast and entrenched evil was in the world. He would shelter her from it, whether from her people or his. He bared his teeth in the dark, feeling his power surge in anticipation. Absurdly, he wondered if this feeling was paternal.

17

STEKIN REVEALED

ARTEN

Arten was too weak to hang onto Stekin's back when he insisted they leave the next morning. She had dressed herself, pointedly waiting until he left the room to do so. He hadn't said anything, but his expression had clearly stated he thought she was being unreasonable. She did let him put on her socks and slot her boots onto her feet, since she didn't have the strength afterwards to manage that herself.

They were outside, the midmorning light bright and cheerful, mocking the pain that still cramped through her. She was parched, but her stomach could only tolerate a little water, and the plain bread she'd had for breakfast had nearly come back up again.

"You should leave me," she said, leaning heavily against the house, paint chips and splintered wood digging into her arm. "I can take care of myself until you get back."

"No," he said, icy and deep. She thought his eyes might have flashed, but it was difficult to tell in the sunlight. She shivered involuntarily as the memory of a caved-in face and dead eyes forced itself up. *He won't hurt me,* she chided herself, but the image stayed.

"But no one's coming," she protested. Stekin had told her more of what happened, how the woman had died, how her son was not returning.

"No," he said again, and she could tell he was making an effort to be civil by the way his teeth sliced the word from the air. "I will carry you," he declared, and her weak protests were ignored. He lifted her in his arms, as though she weighed nothing, though it had been years since her father had been able to lift her so without complaint. "Try and rest," he said, then nothing more.

He all but ignored her as he strode back the way they had come. She felt awkward, being held like a child by someone she barely knew, but when she realized he treated her only as though she were another pack, she relaxed. His arms kept her tight to his chest, absorbed the impact of his footfalls, and his gait was unaccountably smooth. She closed her eyes, dozed. She roused each time Stekin stopped, sipped the water he forced on her, relieved herself if necessary, then dozed again. In the afternoon, they reached the house where she'd previously stayed.

Stekin set her on her feet beside the door, kept a hand on her shoulder to steady her, knocked. She was impressed with the time he'd made, wondered if he had used power to achieve it but for some reason doubted so. He didn't look at her as she watched him, knuckling grit from her eyes. He didn't look tired, didn't look like he'd hiked fifteen miles, much less carrying a person and in good time. He looked alert, intense. *Like a hound on a scent.*

She attributed it to the poison still filtering from her body when the next thought struck her: *He's not so mean looking when you take away the superior disdain.* Still aristocratic, with the long nose and every angle sharp. '*Rich enough to afford a good shave*,' her father had said often of his wealthier customers. She hadn't understood what he meant until Deric and Juro had started shaving, and she'd seen the scrapes and rashes left by over-used blades and inexperienced hands. Most of the men in her village wore short-cropped beards once they were old enough to grow them out. But Stekin's face and throat were as smooth as her own. Something nagged at her, but the door opened and she forgot it.

The entire family was home, despite the early hour. They were dressed more nicely than the glimpse she'd had before, sitting in their common room, reading and sewing and—*It's Saviorsday*, she realized. They'd run together, the days, the houses, the people answering the door after dark, the cells all variations on the same theme. She barely recognized the man who had led her to the stone outbuilding that doubled as a shed, was alarmed at how complacent she had become.

They were all staring at her, a mixture of horror and fear, while trying not to. Stekin was trying to engage the adults, to get their attention, but they kept exchanging worried glances at each other, at her.

"I'll wait outside," she muttered. "No, it's fine," she put a hand on Stekin's arm, halting the brisk indrawn breath, "really."

"Very well," he said quietly, but she heard the shards of ice underneath.

She let herself out, stood in the sunlight, in the yard. In the open. Not scuttling for the trees, not darting for a cell. Alone.

It felt foreign, especially because she knew that perhaps a month ago this would have felt normal.

Before I was a fugitive. Before the person who owns me killed a dedicate. Before the workshop men. Before a demon who was not-a-demon had come into her life. Before she had become a source to his power.

Will there be an after?

The exposure was too much. She found a groomed tree at the edge of the sparse woods, settled under its boughs.

This network leads somewhere. There are people on the other end, people like me. If Stekin is to be believed. As are his people. Not-demons. Not demons, but what? Amassing our power, to what end?

She imagined dungeons, armies of demonic forces pooling, poised to invade. She imagined pens where sources were kept like cattle while tall, grotesque creatures came by to inhale power from them, leaving them collapsed atop one another, licking their distorted mouths as they glided on. She imagined a cave, full of glowing, hungry eyes; imagined Stekin prodding her onwards; imagined discovering there were no other sources just as the eyes grew teeth and descended on her in a rush of wings and snarls.

She shuddered, forced herself to think of something else.

She looked towards the house, wondered what was happening inside. Wondered if people would look at her like that for the rest of her life, *If I have one.*

She reined her thoughts away from a terrifying future again.

People do what he says. Even those people he made clean their cell, they did it, then *challenged him. Even my parents. Even me,* she thought with a jolt. *For my parents, it was money. For me... well, it's safer with him than without, it seems. Even if that makes me naive. But what about these people? Why do they listen to him?*

She thought back, remembered talk of an oath. Remembered how they humbled themselves when he said something—what was it? *The kaz*, she remembered. He wielded the words as though they meant something. *To these people, they must.* She resolved to ask him about it. And didn't have to wait long.

He emerged from the house. Skittish eyes followed his movements from behind the curtains, from the closing doorway. His expression was brooding, his mouth a hard line. She looked away before he noticed her scrutiny. He approached, folded himself to the ground beside her with a rustle of cloth.

"They will purchase some tonic to restore you," he said without preamble, "and some journey bread. Then we will depart."

"We're not staying here tonight?"

"No," the word rippled from him, resonated too long in the air. She wondered what they had done to anger him. "I will carry you," he added into the silence, absently. As though it didn't need to be stated.

"What are you?" she asked.

"Your guardian," he said, remotely, evasive. "More than that, you will decide for yourself." *Whatever that means,* she wanted to grumble, but kept it behind her teeth. She didn't have the energy to try and extract more of an answer from him.

"What is the kaz?" She felt his eyes slide to her, felt the skin of her face prickle as he looked at her. Flushed under his regard.

"My title," he said, then, "What are you asking?" She flushed more at the approval in his voice, hoped he didn't notice. The woman and her son left the house, walking down a well-tracked path with quick steps. To get their supplies, Arten guessed.

"Why do these people, the ones in this network, get quiet and do what you tell them when you say your title?"

"They swear an oath to the network council, the sources that utilize it, and to the kaz when they agree to become a node. The oath to the kaz is unnecessary, but reprisals from an individual are more reassuring to your people than reprisals from a committee." She saw him shrug.

"Reprisals? You're an enforcer of these oaths for this network?" It fit. Her stomach turned at the thought. It was too much like a temple officer.

"I have acted in that capacity, yes, but that is not my primary function. My involvement in the affairs of the network has been minimal in recent decades." He stopped, and she thought he was done, but then he spoke again. "Even before I left to find you, I was negligent of the network. It has existed a long time, has performed its function adequately. I did not question whether adequacy was enough. I am at fault for all that now plagues it. Do you understand why I must address the wrongs as I encounter them?"

Was that a hint of plea behind the chilly words?

"Yes," she said. "But what wrong have these people done?"

"They have done no wrong."

"Then why are you angry with them?"

"Ah," he said after a moment of thought, "you have mistaken my demeanor for anger."

When he wasn't going to say any more, she pressed, irritated, "Then what is it? What happened in there?"

"I informed them that the next node is no longer in the network and gave them new instructions to relay to the sources that come through. I made the requests for supplies and for their hospitality. The first they granted, the second they denied."

"What?" she cried, "Can they do that? What about this oath?"

His voice turned amused and bitter, "The oath, as they reminded me, states that a source must be granted one night in their care and no more save to spare the source from capture or death. And you are no longer in danger, so under the terms of the oath, they cannot host you again." She glanced over, saw his sharp smile. "A clever woman in that home."

"And you're not angry?" she pressed, disbelieving. *She* was angry—to deny her a safe place to sleep just because they'd already given her one? She thought it was petty of them, and high-handed to decide that she was not in danger. She had nearly died two nights ago!

"No. They are within their rights. I do not fault them for their caution."

"Well, I do!" she said hotly.

"Do you? What do you know of their lives, their fears?" his words were frosted with disappointment. "Every moment we linger is a moment someone could happen by and see us. Every item they give to us could be traced back to them, every purchase on our behalf could rouse suspicion. Why do they need an antidote if none of their family were poisoned? Why do they need travel bread if they have no visitors? The temple is eager to investigate all mysteries, no matter how small."

"I...hadn't thought of that," she admitted. Perhaps the fear when her hosts looked at her wasn't entirely because they were afraid she was going to burn down their house.

"Do you know what a compulsion is?" The way he asked

told her that she didn't. "May I demonstrate?" She agreed a little nervously. He shifted to face her, put his hands on either side of her face, chanted a brief stream of words. "It is done," he said. "Now, indulge me. What is your name?"

Arten, she thought, tried to say. "I don't know," her voice said, neutral and calm.

"What is your name?" he repeated.

Arten! "I don't have a name," she heard herself lie in the same even tone.

"What is your name?"

Arten! Arten! "I don't have one."

"Do you know someone named Arten?"

Yes, of course. "No."

"Are you certain?"

"I don't know anyone named Arten," her mouth lied again. She sounded confident and adamant, not as scared as she felt.

"That is enough," he said, placed his hands along her face and chanted more words. "Now, what is your name?"

"A-arten," she said, shaky and confused. Gulped down her relief.

"How are you?" he asked, genuinely.

"That was awful." She shuddered. His hand went to her forehead, rested there while his fingers curled over her head. It was an absurd gesture, and equally absurd that she found it comforting.

He didn't apologize. "Each family, down to the children," he said instead, "is placed under a compulsion to protect the network. They cannot speak of it or of the people that come through to any but one of my people, someone under the same compulsion, or, within limits, to a source. There are things they can say to people they think are in danger but doing so might lead the temple to their door." Arten shuddered again. "If the temple should find them and question them, their answers are much like your own just now." He took his hand away.

"If they never say anything, though, it wouldn't be so bad. The compulsion wouldn't...change their words if they weren't talking about it?"

"That is accurate. If they are suspected of harboring a source, however, the temple will question them. Will question their family. Your friend, the Swain girl"—Arten startled to hear the name—"would stand up to questioning, but if her brother were being beaten in front of her and she were told the truth would save him from tortures and fires, and she had that truth, she would want to give it. The compulsion would prevent that. She would have to watch while the dedicates and investigators tore her family apart, perhaps maimed them, perhaps killed them. All the while, physically unable to speak the truth. And, if she were unfortunate enough to survive, she would have to live with the guilt of that after."

"Has that ever happened?" she asked, appalled.

"Many times."

"Why...why would anyone agree to that?"

"Many have lost family to the pyres, like your neighbors. We relocate them to somewhere they can find work, somewhere that is useful to us, with their consent. Some just disagree with the practice, some want to save the wretched. Some just need the money."

"What money?" Her wandering attention jerked back.

"These people provide us a necessary service. Did you think we do not compensate them for it?" His statement had the easy disdain of a merchant accused of selling inferior products. And it was exactly what she had thought. "You have seen the shabby lives most of these people lead. How did you think they paid for the bunkers, for the food, pittance though it usually is, that they give you?" His words turned hard, "People are not generous or kind without cause, Arten."

Her stomach clenched, the Words bucked. "How much?" she asked through teeth clenched against pain.

"One to three gold pieces per year, depending on the relative costs in the area, and all costs reimbursed."

Arten didn't understand the vehemence of the feelings that had seized her, or why the Words were angry. She didn't need to in order to clamp down on both, to push them aside, to breathe deeply and evenly through her nose trying to calm her stomach. Stekin rose, picked up the bow and quiver, and left without a word. As soon as he was gone, she lost control of her stomach and heaved water and chyme out over the tree roots.

"You are unhappy," Stekin observed from where they crouched behind a rocky protrusion. Arten bit back a snarl. Her patience with him had nearly depleted in the week since her illness, since he had revealed the truths about the network.

Of course I am, she ground her teeth. *I am bought and paid for several times over. You've created a network of people whose minds are enslaved to funnel those like me to your lair.* She was not brave enough to say any of those things. "So?" she snapped.

"So, ask me what you wish to know." He was reasonable, unaffected. She wanted to kick him for it.

"How rich *are* you?" she demanded. She'd done some figuring and, with the number of houses she'd stayed in already, and the estimate she'd extracted from Stekin that she had visited about five percent of the network, Stekin and his cohorts were paying more than five-hundred gold to keep the network running each year. Each year! And it could easily be over a thousand. Not to mention the costs of building the rooms, reimbursing expenses, paying people to come by and distribute the payments!

No wonder he didn't blink at sixty gold to buy me.

"I have enough to meet my needs and those of my sources," he said unhelpfully.

"What do you do with us that justifies that much expenditure?" she pushed.

"As I have said," he snapped, "nothing without your consent." He stalked off, leaving her to wait for dark.

She glared down at the log cabin, refusing to watch where he had gone. *What right does he have to be upset?* she thought caustically. *Why am I even helping him? He's got money, he can pay someone to come out and inspect his network for him. He could pay someone to go through it pretending to be a source and ferret out all the bad houses, if he wanted. He could...*

Demonsfire. He has. That's me. He's bought me. And sent me through his network.

Her anger intensified (she disregarded the small protest that she had insisted on continuing when he had offered her an out), stoking the Words in her gut. They had escaped, and he'd drained them away, that evening after they had been given the antidote and denied lodgings. He'd continued carrying her while she slept off the fatigue that invariably followed. It was past time for them to escape again, if Stekin's frequent glances through her were an accurate forecast.

She wished they would burn him.

For all his talk of consent, it's not like I have a choice. Burn or don't burn. And I'm not ready to kill myself just to spite him. She wondered if he could set a compulsion to prevent her from doing so. Not for the first time, wondered how far compulsions went, if she would be subjected to them once they reached their destination. But he had not yet placed one on her, aside from the demonstration.

If it's so important that I follow him, important enough to buy me, surely he would also use the power he has to compel me to go. Maybe he can only compel words not action. And he knows that if he puts one on me, slave or not, I will not be his network ferret.

She was so focused on being angry at him, she didn't notice the sweat forming on her brow, even though the heat of the summer had started to break, didn't notice the rising of Words that had retracted their claws and pushed upwards with deceptive calm, didn't notice Stekin return. A hand on her shoulder startled her. She jumped and whirled, glared when she saw it was him, then paled as the Words launched for freedom. Their calm shattered, they ripped and tore their way out, hot currents buoying them across her tongue.

Stekin seemed to know the instant they won. His fingers dug into her shoulders, holding her rigidly in place, driving her weight heavily into her heels. His eyes were blazing, his jaws stretched wide as he leaned over her. The Words scraped past her teeth and he drew them in, with that inhale that did not draw air.

The golden shafts of dying light caught him, casting his face in beatific glow, glinting off his teeth. She stared up at him, transfixed with horror and disgust. Her stomach turned over, and the rest of the Words disgorged from her throat in a tight ball. They were gone, but he still loomed over her, tensed with purpose, drawing at...

There was a pressure somewhere inside her, building,

insistent, pulling. Something gave to the pressure, shifted the smallest fraction, rose minutely. Towards Stekin's intense, eager jaws. It shifted again, with a small tearing that shocked through her, lighting her nerves afire. She didn't know *what* it was, but she knew in that moment what it *was* —vital.

She couldn't think, couldn't move, her entire being focused on that thing inside her that she had never known before, that precious thing that was in danger. She tensed around it, every muscle braced against Stekin's pull. It slipped again, the rent widened, agony screamed through her. She wasn't breathing, forced her lungs to start again with a grunt.

Abruptly, the pressure vanished, sending her staggering against the immovable grip on her shoulders. When had she gripped his wrists? Her eyes refocused. He was looking down, through her, his expression something she hadn't seen before. She didn't have time to think about what was written there because his eyes snapped to hers. She wrenched her face away, unwilling to let him force that connection on her. She remembered too clearly, the feeling of him peering into her depths, of the way the Words had responded to him with violent joy, the feeling of her soul exposed for scrutiny, her secrets and shames cracked open and laid bare.

She didn't realize she was shaking until he released her shoulders and her legs trembled too much to support her. He caught her before she fell, but she shoved him away, braced herself against the rock at her back, the other hand gripped the hilt of the dagger which now separated them. She could still feel his thumbs where they had dug into her shoulders, the four points of his fingertips ached only marginally less. It was easier to focus on the bruises than the rest.

"Arten, look at me," he asked.

"Get away from me," she rasped, dry and ashen. The dagger point shook with the physical shock that always set in after. He just had to wait for her to succumb to fatigue and she would be powerless to stop him from doing whatever he wanted. From taking it, that precious thing, whatever it was.

"Very well," he said. She heard the scowl, knew he was giving her that sharp frown, didn't look up. He left as quietly as he had come. She slid to the ground, wrapped her arms around her legs and put her forehead on her knees. She wondered where her body found the moisture to form the tears.

What just happened? she wondered, when she could think again. She probed gently for the thing inside her, but she could no longer find it. The pain had faded to a dull discomfort, but it was nebulous, and if she hadn't just experienced it, she wouldn't have even noticed it. *What was that?*

But then she knew: the wellspring of her power.

He was going to take it! She felt the panic rise again, felt herself hunching around her chest. *Why did he stop?* More importantly, why did she care? *All I've wanted was to find a way to neutralize the power so I can go home. Stekin can take it away...* But the thought filled her with dread. *No, he can't! He can't have it!* Hope and revulsion flashed through her in rapid cycles.

Eventually, she calmed herself enough to drink. The gourd emptied but was not enough to slake her thirst. She roused herself once dusk had faded and tripped and stumbled down the hill to the cabin. She'd taken her pack with her. Its weight was a comfort against her exposed back. She knew Stekin watched her, but not from where.

The couple admitted her, let her into the cell under the common room floor, carved out of the stone under the house, gave her the dregs of their supper. She forced herself to eat it, forced her body to keep it down. Every mouthful from the hand of one of her hosts was a battle since the old woman. Tonight, she didn't do it for Stekin, or for the faceless future sources who would come after her. She did it because she needed fuel to fight the fatigue. Because, tomorrow, she would be alone with Stekin again. And she needed all the energy she could muster against him.

Needed the energy to stop herself from falling at his feet and begging him to take the Words away for good. From attacking him before he could do so.

Sleep trounced her before she finished the gruel. She slept deeply, dreamt of teeth in a dark cave, overwhelming her, of talons piercing through her shoulder and pinning to her to the floor as emerald fire burrowed into her, the cold of it more painful than her Words had ever been, of an invisible force ripping away her insides, hollowing her out. She woke, shivering, pulled on the warm trousers and shirt over her dress, and fell back asleep immediately.

THE MORNING ARRIVED TOO SOON. Her limbs were heavy and uncoordinated as she dressed in her summer-weight clothes. She ripped a hole in the pocket of her trousers so that she could reach the dagger that remained strapped to her leg. Her hosts looked surprised at her transformation but gave her the promised rations and let her go.

She would have run if she could have managed it. It was

hard enough forcing her legs to climb the endless rolling hills that were her road. She managed to stay alert until the sun was well-established in the sky, keeping an eye and ear out for Stekin. He didn't appear. As the sun grew hotter, and the shade shorter and her limbs heavier, her caution faded. Sheer determination kept her moving, kept her from stopping and putting her pack down.

She paused at midday but leaned against the rock-face that shaded her instead of sitting. Even so, it was nearly impossible to convince her legs to get going again. Once they had the motion it was easier to keep plodding along. Much harder to stay alert for the landmarks. She would have missed one turn had some startled quail not flown, grunting, across her path, jerking her to alertness. She actually walked into the river before she noticed that marker.

She turned right at the river, following it as it dipped south and east. *One mile*, she told herself heavily as the sun disappeared. *Just one more mile.* Darkness fell before she arrived.

She stumbled along and would have missed the house if not for the reflection of squares of yellowed light on the river surface.

Squares meant windows.

Her bleary eyes found them, and then the stones that made a broken path across the water. She somehow made the jumps, stone to stone, without falling into the water, though she slipped and went down heavily on her knee twice before resorting to landing on all-fours. She trudged up the hill, holding her relief in check until she was inside her cell, until she had finished her food, then she let it out. Collapsed and slept.

The next day, she was much stronger, felt the fatigue only at the end of the day. She noticed her surroundings that day. Wondered when the sparsely wooded hills had given way to steeper rocky slopes with scrub trees and tufts of grass and not much else. She was hiking now, mostly east. A mountain range sprawled to the north, not as far away as she remembered it being. In the distance, she once saw snowcapped peaks. Then the heat descended and hazed the view.

She didn't see or hear Stekin all day. *But he's out there,* she was certain.

That certainty wavered while she waited for dark, crouched in the shadow of a rocky overhang while frigid rain pattered around her. The clouds had blown in from the north without warning. She'd dashed for higher ground, remembering the plains, expecting this storm to be worse, with the way the clouds boiled and brooded. The deluge didn't come, just the steady drops of heavy rain. Then, just as the sun was setting, the rain stopped as abruptly as it had begun. She was only somewhat damp, felt foolish for rushing to safety. *He's probably laughing at my stupidity.* She scowled, tramping back down to the house.

But she knew it wasn't true. He never laughed.

Maybe he's actually left, she thought, staring at the dark ceiling in her cell. She turned on her side. *No, he wouldn't. Would he? He promised to keep me safe. Not that he's been that great at it.* She turned again, her skin hot and sticky from the rain.

Wait, did he promise? She couldn't remember. Could only remember that he'd bought her, sent her into this network.

But I decided to keep going after the workshop man. He wanted me to stop.

Another voice protested, *But he didn't stop me after the second workshop man, after the poisoner. He didn't ask me, just assumed I wanted to keep going.*

What would she have said if he asked? She knew, grimaced at the knowledge. *So what, he knows me so he didn't ask? That's absurd.* But was it? He was certainly leaving her alone right now. She'd told him to go away. Maybe he was staying away to give her the space she wanted, like he had on the plains.

That's giving him too much credit.

She remembered his face, the too-wide jaws, the fierce joy, the soundless ripping inside her. She shuddered. *He'll come crawling back when the Words are strong again.* The thought provided no comfort. She wished she had his hearing, to know whether he was outside the house, listening for her call, like he'd promised—or had he?

She was torn between wanting him to be there and wishing he was far away.

Between wanting him to finish what he had started and never wanting to give him the Words again.

She hated her indecision.

HER ANGER DRAINED AWAY over the next few days, replaced by nervousness. It was harder and harder to force the food down, though she needed it, since Stekin had not dropped by to cook for her like he had always done before. Harder and harder to enter that cell, not knowing if she would be let out again, not knowing if Stekin was nearby watching, not knowing if this one or that one was a workshop man. Or worse.

Her directions led her invariably east, skirting through the foothills, slipping through narrow valleys, endless rocks and that unpredictable, chilly rain her only constants. She stopped thinking about Stekin, stopped thinking about anything much at all. She thought she understood why people didn't make it to the terminus of the network. It was a struggle to keep going each day.

One afternoon, she simply stopped. There was no point in rushing to the next house. No point in moving through the network. Stekin was gone. If she kept going, she'd run into his people. People who wanted to drain the Words from her, with their teeth and glowing eyes and wild hunger. She couldn't go back—one day only at each house—but she didn't have to go forwards. She sat in the shade of a towering rock formation, tilted her head back against it, eyes closed. Didn't move, even when the rain started. It would pass. It always passed.

It passed. She let the sun dry her. There was a strong scent of the mountains in the breeze, a promise of autumn. *What day is it?* she wondered idly. *I suppose it doesn't matter. There is no one to celebrate my birthday with anymore.* She would never see Juro again, nor Maruko. Not even Deric. Deric, whom she had so little use for, seemed beloved now that he was gone. Her father.... No, she wouldn't think about him. That was all gone now. She had nothing to look forward to. A lifetime harassed by the specter of the Words, a lifetime of fearing and hoping that they be taken away.

A shadow fell over her. A familiar rustle as someone knelt in front of her.

"You are unwell," he said. His voice was different, stronger, it reminded her of the icy peaks she had glimpsed to the north.

"No," she said, not opening her eyes, not moving. His hand met her forehead, fingers curled through her hair. It was cold, as always. She expected to be repulsed by his touch, to want to brace herself, to draw her dagger. But she didn't. She didn't really care. It was better that way, she thought, not caring. So when they chained her up, or whatever they were going to do, she wouldn't be shocked.

"Yes, you are," he contradicted.

"I'm fine."

"Look at me and say that." He was trying to bait her with that tone. That challenge.

"No." She didn't want to play.

He said nothing, fell still and silent. She only knew he stayed because his shadow still fell over part of her. So she wasn't startled when he said, "I am going to pick you up. I would tell you not to argue, but I do not believe you can do so right now." There was a strain in his voice. She tried to place it. Disappointment, but not his usual disdainful brand. He lifted her, curled her against him as he had when she was poisoned.

Her eyes cracked open against her will. Her pack was on his back, his own absent. The muscles at his jaw bulged and jumped as he clenched his teeth. He was not looking at her but picking out a path through the hills. She closed her eyes again. *It begins,* she thought. Wondered where he was taking her. Didn't care enough to ask.

HE CARRIED HER NORTH, deeper into the hills. She watched over his shoulder as the terrain disappeared behind them. *It's probably pretty,* she thought, unable to see anything but rocks and dirt and scrubby plants. The rocks were redder than they had been, streaked with green and yellow in places. She wondered what they would look like in the rain. When the rocks grew boring to look at, she stared at his shoulder, at the embroidery on his short, upright collar, at the patter of life under the skin of his throat.

I wonder if they die the way we do. Clearly, he has a heart, a pulse, a throat. If I plunged my dagger in it, would that kill him? Likely it would.

But then why would he give it to me? They surely won't let me keep it.

Her eyes traced his ear, his jaw, his cheek. *He looks human, but he can't be.* She didn't pursue the thought because another one had caught her attention, one she had put aside weeks before. Involuntarily, her hand came up, fingers touched his cheek, his jaw.

He jumped, stumbled, but recovered. The look he shot her was so unnerved she thought she normally would have laughed. *Frightened of me? That's new.* He cleared his throat and found his stride again, but his arms and shoulders had gone rigid. The skin under her fingers was smooth and soft. She pushed her palm along the skin of his jaw, back to front, expecting to feel the rasp of whiskers underneath. But it was like touching her own face, though with his unnatural coolness.

"Please stop," he said, uncomfortable and stiff. She ignored him.

"You don't shave."

"No." He darted a glance at her, nonplussed, then away. He bared his teeth as she moved her hand over his chin. She saw the muscles in his jaw flex as he clenched his teeth together.

"You don't have any facial hair at all. Not even a little," she wondered aloud.

"No."

"And your hair, it doesn't grow, does it?" she had turned her attention to his head, was touching the hair there. It was unexpectedly stiff and springy, more like a mane than anything. She ran her hand through it, watched it spring back into place.

"No." He cleared his throat again. "I have learned it is rude to—" he searched for a phrase, settled on the distasteful, "*pet* people without their permission."

"You pet me," she pointed out. Curled her fingers in his strange hair in imitation of his gesture.

"I suppose I do," he admitted. "I did not realize it was an unwelcome gesture."

She shrugged but dropped her hand. Her ambivalence made her bold, and she asked again the question he had been avoiding. "What are you?"

"Have you given up on working it out?" He sounded amused. Sounded like he was trying not to sound uncomfortable.

She shrugged and went back to watching the terrain disappear over his back.

"We are only a few days from the terminus of the network," he said. He ignored her muttered, unenthusiastic reply. "I can show you, if you would like, our destination." There was a hesitation in his gait, but not his words, as he continued, "I can show you what I am."

"Do it or don't," she said, "but don't expect me to beg you. I'll find out eventually."

"Do not mistake my reticence for artifice," he snapped, cold as the winter wind. "Though from one who cannot appreciate the danger in which those who have sheltered her have placed themselves, I cannot expect an appreciation for the danger in which I place myself with such an offer." In her periphery, his eyes flashed. She glowered at his shoulder.

"What danger?" she scoffed, drawn a little out of her indifference against her will.

"Tell me," he hissed, "did you determine what manner of being I am in all our time together?"

"Clearly not."

"That is because for more than five hundred years, my kind has been in hiding, erasing evidence of our existence, waiting for the pathetically short and selective memories of your kind to forget us."

She responded to his bitter ice with frost of her own. "There's no call for rudeness."

He struggled, jaw jumping, then mastered himself. "Your point stands. You have my apologies."

"Sure," she said, rolling her eyes. They crested a ridge and he descended sideways down a steep, scree-covered slope, eyes scanning downhill. "So, what *are* you?" she asked when they were nearly down. His vehemence, his claim, had sparked her interest. He stepped away from the slope, onto the relatively-even hard-packed ground. Lowered her to her feet.

He stood there, half an arms-length away, studying her. She shifted under the scrutiny. "Why do you not look at me?" he asked. The wind didn't reach down here, and the rocks around them amplified the words, making them fill the space despite their low volume.

"Why do you think?" she said, defensively, crossing her arms.

"If you answer my question, I will answer yours," he offered.

She thought about it. Wanted to tell him she could wait, but the curiosity burned in her again, her lethargy was passing. And her fear. He had not tried to take the wellspring of her power, had not changed at all from what he had always been. The monster of her nightmares, of her thoughts, of her memory of that one moment, was not here. "Because when you look at me, you...do something. See into me. Rile up the Words. It's...it's...," she shuddered, didn't have a word for it.

"Invasive," he supplied.

"Yeah."

He was quiet. She stared at his hand, which was twitching slightly. "You have my apologies, Arten," he said at last. Whatever she had expected him to say, it wasn't that. "Your reaction is justified. What I did was intrusive and, among my people, is considered a violation. You are owed reparations, and I will make them to your satisfaction."

"Why did you do it then?" she demanded, bristling automatically at her lack of comprehension of his words.

"I have no satisfactory justification. I can tell you that I was excited to finally find you. I had been looking for you since the moment of your birth, and there have been many false trails and dead-ends. I wanted to know if you were the one for whom I had been searching, I needed assurance that my long search was over." His hand twitched again. He curled it into a fist by his side. "The second time was an accident. I did not intend to look so far."

He knelt, folding silently to his knees on the rocky dirt. She flicked her gaze to the side automatically.

"Arten. Look at me, please."

"I'd rather not," she muttered, distinctly uneasy with his face near her level.

"I will never look so far again. You have my word."

"I don't even know what you are, your word means nothing."

"My word has kept my people alive and hidden for hundreds of years. It is the currency of most value where we go." His voice was stronger, resonant in the air.

"You're lying," she said, heard the tremble in her words.

"I am not."

"But you can't... *Hundreds* of years? It's impossible."

"Look at me, Arten." The confidence, the command in that voice.

She looked.

His eyes were bright, but naturally so, and hard and earnest. It was an intensity she had seen once before, but this time he didn't force his way into her core, didn't sift through her secrets. He held her, like a rabbit pinned under a cat's stare.

He said, his voice ancient and unusually grave, "I am the oldest of my kind and have seen more than six hundred years. I have lied, and killed, and stolen to keep our existence forgotten. I would like to tell you what I am. I believe that you will not betray me, that you will keep this secret, and I will not compel you to do so."

Arten knew there was a threat there, one he had chosen not to voice. *He'll kill me if I betray him, and any others I involve.*

He must have seen her shiver because he added, "If you are not ready, I will wait until we have arrived. As you say, you will know soon enough."

She didn't know what to say. For the first time, she saw the depth of years in his eyes, saw a weight there and a sadness. Something crystalline underneath. Her mouth blurted, without consulting her mind, "But you don't look old."

His smile was sharp and tight. "This is just a body, Arten."

Just a body? What is he that he considers people just bodies? She could think of nothing, nothing but a demon. She had to know. "Tell me," she said, steeling herself.

This smile was fierce and toothy. His eyes flashed with

approval. "I will show you," he said, rising to his feet smoothly. "Do not look away."

She couldn't have if she tried. As he stood, he loomed, larger and larger, even as he stepped away. The irises of his eyes burned even in the bright sunlight, held her in place. There was a flutter of blue in her periphery, but she had no thought to spare for the robe that had dropped to the ground because his shape was changing. His neck stretched and elongated as his nose grew and curved down into a muzzle, his cheeks dropping away from the sharp peak of it, his eyes shifting to the sides as his forehead broadened.

That snapped his line of sight, and she scrambled backwards a pace, tripping and sitting heavily on the slope. Loose rock slid from under her hands and heels. Her mouth dropped open. She shut it.

She watched his shoulders, which had pushed backwards and close together, as they split away into wings, which he drew back, swaths of skin and ribs pulling away from his back to form together into membrane and wing spars. His arms elongated, limbs turned into scaled echoes of themselves. Fingers became strong, deft claws, wrists fell back and up. The pink flush of blood in his skin faded and it took on a deepening blue cast, rippled in sharp waves until those ripples solidified into scales.

"Do you know what I am?" The cadence was the same, but the brittle chill of it was exaggerated as his longer vocal chords and deeper chest conveyed the layers of sound his human throat had not been able to produce.

"You're...you're a dragon!" she whispered, then shook head back and forth slowly, the reaction building. "No, no, you can't be. Dragon's don't exist." The eyes he turned on her were emerald, unchanged, and bored into her. The

Words clustered high in her chest, responding, and she shoved them down.

The expression on his scaled face was so like the one she had come to know. The one that said, *You are being obtuse,* and, *Don't waste my time.*

"It's you," she said in wonder, accepting what she hadn't known was in doubt until just then.

"It is," he said, in the flat and factual tone he gave in answer to questions. The one that frustrated her. *Like he doesn't understand what kind of response is needed. Maybe he isn't being intentionally frustrating, but he really doesn't know.*

"Oh," she said, tearing her eyes away from the line of his mouth where sharp teeth had flashed. The Words churned, scrabbled, skittered in excitement. She pushed at them ineffectively. *Not now, not now, not now,* she pleaded. They didn't listen. But when Stekin lowered his head to her level, his jaw as long as her arm, they stopped abruptly. She leaned back involuntarily, sweat prickling on her spine as small sharp-edged rocks pressed against it.

"I am going to pick you up now," he said, teeth slicing the air, biting the words around his lips, mere feet from her head. The oddity was familiar and, for some reason, reassuring. "You must not flee or yell."

"I won't." She bristled, insulted. But when he reared back, wings flared, and reached for her, only her pride kept her from doing just that. He gathered her into his scaled arms, claws caging her shoulders and thighs, a parody of how his human form had so recently carried her.

"Hold on," he growled, and she was forced to clamp her arms about his thin neck as he leapt from the ground. His wings snapped open, caught the air, great beats lifting them higher and higher. Her stomach lurched as the ground dropped away in the nauseating stroke of his wings. She closed her eyes and pressed her forehead against his neck, felt the blunted edge of scales dig into her flesh.

"Do not be sick on me," he warned, and she forced the bile down. Didn't mind at all that the scales made his normally cool skin seem even colder. Used it to leech away the heat of her racing anxiety.

The sawing motion, the taunt snap of wings, the sickening lurches of her gut comprised her world until, finally, it didn't. They were gliding.

"Open your eyes," he commanded. She gulped great breaths of frigid air, only noticed how cold it had become when she started shivering. She forced her eyes open and immediately yelped and plastered herself against him, clinging to his neck with all her strength. The ground was far below, so much farther than she could have imagined. It swam in her vision. "Not down," he said urgently, probably fearing the turning of her stomach, and rightly so. "Out. There."

He caught her eye, pointed with his muzzle. She followed the line. Behind the ridge of a tall mountain she saw the easternmost curve of a valley, flanked on all sides by a series of jagged ridges, some of which still had snow sprinkling the peaks, despite the time of year. There was a thin sparkling line—*a river!* she realized, amazed—that wound down from the innermost mountain and cut south and west across the valley before it disappeared from her sight. She squinted against the sparkle and the distance, and then made out—"What is *that*?" she called loudly, over the air rushing past them.

"My city," he said. Something shifted in her perception with his words, and she understood what she was seeing. Tiny buildings packed together, tiny bridges. A trace movement—Could that be people? "We must return," he said, "we are too close to the humans, I may be seen." Then he was dropping, leaving her stomach in the clouds, and she squeezed her eyes shut again.

She didn't notice when they landed, just clung tightly to his neck and breathed with deliberation to keep herself from losing her breakfast. She felt like she was falling, yelped, and tightened her grip on him. Realized it was skin against her forehead, arms, not claws, supporting her. Then realized he was naked. Jumped away. Fell to her hands and knees when her legs failed to remember how to support her. She felt a wave of relief to have the stable ground under her palms, then heaved her stomach dry as her body rocked to remembered wing-beats.

A shadow fell over her, and she looked up. The familiar angular face, the long robe wrapped around his gaunt frame, so familiar and so foreign. A long strong hand extended, human though she now saw it in scales, and he helped her to her feet.

There was a queer expression around his eyes as he said, "Everyone is sick the first time." He rested his palm on her forehead and raked his fingers carefully through her hair. The gesture grounded her, made him real again.

"Why—why not just tell me?" she managed, shakily.

"I wanted you to see where we are going. To show you that it is not as bad a place as you think." She heard the faint echo of brittle resonance in his voice.

"How do you know what I think?" she asked, frightened.

"I cannot read your thoughts, if that worries you. Your expressions are enough. You do not hide your distrust of me when it strikes." She felt a stab of guilt at the bitterness in his words.

"I'm sorry," she said. His fingers stopped, he withdrew

his hand. She wondered if she had offended him somehow. Before she could ask, he gave her a choice.

"I can take you there, tonight, and we will be finished with this journey, or you can continue through to the terminus of the network."

She wanted to be done. Wanted to go to that city, to meet the people, to see them walking across their bridges, living in their houses, knowing they were alive and real and fine. "How many more stops?" she asked, dully.

"Seven," he said, impassive. She shuddered. "I can send someone else through."

"If we're going to find out the reason your sources are disappearing, it will be in one of them, won't it?"

"That is likely."

Meaning, I am almost certainly going to be poisoned or captured or murdered by someone in the next seven houses. Her skin crawled, and she was glad her stomach was empty. "I'll do it," she heard herself say with more conviction than she felt, "on one condition." He looked at her expectantly, waiting. "Give me your word that I will make it out, guarantee me you will *get me out* each morning."

His eyes flared, approval, delight, and she met them unafraid. "You have my word. I will always protect you, Arten." His knuckles brushed her cheek, and she didn't flinch.

"WHERE DOES YOUR TAIL GO?" Arten asked, trailing Stekin through the narrow ravine.

"That is a rude question," he said and offered nothing further.

She supposed it could be, shrugged and asked instead, "How do you look like a person?"

He snorted his contempt. "I reveal to you the best-kept secret in your world and all you want to know is transformation logistics?"

"You never answer my real questions," she shot back. It had taken her surprisingly little time to adjust to the idea of him being a dragon. *Better a mythical creature than a demon*, she decided. She supposed it wasn't much difference from not-demon to dragon, and she was well-accustomed to thinking of him as *other*, by this point.

"Very well," he said, clipped and brusque, still leading her onwards, "ask them."

The question that had haunted her these long weeks, that had swirled up each night when she was locked in a new cell, presented itself immediately. She hesitated, uncertain. *What's the worst that could happen?* she thought, defiantly. Remembered the flash of teeth, scaled hands the length of her arm, white bone and pulped flesh of a broken face under a staring eye. *At least it will be quick.* "Why me?" She thought he might not have even heard the tremor in her words it was so slight.

"In what respect?" he asked, pausing, turning to look back at her.

"You bought me, you've protected me. And you say you've searched for me for years. Why? Why *me*?"

He stopped, considered. "You are unique. At first, that is what drew me. When I witnessed what I now know was your birth, your power called to me. Only me. Why?" He drooped his shoulders in his semi-circular shrug. "A mystery. One that frustrated and tantalized me for nearly thirteen years.

"Then I found you. Your power came earlier than any

other source's has. Power that called to me so strongly I was not prepared to resist it and violated the privacy of your soul. And there is the nature of your power. It is not uncommon for a new source's power to be wild, but yours... It is like a flash fire, like sheering cross-winds. Every time it flares, I must battle it." His eyes were wild, glowing, his teeth bared in exhilaration. "It is glorious. I almost regret that you will tame it." A skittering of fear danced up her spine.

He sobered immediately. "It is best that you do, however, and quickly. I went too far last time, Arten. Your power is— intoxicating. Invigorating. I pulled too much, I could have harmed you. It was a mistake and one I will not repeat, you have my word."

She felt an intense relief deep in her core, a relaxing of tension she had been carrying for days. Yet also crestfallen. *He won't take them away permanently.* She didn't know why that bothered her, except he hadn't given her the option.

He's always wanted the Words, I know that, she told herself, but it didn't fill the hollow inside her. *I guess I just hoped...maybe he meant something with all his talk of choice.* She wanted to be more than just a glorified power pond.

The edges of cold palms pressed against her jaw, lifting her head from where it had drooped, long fingers curved around behind her ears. There was a feather-soft brush of a thumb at her temple. "Arten," he said, "your power is unlike anything I have seen in my considerably long life. But it is such a small part of what makes you truly unique. You are so young and frail, and yet have more courage than most of my people. Despite your fear, you have continued to endanger yourself to help others. Knowing what awaits you tomorrow, you have not begged me to fly you to the city, as so many would without shame. I barely know you, yet I am certain you are worth knowing better."

He frowned, his thumbs touched the edges of her eyelids, drawing away moisture. "I have upset you."

"No." She rubbed at her eyes and swallowed, but the hard pebble in her throat didn't budge. "I wouldn't be brave if you weren't here to save me. I'm a coward. I'm afraid every time. In...in every cell. With every bite of food they give me." She felt craven and small, admitting her failure on the heels of his praise.

"I very much doubt you would behave differently without me," he said, his smile sharp but not unkind. "And your fear makes your deeds all the more admirable." She didn't believe him, but his words filled an emptiness inside her all the same. "Now, come, you are hungry." He drew his hands away.

She followed, quietly, thinking. *If I wanted to change my mind about going back into the network tomorrow, I certainly can't now. Not after that speech.* She wondered briefly if he had said those things intentionally so that guilt and shame would drive her to finish the task she had started.

No, she decided, *I don't think he would. He gave me the choice.*

Another voice whispered, *But you haven't said no yet.*

That was true, and part of her worried what he would do when she did. But another part remembered him saying, *'My word is the currency of most value where we go.'* He'd given his word to protect her, and she was willing to make the case that also meant from him.

That sent her thoughts in another direction. To the city, the people there. What did they do? Were they all like her? They didn't seem to be chained or penned up, like she'd imagined, but milling about unworried, like the people in Laird after the merchant's fair ended.

The memory made her eyes sting. She saw her father's

face, heard his laugh, smelled the hot sweat of the horses for just a moment. *I'll never see him again.* The thought smashed into her, *I'll never go to the fair with him, he'll never finish teaching me how to bargain.* She'd never swim in the river with Juro, never listen to Maruko play her hand-harp, never know if Deric found his patron. She may not be going towards a pit of demons, but she wasn't going home, either.

She had been able to march towards despair and pain and torture with no issue. But knowing she was going to that normal little city was too much. She hadn't thought about the future, hadn't expected to have one. Now it stretched in front of her, devoid of everyone and everything that had given her joy and meaning.

Stekin's hand on her shoulder made her jump. She had stopped, was doubled over, clutching her chest and abdomen, her body reacting instinctively to what she had been too preoccupied to notice. The Words lunged, broke free. Stekin's wide jaws pulled them in, snapped around the dregs. She saw other teeth, another face, scales and a horned ruff instead of hair. That made it easier, somehow. And there was no pulling at that place in her core.

She wouldn't let him carry her but leaned on his arm for support as she listed along the ravine. When they finally reached the niche in the rocks where he stopped, she sank into the shadowed shelter gratefully. Stekin's pack was there, propped against the back wall. Unlike where they had weathered the storm on the plains, this one had a roof of a slab of fallen stone and was wide enough they would both be able to lie down with room to spare. She curled up and slept with the speed and depth she only ever achieved after the Words escaped.

When she woke, it was dark. Stekin was outside, sitting near a small fire, roasting strips of meat over the flames. He heard her sit up, brought her some of the strips and her bowl with some mushrooms and soft-cooked root vegetables inside. She managed a thanks and tore in. It felt like ages since she'd eaten. Certainly anything this good. *I don't have to wonder where the rest of the meat went anymore. I wonder where it goes when he changes to human.* She didn't pester him with the question. Clearly, *transformation logistics* was on the don't discuss list, *for now, anyway.*

The night air was chilly and humid, the rocks outside damp from a rain she must have slept through. She came out and sat by the fire, warming herself. She watched the flickering flames, wondered if she would ever watch a fire again without imagining herself at the center of it.

"How many slaves do you have?" she asked.

"I have had servants in my employ," he said, "but no slaves."

"But I'm your slave."

"You are not my slave, you are my source."

"Isn't it the same thing?" she dared ask. "I mean, it's not like I can't give you my power. The Words come whether I want them to or not. And you bought me."

"Once your power is tamed, you will have more choice in the matter. It will still build and need to be released, but it will not control you as it does now."

That didn't really answer the question. She frowned. Stared into the flames until she had enough courage to say, "What if I don't want to be a source? What if I don't want to give my power to you?"

"You must give it to someone," he said, unconcerned. "Though," he amended, "I had not thought you would not wish to be source to me. I suppose," she heard a small growl under his words before he controlled it, "you may choose. It is irregular. The dragon has always chosen the source." His words turned thoughtful. "This may provide a solution to keep them from fighting over you. I will see it is done."

She swallowed hard. "Fighting over me?"

"You are unique," was all he said, something hard under his words.

A slave with a choice of master? It was odd. But then, Stekin was odd. *Odder than I knew this morning.* Regardless, she didn't like the sound of it. But the fatigue hit her, and she crawled back into the niche to sleep.

18

A CHOICE REGRETTED

STEKIN

S tekin turned her power inside him, calming it, claiming it. It sizzled and spat, and he buried it in thick bands of his own. He watched the embers flickering in his fingers, swirling in his hand, cascading down his arm, tiny sparks of defiance. Watched as they cooled and stretched and faded. Merged with the nearly-invisible currents of his own power. He had never seen the process before, not with any of the thousands he had sourced from. His skin felt stretched, tingly, his sinews thrummed. Even that was stronger with her. He felt the diamond wings inside him stir, curled his power around his core. The scent of ancient ice ebbed away, and he gladly let the thoughts of a home that no longer existed flow with it.

What was she, what property did she possess to affect him this way? To awaken what was better forgotten, to create echoes of what had been lost so long? Even practiced healers had to concentrate to see power in another, but with Arten, he could not unsee it. He had ranged away the past few days, giving her space. But more truthfully, keeping his distance while he processed the guilt of what he had nearly done and internalized his resolve to never put her at such risk again. He had also tested the distance from which he could sense her. Now that her power was fully wakened, it had only begun to dim to his sight when he had ranged ten miles.

He watched her, beyond the fire, sleeping. Even drained, he could see the wellspring knot deep inside her. A beacon, a flame, that drew him inexorably.

I cannot let her source to another. They would not appreciate her value, not as he did, would not see her potential. *I will give her the choice I have promised, but she will choose me. Until she has tamed her power, it is moot.* He might be the only one skilled enough to contain and transmute it at this stage. It was not a matter of strength, but experience, and of all of his people he had the most in that area. Even Nhemith, the last one remaining who had also lived through the Sundering, did not rival him in that.

I have some time.

Arten shifted in her sleep. *She is so young.* He felt a stab of conscience. She had asked for the truth, and he had given her only part. When he had first seen the flare of her life, the thing wound deep at his core, the thing that had kept him alive through the Sundering and the long years since, had gone still. Alert. Predatory. He needed her, even if he did not yet know the reason. His bones practically shuddered with the certainty of it. He may despise the thing that necessity had wrought within him, but it was never wrong.

He *needed* her.

He needed *her.*

But she was so fragile. He could not let her break. He could not tell her the whole truth. Not until he understood her purpose. Not until she trusted him, was willing source to him. *You wish to protect her,* the thought snaked through him, *but who will protect her from you?*

I should send word to Nhemith. He set the other thought aside. *I am close enough to reach her now. We will arrive in under a week, and there is much to prepare.* And thirteen years of events to hear. *I hope she is in a reasonable mood.*

Stekin borrowed the little pad of paper and dry ink packet from Arten's pack. He had been intrigued by it when he had rifled through her pack on the plains the night she had spent at the grief-stricken farmer's. The night he had read her last journal entry and seen what she thought of him. The memory still flushed him with guilt and an edge of despair. He had understood her prickliness after that, but it cut him deeply each time, knowing she was evaluating him, weighing his merit, bracing herself to bring down his city and his people. He pulled his thoughts away, back to the task at hand.

Dry ink was such a novel idea, and so practical. He wondered where the Tsyaro boy had acquired it, and why its use was not more widespread. He had known it was from the Tsyaro boy, the scent of him had seeped into the oilskin wrapping. It was something he had carried with him for some time, *A personal gift. I wonder if she knows.*

He struck down a brief message, folded it neatly with the long fingers of his hands.

These hands, so perfectly suited to writing and other delicate tasks. Given the choice of it, would he give them up? He flexed his fingers, remembered the dance of her power within them.

That may never happen, he reproached the fanciful thought. He quickly summoned his newly-bolstered power. With a brief word, the paper vanished, taking with it more power than he liked to spend.

19

THE LAST ROAD

ARTEN

*O*nly four more left, she thought, loosing a shaking sigh of relief as she left the third house behind a ridge. Stekin's blue robe caught her eye, and she felt some of the tension leave her shoulders. He waited for her to change, then fell into step beside her as she walked on.

"That house, it gets a lot more people in it, doesn't it?" she asked as they slipped into the shadow of a pine grove. The foothills were giving way to the mountains, and the rocky slopes sported more trees and grassy meadows now.

"Three lines of the network combine in that node, so your assessment is accurate. What sparked your enquiry?" A month ago—two months ago?—the answer would have bothered her. Would have made her wonder if he was talking down to her, commenting on her ignorance. But now, she was used to it and took no offense.

"They were really nice," she said, heard how lame it fell, and tried again. "The cell was clean, had fresh straw in the pallet, a pillow, they even washed the blankets. And they gave me a basin of warm water and some real soap for a bath. The food wasn't just burnt scrapings." She didn't add that they hadn't looked at her with that mixture of fear and resentment that had become her customary greeting. And her cell hadn't felt quite so small, or quite so dungeon-like.

Which, of course, had made her suspicious and paranoid and she had barely slept at all, despite her relative physical comfort. She had half-expected the boy who let her out of the cell to lure her into some trap his parents had laid. When she'd heard footsteps running after her, her heart had slammed against her ribs, and she'd sprinted a few steps. Until the boy's plaintive call for her to wait, that she had forgotten something, had slowed her.

Her breakfast, apparently, and a sandwich for later, wrapped in a scrap of cloth and tied neatly, and a fresh apple beside. He'd handed them to her, wished her luck, and scampered back towards his house.

She looked down at the apple in her hand. *No, it doesn't make sense that they would poison me after treating me so well.* But then, it didn't make sense that the old lady had poisoned her, either. *Best to get it over with before I praise them too highly,* she thought and took a bite of the apple. She wanted to offer Stekin half but thought better of it. *If it's poisoned, I don't want him getting sick, too.*

By noon, she had decided the apple, the sweet (if stale) pastry, and the bits of sandwich she had sampled were not poisoned. She offered the remainder of her sandwich to Stekin, who declined. She felt his eyes on her while she ate.

"The food makes you nervous," he observed. "You need not eat it."

"I want to know," she said, grim, ripped off another bite.

"I am offering to test it in your stead."

"No." He inclined his head in silent question. It was still

strange that he listened to her when no other adults had or would. "If you get poisoned, I wouldn't know what to do. You clearly do. Besides," she said around another mouthful, "sometimes it's actually tasty." *Once I know it's not going to kill me.* It was all ash before that point.

"Very well," he conceded.

Not much farther from where they had rested for lunch, Stekin's light hand on her shoulder halted her. She looked back at him, followed the line of his sight, up the hill she'd been climbing, to the top. A woman perched atop a boulder where the trees had thinned, light pooling around her. She sat as though she were on a throne, her bearing elegant and regal. She wore a mist-gray robe of a thin, rippling material that shimmered in the breeze. The woman's gaze was riveted on Stekin, just as his was on her. Arten felt a tension between them she didn't understand. She looked back at Stekin.

His face was hard, his voice more brittle and biting than usual as he said, "Nhemith." He inclined his head a little, not breaking the eye contact. The woman didn't respond, not immediately, and Arten thought she saw Stekin's jaw tighten.

"Kaz Stekin," the woman said at last, formally, inclining her head to him, more deeply than Stekin had. Arten felt, more than saw, Stekin relax. Wondered how she could tell the difference when he always seemed rigid. "I am pleased you are not dead," the gray woman continued, easing into more natural tones. "I hope you have not developed...*tastes* while you have been away."

"Do not be vulgar, Nhemith," Stekin snapped from behind Arten. His hand tightened on her shoulder, and she turned to him. He didn't look at her, his eyes, almost entirely pupils, were fixed on the woman atop the rock.

"Please leave us, Arten. I will rejoin you before this evening."

"Sure," Arten said, glancing between the two of them. Each impassive and unmoving, each wholly fixated on the other. She scrambled up the hill, giving the woman a wide berth, and down the other side. At the bottom, she paused behind a screen of tree limbs and bushes.

The woman, in her column of light, was still sitting on the rock, unmoving. Stekin's head crested the hill. *I should keep going*, she thought but stayed. *What is between them?* she wondered as Stekin approached. The woman stood. The way he looked at her, Arten thought he might kiss her when his hands reached for her face. Arten looked away, embarrassed. When she dared a glance back, they were not kissing, but had each laid their hands along the other's jaws, as Stekin had done with her a few days earlier, and were just looking at one another, their heads held high, almost haughty in their angles.

Standing next to her, Stekin looked positively shabby. Arten saw the grimy stiffness of his robe, the places it had snagged on brush and rock or under her own clumsy step. His feet were reddened with dirt, the sandals worn and cracked, straps stretched and thin with age. His pack was battered, stained, his bow in need of a new case, his quiver nearly emptied.

In contrast, Nhemith was soft and flowing, her robe rippling around her like the delicate evidence of an insect skimming over water. Her graying hair was swept up in an elaborate coif, her bare feet as clean as the rest of her. She was as beautiful as he was haggard.

When had he become so? Arten saw him again, when he had entered the shop, across from her mother laying out a line of gold. He had seemed untouched by life in the way only the wealthy managed. That was gone now.

"I am glad you live," Stekin's voice wafted to Arten where she hid. It didn't sound like someone greeting a lover, not even someone greeting a friend. It was wary and neutral and didn't sound particularly glad.

"Is that the one you left us for?" Nhemith's voice was *definitely* not friendly. "I hope she is worth it."

"What has happened?"

"Before we get to that, you should know your *pet* is not fully trained. She is observing us."

Arten bristled. *I am not his* pet! She wanted to storm out and shout it, but that would prove the woman right.

"You are being rude, Nhemith," Stekin said, his words as sharp as his frown.

The woman laughed, a rich sound but backed with an edge. "I had forgotten how pompous you can be, Stekin. Thirteen years living amongst their kind, I expected you would have unbent a little." Her angles and hardness vanished, and she pulled Stekin's face down to hers, pressing their foreheads together. "I *have* missed you." Arten looked away, face heating.

She heard Stekin agreeing, "Yes," as she crept away as silently as she could. She was curious, wanted to know what Stekin would learn from this woman—*no, dragon*—but not enough to intrude on whatever private moment they were about to share. *Is that his wife?* she wondered, as she continued towards her evening destination. *He's never mentioned a wife. He's never really mentioned anything about himself. I suppose he could be married... but who would leave their family for thirteen years?*

Someone, she supposed, for whom thirteen years was

nothing. Someone who had lived hundreds. *'I am glad you live,'* he had said. *How long do dragons live?* she wondered.

HE REJOINED her a few miles from her destination. He was quieter than usual, which was an impressive feat, and while part of her wanted to respect his privacy, the larger part was burning with questions.

"She's a dragon, isn't she?" she asked, unable to contain herself any longer.

"Yes."

"She didn't seem as surprised to see you as you were to see her."

He answered the question underneath. "I asked her, several days ago, to meet me. I did not expect her to take so long about it." He sounded equally irritated and suspicious.

So, of course, Arten wanted to know. "Why did she? Take so long, I mean."

"She was vague on that point" —*Not at all like the other dragon I know*— "but I gather there has been change in my absence." He sounded so brooding she didn't need clarification to know he hadn't liked the news.

"Is everything okay?" she asked, meaning, *Is it safe?*

"It will be," he promised, grimly. "I have been away too long, that is all."

"Is the network in worse shape than you thought?"

"No, Nhemith was unaware of the problem we chase, but she has promised me new data tonight."

She frowned. *If they don't know about the network, what does it matter how long he's been gone?* He looked over at her, seemed amused by what he saw.

"You once thought me a thug," he said, "what function do you now think I fill?"

She hesitated, wondering if this were a trap or test of some sort.

"Tell me," he asked.

"Well, I think you're some sort of supervisor or clerk, I guess. Like the people who keep the roads repaired and make sure our temple tithes are correct."

He made a thoughtful noise. "That is well-reasoned but incorrect." He seemed like he was trying to be kind. "I am the kaz, as you are aware, but I have not told you what that means to my kind. It is a title bestowed on, typically, an elder, one who is trusted within the community, whose advice is sought. The humans think of it differently, and I have given up correcting them.

"That Nhemith acknowledged me as kaz is significant. It means she still trusts me despite my long absence, and others will follow her example." He paused. She felt his eyes on her, glanced over. He looked serious, slightly concerned. "It is important for you to know that I am of high standing in the community because my behavior and my actions set a precedent and are noted. And so, by extension, will yours. Do you understand?"

She flushed and looked away. "You mean that I should behave like a well-trained pet." She didn't try to hide the bitterness that came out.

"No," he said to her chagrin. "I mean only to warn you that where we go, people may ascribe unintended meaning to things you and I do and say."

"People like Nhemith?" she hazarded.

"Precisely."

"I thought Nhemith was your..." she immediately thought *wife*, but corrected herself in time, "friend."

"Nhemith has been a friend to me in the past. The relationship between us now remains in question."

Whatever that means, she thought.

THE NEXT THREE houses were all of a kind with the previous one. Hospitable, generous, clean. But Arten couldn't enjoy it. With each house, the likelihood that something terrible would happen to her increased. She hadn't eaten last night, or this morning. When they'd released her, she'd seen concern in their faces. She knew she looked terrified, knew her hand was twitching over where the dagger lay under her dress. But they let her go. Her legs had lost integrity as soon as she sighted Stekin, and she'd fallen to the ground, shaking.

"No," she said, "it's okay, I'm okay. I'm okay," she repeated a few more times for herself, fisting her hands in the pine mulch to stop them from trembling. "It's..." her mouth went dry, "it's the next one then," she said, shuddering at the ominousness of her tone.

"It appears so," he said from above her. "You will bypass it. I will investigate on my own. Before you argue, you agreed that I may deem the situation too dangerous for you to continue."

"Okay," she agreed, feeling small and cowardly for not challenging him, for not making a show of wanting to continue. *I thought I could finish it, but I can't. Demons, I can't!* She was shaking again but now from shame.

"Come," he said, offering her a hand up. "I will tell you the way to the gatekeeper's. I must question this family, then I will get answers from the last node." A growl rolled deep in his chest. He stopped it with a visible effort. He gave her a route that angled away from the one she had just been given which, he said, would cut the corner off the last node and place her on the route to the gatekeeper's. If she pressed, she could reach the gatekeeper's tonight. "I will rejoin you on that path. I will find you once this is resolved. Do not wait for me."

She didn't want to know what he was going to do to them, didn't ask. Just accepted the metal box that contained the remnants of some rabbits his bow had brought down and parted ways. She felt lighter, buoyed by relief, her legs pushed her over the sometimes rocky, sometimes forested ground. She was making good time, wanted to reach this gatekeeper tonight and so pushed herself harder. Stekin had promised her the gatekeeper would not put her in a cell.

He said the gatekeeper isn't a person, but what else could keep a gate? She kept her thoughts focused on the mysterious gatekeeper, on what might await her on the other side of said gate. Anything but the prickling to her right, as she angled away from the last node, anything but the people who might be there and what answers Stekin would soon be getting.

She did learn why the last node existed, why this shortcut wasn't part of the normal route, around midday when she had to scale a daunting series of steep ravines Stekin had referred to as "the cuts." *More like the gouges,* she thought as she took a panting rest at the top of one. They seemed interminable, but there were actually only four. Like a giant hand had swept down from the mountains and furrowed claws deep into the rock, scraping it away. She shuddered at the image.

Don't be silly, she chided herself. *If dragons got that big, they wouldn't be able to hide.* Stekin, even in dragon form, would have fit easily into the bottom of one of the cuts. *If something like that were out here, he wouldn't send you this way,* she reminded herself.

That was not entirely reassuring, and she was glad when the cuts were finally behind her.

She reached the trail in late afternoon. It was a proper road, relatively even, wide enough for a cart to traverse but just barely. She noticed the wall first, carefully constructed, and followed the line of it up to where it supported the road. She scrambled up the hill and surveyed it, marveling.

In some places, the road had been supported by walls that artificially widened the path. In others, the mountain had been cut away to create the width. She'd never seen anything like it, wondered how the walls didn't fall down, how the mountain had been carved like that. Itched to question Stekin, but her cast around revealed he was not yet here.

I wonder if dragons built it, or humans. It must have taken a long time to build, even just this part. How long is it? Who uses it? She let her thoughts spin down those paths, so that they didn't think about what was now at her back, or about what Stekin was doing.

By evening, the novelty of the road had nearly worn off. She was still struck by the beauty and ingenuity of it in places, of the sweeping vistas it offered, sometimes of the mountains, sometimes of the foothills, as it twisted and wound up and up, clinging to the sides of peaks and the narrow valleys between them. She stopped in late afternoon, when the road crossed a stream. A stone bridge spanned the gap, already wrapped in shadow. The water had cut a gap in the mountainside, and steep golden light poured through at an angle too flat to reach below the surface stones of the bridge.

She slipped down the moss-strewn slope to the thin, fast

rush of water below. She cooled her hands and shins, abraded in her uncontrolled descent, in the water, and drank deeply from it. It was icy and tasted clean and fresh. She emptied her gourd and plunged it into the water, her back to the bridge's stone pillar to brace herself against the pull of the current.

That's when she heard the scream.

20

THE LAST ROAD

STEKIN

S tekin knocked politely. Even if he planned to disembowel the man later, there was no need for theatrics. Inside, a person moved, dragging a foot behind them.

An old man opened the door, leaning heavily on the frame. His left leg did not support him, and Stekin knew the scar that ran down the right side of his face and had taken his eye had a twin that ran up the left side of his body. Stekin had not asked what caused the injuries, but they had been neat—blade work. The man had been young then, unwilling to lose his life, unable to support himself in a profession that had been primarily physical after the damage to his body.

Stekin had seen the opportunity and taken it. Had the man patched up, moved here. Kept him comfortable, well-fed, warm in the winter, reasonably entertained. In return, he sheltered the sources, kept their secret. He was the culmination of the network.

And, perhaps, a snake.

"Jackson," Stekin greeted, frostily.

"Kaz," the man nodded, then jerked his head over his shoulder. "Best come in." Stekin followed silently as the man stumped inside, settled himself into a chair, stretching his useless leg in front of him. He rubbed it with a grimace. "Almost wish you'd chopped the damn thing off," he muttered to himself. Then his voice went hard, businesslike. "So, you're back, are you? Did they find him, yet?"

"I am," Stekin said, folding himself into a chair opposite Jackson. "Whom are they attempting to find?"

"My replacement." He grunted as he hit a sore spot on his leg. "I'm glad it's you. Was thinking I wouldn't see you again before I toddled off, and that'd be a damn shame."

"Where are you going?"

"Demons," the man swore, "I'm dying, Kaz. Can't you tell? This busted up body's finally quitting. And I'm ready to let it. Just been holding on `til you bring someone else in. Then I'll take my potion and be done." The man scowled, squinting at Stekin from his one eye. "But you don't know that. So, you're not bringing my replacement. So, why *are* you here?"

"I have some questions to ask you."

"Well, get on with it then. I don't have much time left." He grunted.

"How frequently do sources come to you?"

Jackson thought and answered, "`Bout two a month. Less in the winter. I figure we lose some to the cold then. Or maybe they're just not willing to set out and get snatched up by the temple." He shrugged and responded to Stekin's raised brow with, "I got a lot of time to think out here."

"How frequently do you send them on to the gatekeeper?" Stekin asked, neutrally.

"`Bout two a month, less in the winter. Like I said." The man's face twisted in confusion.

"How frequently do you think the gatekeeper is activated?"

"I'm guessing," Jackson said slowly, understanding spreading grimness across his features, "less than that."

"You are correct. Nhemith has updated me on source acquisition numbers since my absence. There has been a decrease in source intake, hovering around ten percent less than average, starting twenty-three years ago. Five years ago, that increased to nearly fifty percent. Can you explain that?"

Jackson swore. "Twenty-three years? Demonsfire, Kaz, this has been going on for twenty-three years and you're *just now* asking me about it? What is happening to all those kiddos who come through here if you're not getting them?"

"Is it correct to infer from your statement that you have noticed no such decrease?"

"No. `Bout two a month, less in the winter. Every year since I've been at this post."

"I must be direct. Are you in any way harming them?"

"No." The man growled. "Never. I make `em clean up, since I know you lot can be snippy about the smell, and I keep `em for a few days if they've got a cold or look like they're too beat to make it or the weather's rotten. That happens more in the winter. Gotta treat a few for frostbite now and then, and I won't send `em out `til they're recovered. You talk to that healer you send down here, he'll tell you what I'm asking for and how often. They usually perk up after a day or two of some hot food and a warm bed. Then I send `em on. Been doing this, what, forty years? Never had one die on me, not a flare-out, nothing. I take good care of all of them, even the shifty ungrateful ones who steal from me. And I don't like your accusation otherwise."

Stekin could tell the man was being truthful, or was a confident liar. *Given his physical condition, which I know is genuine, I doubt he could overpower enough of them to make up the numbers missing.* "You will not mind if I inspect your property," he said, standing. He liked Jackson, and for all that he believed him, Stekin must verify the man's words.

"Knock yourself out," Jackson said gruffly. "You know where everything is. You know where to find me."

Stekin left him sitting in the chair, glowering thoughtfully at his aching leg, and went back to inspect the saferooms.

Jackson had two because of the high volume of sources he supported. The rooms were tidy, the floors had been swept but not scoured, and there were lanterns and blankets and fresh bedding in each. They smelled somewhat fresh, a little of old sweat and the faint residual miasma of scents that accompanied any new source: fear, pain, excrement.

They were acceptable.

The food and medicinal stores were in order. Nothing unexpected, nothing missing. *Poison would have been his easiest weapon*, Stekin knew.

After that, he inspected the grounds thoroughly. There were no graves, marked or unmarked, the only decomposing things he found were a couple birds, probably killed by the man's cat. An inspection of the shed revealed nothing suspicious, a ladder, some tools in the expected line of his use. No blood, no pain. No secret rooms there or in the house. In the end, he was satisfied.

And yet, completely dissatisfied.

"I believe you," Stekin said to Jackson, who had stumped after him to the door. "I will check into your replacement. And I will be sorry to lose you. You have been of great service to us." He inclined his head in respectful appreciation.

"So, what's happening to `em, then?" the man asked,

grim and angry. The long angle of late afternoon light cast his scarred face into menacing lines.

Stekin's power rippled anxiously. "I will let you know when I find out. Please excuse me." He left without looking back. As soon as he was away from the house, Stekin gathered the ends of his robe into his belt and ran.

Because if Jackson was not taking them, then someone else was. Someone between here and the gatekeeper. And he had set Arten along that path alone.

He had not gone far when her power winked out.

21

ERGIN

ARTEN

U pstream, a woman called for help. Arten looked
up, wondering if she'd imagined it, but then it
came again. The hill that the stream tumbled
down was steep and looked as slippery as the one she'd just
descended. She made a quick decision, wriggled out of her
pack, left it and the gourd leaning against the bridge pillar.
Another quick decision and she pulled off her boots,
searched for a place to put them, ended up tucking them
into the waist of her trousers. It made a tight fit, and they
dug into her ribs, but it freed up her hands.

She scrabbled up the slick slope on hands and feet,
fingers and toes gripping anything and everything for
purchase. Sharp rocks cut into her, chipped at her nails, her
hands and feet slid off the slick surfaces, and she went down
a few times on elbow and knee. The woman screamed
again. She gritted her teeth and kept going.

At the top of the hill, Arten paused to stuff her feet back
into her boots and splash some of the blood from her arm.
Enough to determine that the cut from one of her falls
wasn't as bad as it looked, didn't need to be bound. She kept

going but more cautiously. Her hand hovered near her pocket. She was minutely aware of the bite of the dagger's belt and the bumping of its handle against her leg.

Without the sound of the water echoing around her, the scream sounded different, less like a woman and more like an animal.

A tension in her that she hadn't been aware of snapped loose.

She took out the dagger, met her eyes in the reflection of its blade. They looked back at her, rueful. *And just what did you think you were going to do if someone had actually been in danger?* she scoffed at herself. The eyes looking at her turned hard and critical. Her mother's eyes.

She shoved the dagger back into her pocket with a hiss.

She should have turned back. Her mother's voice echoed in her head, telling her to do just that. But she was feeling relieved and tense at the same time, feeling loose but bound up. Like her mind was saying one thing and her nerves another. She needed to... What she didn't know. She needed to do *something*. So, she listened instead to the other voice, the one that whispered, *Let's just go make sure.*

The call grew louder, she was getting closer. It was definitely an animal. How could she ever have mistaken it for anything but? When she finally saw it, she was disappointed, having expected something fierce or frightening. It was just a strange, lumpy bird with iridescent blue and green feathers, a long neck, and a longer tail, arched under its own weight. She edged around the twisted wire that formed its large pen, squatted for a closer look.

"What are you?" she asked the bird, waggling fingers at it through the wire cage. It followed her fingers in an alert way that made her think better of the idea, and she pulled them back. It cried again, moved away, tail tip rustling through the forest mulch.

Seeing the silly bird strut around its pen drained away the last of the buzzing conflict in her. She tried to ignore the echo of her mother's censure. *I should get back.* She sighed. *I don't know how much farther this Gatekeeper is, and I've lost too much daylight following this stupid impulse. I need to get back before Stekin finds my pack and comes after me.* He *would* find the pack, and he would follow her. And she really didn't want to have to explain how foolish she'd been.

She stood up, face hot with embarrassment at the merest thought of trying to explain rushing into danger without a plan or thought.

She turned to go.

She didn't have time to react.

A MAN LUNGED AT HER, closing the few paces between them before Arten could do anything but widen her eyes and start. The bird's cries and its tail dragging along the ground had covered the sound of his approach.

His one arm clamped around her ribs, pinning her arms to her sides, while his other pressed something hard and cold under her nose that had her coughing and gagging, eyes watering so badly she couldn't see. He released her, and she stumbled, fell to her hands and knees, dirt and pine needles stinging against her raw flesh as she retched. He circled her, out of reach, watching. She struggled to her feet, glaring at him. Her hand reached for her dagger, found its hilt and half-drew it, but another gagging fit clutched her. She fell to her knees again, able to think of nothing but drawing the next breath.

A hand closed around hers, crushing it around the dagger's hilt. She cried out in wordless pain. The weapon was torn from her grip.

Something clicked around her wrist. Heavy, cold. Her skin crawled from its touch. Then the other wrist. And she knew.

Demon-metal.

Her vision was already warping, the sound of her captor's shifting clothes was strident in her ears. He squatted in front of her, pushed her head back to look at her appraisingly.

He took out a glass vial and held it under her nose. She held her breath, thinking it to be whatever had set her reeling before, but he laughed, the sound like nails driving through her head, sealed her mouth with a broad hand, and waited her out.

She drew an unwilling breath. This vial wasn't the same and she felt her stomach settle, felt her lungs open up again. *An antidote?*

Her eyes stopped streaming. She could finally see him, through the demon-metal distortion of her vision. He was saying something but the words were now out of synchronization with his mouth. He put the vial away, grabbed the chain between the manacles around her wrist, and stood, tugging her to her feet after him. That was clear enough.

She stumbled behind as he led her away.

He's not a dedicate, she thought, frantically trying to remember how long she had before the metal made it difficult to focus.

He looked to be around forty, and was dressed in leather, like a trapper, wore a long knife at his side, and he walked in a light, rolling semi-crouch. Her dagger was tucked into his belt on the other side, its hilt between his ribs and arm. It may as well have been in her pack by the bridge.

How does he have demon-metal? And how did he know to use it on her?

He twitched the chain, hissed something garbled over his shoulder at her. Her hands stretched in front of her, and she stumbled.

Where is he taking me?

No, don't think about that. Stekin will find me. He'll find me, he has to find me. But what if he didn't think to go up the hill at the river? What if he thought she'd fallen in and searched downstream for her?

I'll call for him. If he's nearby, he'll hear me. He'll come. If he's not… No, don't think about that. I have to call out while I still can. Come on, come on, come on! She drew several deep, building breaths, expanding her lungs as far as she could. She tried to scream his name, thought she might have screamed at least but sound was dampened, and she couldn't tell if it came out at any volume higher than a whimper.

Her captor whirled around and clapped a hand over her mouth. The look on his face was enough to silence any further efforts.

I must have made some sound. Was it enough?

She couldn't depend on it.

He yanked her onwards. She dragged her feet, deliberately stumbled into trees and bushes, trying to get blood from her arm on them.

But it was tough to remember why she was doing it.

Then she had enough trouble staying upright, while the ground swayed under her, that she forgot about leaving a trail. She stumbled and swayed as obstacles underfoot, unseen in the deepening dusk, tripped her.

There was a name pounding through her mind, demanding to be said, and she wanted to say it, but her throat wouldn't cooperate. Her mouth was full of sand.

How long had she been walking? In the weft of her senses, it felt like days.

There was a sliver of black, a crack in the mountain in front of them. No, a cave. She was being taken towards it. It was very important she not go in the cave, but she didn't know why.

She managed to plant her feet, and that was effective for a few moments. Until the man threw her over his shoulder and took her inside bodily.

Upside down, the world spun madly, and she was lost in the dizzying swirl. When he dropped her on the floor, it slowed and stabilized to a rolling list.

There was a click that hammered through her skull. She looked down, saw a lock attaching a link of her chain to a longer, heavier chain connected to a metal eye in the stone floor.

"I'm going to take one of these off," she heard, then saw his mouth move. Tracked his hands to her wrist, where they unlatched the demon-metal cuff.

She was thrown back into reality with an abruptness that made her throat burn with bitter acid.

"If you try to take the other off, they both go back on. You hear me?" He snapped his fingers in her face. "I said, you hear me?"

"Yeah," she managed around the gravel in her throat.

"Good." He sat back on his heels, and his face cracked into a disarming grin. "Well, well, you're something new." She glared at him. "Feisty. Clever of you to dress like a boy. Did it help?"

She ignored his question. "What do you want with me?" she demanded.

"I want the same thing you do, little dove," he said, running a finger down her cheek, "To rid you of the monstrosity inside you."

"What are you talking about?" she said, the Words inside her going cold and still.

"I'm talking about freeing you of the Taint."

"But that's...not possible."

"And who told you that?" he mocked, "Hmm? The person who shoved you," he paused, a brief struggle evident on his face, "down this path? And you believed them?" He stroked her cheek again, said pityingly, "Poor thing."

She thought back wildly. Stekin had said she would flare-out without him to drain the power away. Said the power grew in her like a spring.

Stekin said my power couldn't be taken away.

But he wants it, a suspicious voice inside her hissed. If it were possible to remove it, would he even tell her?

She felt a fluttering of doubt.

But she said, voice quaking, "I don't believe you."

"Fair enough," he agreed. "Though I am living proof that it can be done." He grinned again, his face open and sincere. "I was like you once. Walking down this same road, to a place they told me I would be safe, where the Taint inside me would no longer be a blight on my life." He paused, another struggle strained his features.

"Did you make it? What happened?" she pressed.

"It doesn't matter," he dismissed calmly as he stood and looked down on her. "What matters is that it's gone now. And I have the ability to free you from yours. To help you, as I have helped so many others."

He's the one that's taken them, she realized. *Taken the*

sources to free them from their power. If that's true, then no one has died! He took away their power and they went home.

Can he really make it so I can go home?

"How?" she demanded.

"It's simple. I hook you up to a machine and it leeches away the Taint."

Could it be so simple? "Show me."

He kept one eye on her while he picked up the lantern from the floor, pulled back a canvas tarp from the bulky item to the side of where she huddled on the rough stone. Cast the light on it. It reflected off a metal chair, which sat in a wooden pan. Two large earthenware jars stood on either side of the chair, and hooks of the same metal caught on the lip of each jar and curved away to rest in the pan. The pan, he explained, would be filled with water. The power would go through the chair, through the water, and up into the jars. There was a chemical inside each that could store the power.

"Why?" she asked when he was done. "What do you do with it?"

"Nothing," he smiled.

"Then why?"

"To help people like you. People like me."

Something wasn't right. She was getting the same feeling as she'd had with the workshop man. "What happens to me? After."

"That's up to you," he said, far too reasonably. "You can go home. You can stay here, if you want. I could use an apprentice. Where you're headed," he paused, again that struggle passing through him, "they won't want you without the Taint."

She didn't trust him. Wanted to believe him. "So why all this?" she asked, shaking the arm still manacled in demon-metal at him. It set the world reeling and stretching, so she stopped quickly.

"I couldn't risk you causing trouble so close to the road. They don't know I'm here, see, and I can't risk them finding out."

"Who doesn't know you're here?" she asked, already knowing the answer. Wondering if he did, if he'd ever actually been to the city she'd glimpsed from the sky.

The struggle passed over his face, and his mouth twisted briefly into a snarl, then smoothed away again. "It doesn't matter," he said again.

She frowned. "How did you know I had it? The Taint?"

Again, he said, "It doesn't matter."

There was something about the way he said it that bothered her.

She pressed, "It does matter! How am I to believe you when you won't answer me? How do I know this...this contraption even works? Where did you get it from?" Whatever it was, she doubted he'd thought it up himself. He was a trapper or a hunter, she was certain of that now that the demon-metal fog was gone. She didn't think he would be able to design a machine like this.

"It doesn't matter. What matters," he said earnestly, "is that I can help you."

But she wasn't listening because she'd realized what it was about his dismissal that was bothering her. She recognized it from that day under the tree with Stekin and the strange quality of her own voice as he asked her name. She knew. *He's under a compulsion!*

She kept the realization from her features, schooling them into a thoughtful look. *That means he did make it to the dragons. And now he's hiding this from them. Why? What happened to his power? What does he really want to do with mine?*

She needed to buy some time, get answers, make a plan to get out of here. Which meant she needed to get out of these chains. The manacle wasn't locked, she just needed to distract him long enough to work it free...

"What *is* this stuff?" she complained, glaring at the metal.

"Don't know," he said, but she didn't believe him. "A dedicate found me on my run up here, I took it from him. It doesn't do any real harm, just muddles you up for a bit," he assured her. He seemed regretful as he added, "I can't take it off, you understand, not until you're safe."

"What do you mean?"

"That stuff, whatever it is, keeps you from burning up all your power. If you were to do that, you'd kill yourself and take me down with you, so you see why I need you to keep it on."

She didn't fake the shudder, remembering what it had felt like when she nearly flared-out the first time. When Stekin had ripped the door open to save her. *Stekin, where are you?*

"Can you really take it away? Forever?"

"I can, little dove. A few minutes in that chair and you're free. Isn't that what you've wanted since this all started?" He smiled.

She was tempted. A chance to be normal again? To go home, free of the Taint, free of Stekin?

Then she remembered, that sickening, broken feeling inside her when Stekin had pulled away too much of her power. The terror. She remembered how vital the source of her power had seemed to her afterwards. How had she ever forgotten?

Which made her wonder, *How is this man alive if his power is gone?*

It's a story, she realized, *a lure. Who wouldn't want to go home, especially after going through the network?* Here, just before the gate, how many would turn down the comforts of home in favor of continuing on into the unknown?

"It doesn't hurt," he assured her. Then, when she remained silent, "Why would I lie to you?"

A question she didn't have an answer for. "How do I know this thing works?" she asked, trying to sound small and almost-convinced.

"The fact that I'm here isn't enough?" he offered. When she shook her head, he smiled sadly, like she'd disappointed him. "Alright," he said, "I'll show you."

He held the lantern before him as he walked along the wall. The light followed him, revealed a niche in the stone covered by a patchy leather curtain. He looked at her as he pushed the curtain aside and moved the light to reveal shelves of jars, then set it down. He took down a single jar from the middle shelf, stroked it reverently, then set it gently on the stone floor. With careful fingers, he un-stoppered the wide mouth and tilted it towards her.

Inside, a thick liquid sloshed. It glowed from within its dark home.

"That was from Jona," he said, stoppering the jar again. He lifted it back to its shelf. Touched the neighboring jar. "This is from Amile." He touched each jar, named the source whose power it contained. Twelve of them. "And these are just from this year. The rest I have in the back." He waved a vague hand into the darkness behind her. "All safe."

Arten felt sickened. "What happened to them?" she asked. He was back in front of her again, but his mask had slipped, and she saw a glittering in his eyes that screamed alarm through her.

"All safe," he said, "all free." He smiled, but she saw through it this time. "So, will you let me help you?"

She gulped. *I need to go along with it until I can run.* "Sure," she forced herself to say.

She tried not to flinch when he stroked her cheek again, her hair. "There's one other thing, little dove," he crooned, his hand under her jaw, thumb brushing her chin. His eyes went hard just as his hand tightened, digging into the bone. She felt Stekin's phantom fingers driving into her shoulders. *Stekin, where are you?*

"How," he hissed, "do you know Kaz Stekin?"

She panicked. She *had* said his name. And this man had lived with the dragons. *Stupid, stupid!*

Her thoughts and her eyes flashed to her dagger, still shielded by his arm.

His own knife was in reach, that side now exposed with his hand gripping her jaw. But he knew how to wield a blade. Even if she grabbed his, she doubted he would hesitate before using her own to end her.

"You're hurting me!" she cried stupidly, stalling for time.

"How do you know Kaz Stekin?" he repeated, his voice deadly, the mask of amiability slipping.

"I don't know what kazstakin is!" she wailed, deliberately slurring the words together as though she misheard them.

"Don't be difficult," he warned, "I heard you calling for him."

"For who?" she cried, thinking of the pain of his grip, of how helpless she felt, focusing on those things so that tears swelled and fell down her face.

"Hmm," he said noncommittally but released her jaw and stood.

She brought her hands to her face, rubbed at the bruised bones. *I have to get away from him.* She glanced at the manacle about her wrist, her eyes picking out the tricky catch in the stolen moment. She lowered her hands and brought her knees up to her chest to screen them as she started to work open the clasp.

"I don't believe you," he said, once again easy in his manner. "You shouldn't lie to someone who is only trying to help you."

"Trying to help me?" she repeated, bitterly, "What part of drugging me, putting me in chains, and dragging me to this place is helping me?"

"The part where I remove your Taint," he snapped, pacing. "Hush now, I'm thinking."

She watched him pace, her fingers still feeling at the clasp of the manacle. She thought she had it nearly figured out.

In her eagerness to get it off, she pinged the metal with her nail.

He lunged, was in front of her in an instant, his hands around her wrists, wrenching them apart.

"You ungrateful wretch!" he barked, and when she looked up at him, she saw something dark and twisted slither across his face.

A black rage that shattered his pretenses.

"You're in league with them," he muttered to himself, "They've found me, they've finally found me." He was working the other manacle around her wrist, immune to her struggles, his hands hard as iron.

"You've done me a favor, girl," he said just before he clinked the second manacle closed. "You're going to help me kill the kaz," she heard just before the demon-metal sent her senses reeling.

22

ERGIN

STEKIN

When Arten's power went dark, Stekin snapped the leathers of his sandals mid-stride, threw off his robe and kit, and transformed. He swept his wings down, leaving evidence in the road, tore into the sky.

If anyone had asked him, he would have said it was a risk he would never have taken. But just then, he was not thinking of risk, he was not thinking of his people, he was not thinking of any consequences save one: what would happen if he was too late.

He angled towards where her power had blinked out, eschewing the road.

Too long, it took too long to pick up her trail. It was the blood that finally alerted him. And enraged him.

He skimmed low over the trees, his eyes picking up what his nose did not, his tail thrashing at the canopy. He overshot, had to circle back. He was moving too quickly in the air, and the deepening twilight was working against him.

He landed. Shifted. Hunted afoot.

Blood, a scuffed path, led him to a hill of sheer rock, a

sliver of dark marking an entrance into its depths. He touched the drying smudge of blood at the gap, bared his teeth, and entered. The passage was narrow, he had to twist his shoulders to get through. It wound back and forth a few times before he sensed the dead air of a large space ahead of him. He edged forwards around the next bend, saw the splash of light on the wall ahead. The next turn would expose him to the cavern.

He stopped. Listened.

Two people from the breaths. She was alive and not seemingly in distress.

He stepped into the light.

"That's far enough," a voice said. Male, cocky. It took him a moment to find the owner because what filled his vision was Arten, kneeling in chains. His blood pounded in his ears, his vision flashed with red.

He wrenched his eyes away, saw the man standing over her.

"Ergin." He growled, coiled to spring.

Immediately, the air in front of him was filled with a sparkling wall of dust that drifted down from above the exit to the passageway. He brought up his hand to cover his nose and mouth. Too late. The little he inhaled set him coughing, retreating from the cloud.

He felt an uncontrollable tremor start in his limbs. Alarm filled the place of his rage.

"I said, that's far enough, Kaz," Ergin repeated. "Unless you want a lungful of demon-metal. I've never had demon-metal in my lungs, or my eyes, but I can imagine it'd do a world of damage to *you*."

Demon-metal shavings? It was abhorrent, unthinkable. A measure designed to inflict the most damage possible to anyone with power.

No, to any dragon. Ergin had prepared for his eventual discovery. *The temple wants to burn us, but this...this is designed to torture.* Stekin felt shavings in his throat and nose, felt their sharp edges prickling tender membranes, felt his power recoiling wildly from them. He could do nothing to calm it.

"Release her, Ergin," Stekin said, trying to keep the weakness from his voice.

"I will," Ergin assured, "eventually. First, you're going to help me." Through the settling, glittering cloud, Stekin saw the man move to Arten's side. Stekin's eyes picked out the cord attached to his leg, which appeared to run up the wall, presumably to a mechanism there to release the filings.

"Do not touch her," Stekin growled, tensing.

"Easy, Kaz," the man warned, drawing the cord taut, letting a little metallic dust filter down. He was busy at Arten's arm. Stekin heard the release of a manacle. Heard Arten's sharp inhale, knew her senses were overloaded with the return to themselves.

Ergin caressed her hair, murmuring soothingly. "Here now, look who's joined us," he urged her.

Arten looked up, her eyes wide, saw him. "Stekin."

"So, you do know him," Ergin said, pulling her to her feet roughly. Stekin growled, teeth bared, but did not advance into the room. His legs shook, and he was no longer certain that he could rely on them.

"So what?" Arten demanded. He would have smiled at that if his lungs were not burning quite so much.

"Leave her alone, Ergin," Stekin said before the man could respond, drawing his attention. *I must keep him focused on me. I must create an opportunity for her to get away.*

"I would be happy to, Kaz," the man mocked, "if you were to restore the power you stole from me." He was holding Arten against his chest, a long hunting knife against her collar bone, his other hand clamped around her still-manacled wrist.

"It cannot be done," Stekin said.

"You're lying, Kaz. I have the machine, I know you've made it work before. You're going to make it work tonight. Now. You're going to take her power and give it to me." Stekin followed the man's glances, edging forwards along the wall until he could see the machine.

His stomach twisted in a way that had nothing to do with the demon-metal in his airways.

He knew where Ergin had learned of such a device, knew from whose mind it had sprung, and knew it would never have worked. Not for Ergin. Certainly not to the purpose he desired.

"So that is what you stole," he muttered.

Ergin barked a laugh. "Never worked it out? I thought you were supposed to be the smart one."

"This is what you have been taking them for?" Stekin hissed, his anger sparking against the metal that weakened him. "You fool. Even if you were able to direct the power into the storage medium, you would never be able to use it."

He had been murdering sources for years on a useless hope. A doomed quest from beginning to end.

"That's why you're going to work it for me." Ergin grinned, a twisted thing.

"It cannot do what you want," Stekin snapped, trying not to focus on the tearing in his throat with each word, "which you would know if you had read any further. It was never functional."

"You're lying!" Ergin shouted. The knife edge wavered closer to Arten's neck. She was frozen.

"No, Ergin. That machine brings only death. The most it

ever did was store power for an hour before the chemical suspension broke down. But the power cannot be extracted once it has been bound in the suspension."

"No," Ergin grew even more agitated. "No, you can do it, you can operate it."

"Even if I could, I would not. You are deranged. I knew it was a mistake to let you live."

"You bastard," Ergin rasped, then his calm shattered and the real man emerged. "You demon bastard! A mistake? A *mistake*? You tore out my power and cast me out of your little hideaway. Left me out here to rot."

"You had another option," Stekin said, his eyes flashing.

"I should have taken it," Ergin said, the knife wavered against Arten's neck. "You have no idea," his voice broke, "no idea what it's like. Having it torn out like that. Trying to live, feeling like you're missing half yourself. You demon-spawn bastard, you did this to me."

Stekin dismissed the accusation, dismissed the painful resonance those words caused in him. "So this," he gestured to the machine, "all those sources you have murdered, is to try and restore your power? By stealing it from another?"

"You stole it from me," he spat. "So why the hells not?"

"I stole nothing from you, Ergin, you gave up your power to save your undeserving life."

Ergin ignored him, "You're just going to burn them up anyway. At least I give them some hope before they die."

"And what hope is that? The same hope you gave that last girl before you butchered her, the same hope you gave to all those you savagely attacked?" Stekin growled.

"This is different! I *save* them. From you lot."

"By killing them?" Stekin sneered.

"At least they die thinking they'll be normal instead of

broken husks before their time, tortured by the lives you've stolen them from!"

"Like you are now normal? You are broken, Ergin! You have tortured and killed how many? Hundreds. To get back something you once discarded as worthless."

Arten had been quiet, but Stekin noticed her stiffen at his statement. *What lies did he tell her?*

"Tell me, have any survived your ministrations?" he taunted.

"They were all weak," Ergin growled, a dark madness passing over his features. "Inferior."

"So, none."

"This one is strong, though," the man plowed on. "She'll be the one. I'll get my power back. And you'll help me, or I'll kill both of you." His eyes glimmered, the madness still bright, as he sneered at Stekin, "I've been hunting dedicates for years for their demon-metal. I've got enough to incapacitate you and anyone who comes looking for your sorry corpse." He seemed to remember himself, tapped the flat of his blade against Arten's collar bone again. "So don't get any ideas."

The scrape of blade over her throat sparked something in Arten. Something Ergin failed to see, focused as he was on Stekin. Her fists clenched, her face changed from blank shock into that stubborn, fixed expression she got when she decided on something Stekin was probably not going to like.

Before he could say anything, quick as a scorpion, she twisted in Ergin's grip, shoving his knife away from her throat with her shoulder. There was the flash of another blade in her hand, drawn from his side.

Ergin jolted into action a shade faster than Stekin did. His blow knocked her sideways, interrupting the arc of her blade, sent her dagger clattering to the cavern floor. His foot kicked back, sending a rain of demon-metal down on Stekin, forcing him to retreat into the passageway once again.

Arten went down on top of her fallen dagger, her chains tinkling musically. Stekin could feel the shards of metal tearing his throat as he bellowed, unable to pass into the cavern as the dark, glittering cloud continued to descend. Through it, he saw them struggle for the dagger, saw the gleam of the other knife, which Ergin had dropped in his surprise, where it lay, abandoned to the side.

He will not hurt her. He thinks she is the only one strong enough to survive the machine, Stekin thought, and hoped he was right.

He needed to get through the cloud of shavings, needed to get to her, but he could barely stand. The thick cloud was sending metal back at him, he could feel it in his lungs now.

He felt the scrape of diamond in his core, and for the first time in hundreds of years, embraced it.

Ergin had wrested the dagger from Arten. It went sliding across the floor, scraping over the stone with a sickly sound. Ergin overpowered her, his hands tightened around her throat.

But Arten brought her manacled wrist up with a ferocious yell, sent it slamming into the side of his temple.

He fell back, dazed, shook it off.

Arten lunged away, towards the knife Ergin had dropped, the dagger now out of reach.

Ergin's hand caught her foot, drew her up short. Her arm stretched, fingers scrabbled at the leather-wrapped hilt. He heard the catch of her nails, the ponderous scrape of blade over stone.

Stekin was seized with coughing. Blood flecked the air. The beast inside unfurled, the tremors in his limbs fading.

He heard Arten kicking the man's hand, the slide of her body across stone as Ergin pulled her towards him. Stekin looked up through eyes keener than they had been, to see Arten on her side, Ergin pinning her to the ground between his knees, his hand coming up to twist the knife from hers, the other pressing her neck to the ground.

She brought her manacled wrist down on his hand with short, pounding motions until he released the knife with a hiss of pain.

Then the knife was arcing again, found its mark this time. She drove it into his thigh.

Stekin heard the hitch at it nicked bone.

His eyes glowed as he pulled himself upright, false strength flooding through his limbs. He covered his nose and mouth, closed his eyes and held his breath, went through the glittering, evil cloud. Shards of metal pattered down on his skin, some causing pinpricks of reaction, some inert iron. Then he was through.

He could still feel the metal in his lungs, felt the pain of it, the weakness it was causing, the chaos of his power. But it was no longer important. He strode to the crumpled heap that was Arten and her captor.

The fight was already over, though Arten did not yet know it.

She struggled to get away from Ergin, who had both her arms in his hands, pinning her with the weight of his body, trying to force her freed wrist back into the manacle. He was doing an impressive job of ignoring the blade in his thigh, until Stekin kicked it. He used the blade to lever the man off her.

"Use every advantage, Arten," he said, heard the cracking ice in his words. She had already scrabbled away, and he heard her working at the demon-metal on her wrist.

Stekin crouched beside the man at his feet, ignoring the weakness of his legs, ignoring the hot blood between his toes. "It cannot be restored, Ergin."

Now on his back, Ergin's hands wrapped around his leg where the knife protruded. His heart pushed blood out of his body beat by beat. He had lost too much. Since Arten had stabbed him, it had only been a matter of waiting. "You could have helped me," the man pleaded. "She was strong enough. You could have given back what you took."

"No," Stekin said, "but I can still help you."

Ergin paled, hissed, "Burn on a pyre."

But Stekin had already drawn the knife from his thigh. The blade arced, steel flashing as it caught the lantern light. A thin line of red at Ergin's neck choked off the last word. Grew and darkened as the man's heart pumped the remaining life out of him.

Stekin watched Ergin until the spark of anger and pain in him faded, until the slowing thump of his pulse ceased. He then wiped the blade roughly on the man's shirt, freed its sheath with the expedient rending of the man's belt, and stood.

Arten stared at the corpse, eyes wide, freed and whole. He pressed the knife and sheath into her hands. She stared at it, then at him.

"Come," he said, "We do not have much time." She nodded, tucked the blade and sheath into her boot.

The pain was already reasserting itself. Danger gone, the beast had drifted back into slumber. *Not that it was necessary,* he thought, propelling Arten out of the cave. He rested his forearm on her shoulder, more heavily than he would have liked. *She was magnificent without my help.* He felt his eyes glow with pride.

23

AT LAST

ARTEN

S tekin was heavy and sluggish and naked but insisted they make it to the Gatekeeper right away. They paused only for Stekin to kill the bird.

His coughing grew worse as they went down the road, and he leaned more and more on her shoulder until she wasn't sure how she could bear his weight and still move forwards. But she did. She didn't know how he weighed so much. He had always been thin, but he looked unhealthy, his ribs and spine standing out, his hip sharp. She tried not to think about it.

She tried not to think about a lot of things. Like how it had felt to drive the dagger into Ergin's thigh, the little stutter as it hit the bone. The stiffness of her trousers where his blood now dried to a crust. The dark sash across Stekin's chest and legs, the smears on his hands and feet. The stinging cuts on her arms and hands and the aching one on her side where Ergin's blade had scored her in their struggle. She focused on keeping them moving, on her grip on Stekin's forearm, which kept him from slipping, on her grip on his hip that kept his weight aligned over her spine, on the wet sound of his breath that meant he needed to stop and cough.

They reached a long straight stretch of the road where it ran along the bed of a shallow valley. Midway across, he told her to stop. She placed her hand where he indicated, and he spoke some words. She would have jumped when the rock face disappeared if Stekin's weight hadn't immobilized her. A dark maw opened in the rock. With effort, she got them through the void and into what turned out to be a tunnel. They stopped just inside, after the rock materialized behind them, and Stekin had her put her hand on another part on the wall. The walls glowed, providing a little light, enough to see shapes and rough details.

"It is Stekin," he said, his voice hoarse, "and a source."

He looked like he was waiting for something, she wondered what it could be. Nearly jumped out of her skin when a disembodied voice echoed through the tunnel, "Welcome back, Kaz."

He hissed, irritated, then wheezed, "Send Kylik at once. And Nhemith."

"Are you well, Kaz?" The voice sounded alarmed.

"No."

Nothing further echoed through the rock passage, so Arten assumed his instruction had been carried out. She helped him sit down, leaned him against the wall. Discovered the source of the light was some type of lichen. It was the same color as the liquid in Ergin's jars. She didn't object when Stekin held onto her hand.

"What can I do?" she asked anxiously after another coughing fit had passed.

He spat out blood, then leaned heavily back. "Tell Nhemith," he said, "about Ergin. Tell her...I left our packs on the road... And...do not let them send you away." He squeezed her hand.

She didn't have to wait long. The far end of the tunnel opened up, admitting two dragons. They ran towards them, and only Stekin's grip on her hand kept her from fleeing. One, the smaller, squarish one, didn't even acknowledge her, had eyes only for Stekin. He skidded to a halt, began a quiet song even before he had stopped moving.

"Child," the other dragon, long and sinuous, said, spearing Arten with a stare, "tell me what has happened."

She recognized the voice. "N-Nhemith?"

"As you see," the dragon snapped. "Do not waste my time."

Arten stammered an apology, then sketched out what had transpired with Ergin haltingly, her eyes darting between the three dragons. They lingered on Stekin most. Was he breathing a little easier?

"Demon-metal filings?" Nhemith hissed, a sound that sent terror sparking through Arten's limbs. "Did you catch that, Kylik?" The other dragon grunted but did not break his concentration or the low song that accompanied the subtle motions of his hands. Arten remembered Stekin's hands moving over her shoulder, the chant of his power. *That one must be a healer.*

"He said to t-tell you," she gulped as Nhemith's stare pinned her to the wall, "to tell you that our packs are still on the road."

"Messy, Stekin," Nhemith growled.

He must have been feeling better, because he spoke for the first time since the dragons had entered, "I have cleaned up your messes plenty. Just get them."

Nhemith huffed but placed her scaled hand on the rock where Arten had, requested to the air to open the door. The rock vanished, she left. Arten saw her spread wide silvery wings before the rock closed again. Then there was nothing to do but wait. Stekin stared at her, his eyes bright with pain and offering her something...something solid and timeless. She accepted, and the world narrowed, receded.

STEKIN'S hand tightened on hers, she jumped a little, startling out of her daze. The singing had stopped. She was sitting beside Stekin, still gripping his hand that now dangled from the arm around her shoulders.

"Come, Arten," he said, releasing her to thread his arms through the robe Nhemith was helping him into, her face a mask of abhorrence. Arten was wondering how long she'd been out of it when Stekin's next words stopped every thought.

"It's time to go home."

JURO,

It's been a long day. I stabbed a man, but Stekin killed him. Stekin has demon-metal shards in his lungs, but the healer-dragon says he might be able to get them out. He's not coughing up blood anymore, so that's good. Nhemith insisted on flying him home, so the healer flew me. It was scary flying with someone who wasn't Stekin. But Stekin promised I would be fine, and Kylik defers to him, so I am. I was pretty tired, but now that I'm here, I can't sleep.

I'm here, by the way. I hope I'll be able to let you know that. Everyone kept saying, "It's a safe place," but I didn't know what to expect. After all the stone cells in the network, I expected another stone cell.

I guess that's what I have in a way...a very nice stone cell. A suite of stone cells, actually. Bigger than all our living space. Not as big as yours. But that's just my rooms. There are about a dozen other rooms (not suites, just single rooms), but I'm the only one living here right now. And then there's a gigantic common area. I guess if you have that many people living in one house, you need a big space for them to spread out in.

Then there's the kitchen, and the bathing pools (indoors!), and even a library. With all of that, it's way bigger than your place. You and Maruko and me and your horse could all live in just my suite without getting in each other's way. But it's going to be kind of empty with just me here.

It's nice, once you get past the stone box. I get it. If a source flares-out, they didn't want them taking down the whole place. But I feel grimy and closed-in just looking at the walls, no matter how far apart they are. Kylik, the healer, says to open the windows, that it will help. I'm going to try that tonight, while I sleep in my real bed, with real pillows and clean bedding. Stekin's even getting servants to come and make my meals and do my washing. I told him it's fine, but he says he has to set the standard or something. Turns out, he's not just some stuffy administrator but actually important.

Well, I won't be here long, so I guess I'll let him spend the money if he wants to. (Seems like he's got a hoard of it.) He says he's going to find someone to teach me to tame my power. It's wild. He's said that before, but I still don't know what it means other than I need to tame it. Once I've done that, I have to pick which dragon I want to source. Which one I want to own me, basically. Which is more than I thought I'd get. Tomorrow I'm going to have to find out what this place is like. It's the middle of the night—well, it's probably closer to dawn now—so everyone was asleep when we got here.

So, lots to investigate. Lots of questions to answer. I think you'd be proud of me, though, for getting away from that man. Once I knew he needed me for the device, I just...acted. He'd killed all those people—not one of them survived his process. I need to ask Stekin about it, about what happened to his power and what Stekin's role in it was. Maybe tomorrow.

You'd also be proud of me for not piddling myself when those dragons came up to us today. Demons, they're big. Stekin is practically a runt compared to Nhemith. And he could eat me in two bites.

I just realized Stekin probably wouldn't want me writing all this down. I mean, it's the biggest secret in the world. (If you could hear that, you'd laugh, I think I can pull off a good impression at this point.) So, this might be the last time I write you. Not that you'll ever see it. But...I just wanted to say, before I go... Thank you for giving me this. For what you do for people like me —sources. For being a good friend, and for fixing what had gone bad between us before it was too late.

I miss you, and Maruko of course, but...I don't think of you as often anymore. I guess I don't need the thought of you to give me courage. The more I think about home, the more certain I am that I can't go back. That whoever I was there is gone, and I'm turning into someone new.

Sure, I'm still afraid, but when that man—Ergin—captured me, I did something about it. I don't know how many other sources he's captured (Stekin said hundreds), but I'm the first one who's gotten away. And you didn't do it for me, and Stekin didn't do it for me. I grabbed the knife, and I fought him off, and I got away. Stekin might have killed him, but I didn't need anyone's help to save me.

Stekin gave me that knife. It's on the table beside my bed. I didn't want it at first, but now I'm glad he did.

He also gave me my treasure box tonight, the one I hid in the wall. I didn't even know he'd been carrying it this whole time. I don't know how he found it, or what made him look, but it was kind of him. (And that was before he even knew me. I'm pretty sure he's a decent guy—or dragon.) I went through it but all that stuff inside that was so important to me felt like I was sifting through someone else's life. Memories, mementos from our adventures. But, like I said, I don't think I'm that person anymore. (Which makes me wonder who I am now.) So, I guess what I'm saying is...

I loved you, Juro. And goodbye.

AUTHOR'S NOTE

Thank you for reading *Dragon Source*. If you enjoyed it, please leave a review at your favorite online retailer. Reviews help other readers find books they like and let them know that, yes, this book has dragons. Reviews help new authors, like me, immensely.

Arten and Stekin will return in *Dragon Slave*, book two of the Reunification series, available Summer 2020. Follow me on Patreon (Patreon.com/BirminghamGlenn) or Twitter (@BirminghamGlenn) to get the latest updates. *Dragon Slave* will follow Arten as she explores the dragon city and decides whether she must deliver on her promise to burn it all down.